# CORONATION

## LEE F. JORDAN

author of *Hell's Doctor*

Black Rose Writing

www.blackrosewriting.com

ISBN: 978-1-61296-099-9

PUBLISHED BY BLACK ROSE WRITING

www.blackrosewriting.com

Printed in the United States of America

*Coronation* is printed in Chaparral Pro

# ACKNOWLEDGMENTS

This book could not have been written without the support of my family, which never ceases to amaze me. I owe a special thanks to Mark Primeau for his insight and thoughtful suggestions that made this book considerably better.

I owe a sincere thank you to the genius of a rising young star, Landon JP Ginn, for his superb cover, spine, and back art. (www.landonginn.com)

I am also blessed to have the considerable talent of Cat S. Ginn and her wonderful artwork and friendship throughout this novel. (www.catginn.info)

Contact the author directly at www.leefjordan.com

This book is for my brother, Steven A. Jordan.

# PROLOGUE

He was close to vomiting. His palms were clammy and bullets of water masquerading as sweat started streaming down the side of his face two minutes ago when he first glimpsed the scene. *Ghastly*, was the only way to describe it. Quickly, he turned his head away and coughed into a closed fist before wiping his brow. He wouldn't look again until he composed himself.

Shaking his head and then mustering strength from nerves that had just been shattered, Commander Gary Bryant turned to the man standing at the rail next to him. The man was dressed in his Navy whites with an open collar, and at the moment, a completely open mouth.

"Morrison." No response. "Morrison," Bryant said with a little more force in his voice. He had to be careful. This was the radioman's first deployment and he was in a vulnerable state. Gently, almost like a father cradling his son, Bryant touched the arm of Morrison. "When did we receive the last communication from them?"

Morrison tore his eyes away from the carnage in front of him. He had never seen anything like this. The recruiting officer told him he'd see some things that would stick with him for a long time. But *nothing* like this. This shit did not happen. "Sorry, sir," he muttered. "Two days ago." Morrison pulled a wad of paper from his back pocket and consulted it in an effort to forget, if only for a split second. Take his mind off of it.

"Bently. We're going to need to take pictures and record this." Bryant turned to his Executive Officer who had just vomited all over the steel floor of the first deck. Unlike Bryant, Bently couldn't stop the nausea from overtaking him completely. He paused for a moment and looked at Bryant again and then turned away with a green face and threw up. It was dry heaves by now. Nothing left in his stomach to eradicate.

Bently wiped the back of his sleeve across his mouth and turned to his commander. "Sir, what in the fuck happened here? Sir?" He was close to crying.

"Don't know," was all Gary could manage. He turned back to the vision that he knew would haunt him the rest of his life. He mumbled his words, not really speaking them.

Bryant turned to his left and pulled his stiffly pressed cap down a little tighter over the top of his bald head. It normally sat pushed back and inviting, but not now. Maybe not ever again.

He walked past the first row of enlisted men. Each of them was dressed in their khaki pants and blue shirts. Collars were open and revealing a white or blue Navy issue undershirt. Belt looped over on itself at the correct angle. Shoes polished to a tight sheen.

Behind the first row was the second row and as Bryant walked between them he could see a total of four rows of six men apiece. Twenty-four men. All that was needed to power this nuclear submarine, the *USS Nevada*. A skeleton crew at best for something this size and with this tonnage, but he knew that the men were highly trained and could handle anything that was thrown at them.

Perhaps not *anything*.

Gary had seen dead men before. Any commander with his time in had seen the ravages of war from both sides of the aisles. He had given it out and seen it handed back.

But this was different.

Perhaps it was terrorists. He hadn't heard of them hitting anything of this size, but to possess a nuclear sub from the United States could make whatever sect owned it an instant world power.

Perhaps it was some kind of mustard gas or bio-medical agent filtered in through the air system. These subs could spend weeks at sea, under their own power and were almost self-contained. They could leave port and not touch dry land for months. Not even for supplies like food and clothing. Exactly like the Navy envisioned so long ago when these really big submarines were originally commissioned.

Mustard gas could be nasty all by itself. Bryant had come across some Iraqi soldiers who had been exposed to mustard gas that their flame retardant suits couldn't repel. The soldiers had burned from the inside out like someone had placed them in a microwave and set the heat to popcorn strength. The men had literally melted in their suits. Bryant had witnessed the medical examiners trying to scrape some of the more apparently recognizable parts off the insides of the suits. After using both putty knives and a vacuum to clean the mess, the doctors had just given up and grabbed a wad of duct tape. They would alternately stick it against the suits and then put it in a bag.

Whatever it picked up was better than nothing.

But he knew as he walked among the four rows of the enlisted men, this wasn't a bio-toxin agent. It wasn't terrorists, nor was it a fuckup from the manufacturer.

Twenty-four men. Twenty-four dead men.

This was something *different*.

"Two days you say, Morrison? No contact at all for two days?"

"Yes sir. According to the records. Just the call from the New York Port Authority reporting the drifting sub."

Morrison had received the call this morning. The sub was listing in choppy waters just off the coast of New York. The Port Authority had sent a couple of Coast Guard ships to investigate and they reported the ship appeared to be abandoned. Impossible, Bryant knew.

"I want this entire area sealed. Pull the sub into dry dock and wrap it with yellow tape. Until we get a chance to go over this with the forensics team, no one, and I mean no one, touches this."

"Aye, sir," Bently nodded. He had regained his upright form and strode towards his commanding officer. He was going to try and save some face here if possible. He was always the professional, but in this case he couldn't get out of the conn room fast enough. The stench of the freshly dead had worked itself up under his olfactory senses and was slowly crawling through the inside of his nose. It reminded him of rotten, maggoty cheese. He consciously tried to stop the advancing aroma from reaching his brain, telling himself that he had smelled dead men before. He could control it.

"What do I tell the Admiral about his sub?"

Bryant stopped midway between the rows of dead men. He did not relish the conversation with the Admiral about why he couldn't use his new sub, but he really hated the letters he'd have to write to the wives and families. He couldn't even tell them what killed their fathers and husbands and sons.

"I don't give a shit about the Admiral, Bently. Just send the message. Dry dock. No one touches the *Nevada* without my express authority."

Bryant retreated to the front of the sub. He surveyed the bodies of the men in front of them. He had no training for this.

Twenty-four smartly dressed, newly enlisted men hanging by their necks from nylon ropes in the foredeck of their newly commissioned nuclear sub. The captain of the sub, a man named Joe

Brown that Gary had served with a long time ago, and Brown's second in command, his executive officer, were hanging in the first row. With every lurch and list of the sub, the twenty-four bodies would swing back and forth slowly from the rafters.

None of the men had struggled. None of them had marks like they tried to resist. It looked to Gary like they had all made their own individual nooses. One of the men overpowering the rest of them? Impossible. Mass suicide? Simply impossible. Simply fucking impossible. His Navy-trained mind could not accept that.

"Sir," Bently was trying to climb the ladder from the deck and get out into the fresh air. "Should I mention their faces?"

Bryant had seen them. He had deliberately avoided thinking about them. It just couldn't be.

Each of the twenty-four swaying bodies was *smiling*.

"Don't bring it up to anyone," Bryant said. Somewhere outside the submarine, the only sound he could hear was the gentle listing of the waves against the hull. No longer able to control it, Commander Gary Bryant fell to his knees and vomited.

# CORONATION

# Book One

## Inception

# CHAPTER ONE

*I am Evil.*

*I am the embodiment of all that you have ever feared. I am the carnage that hides in the recessed corners of your mind and awakens you sweating in the dead of night screaming as loud as you can. I am the terror that brings forth images from the tombs of your subconscious; that sends shivers up and down your spine; that causes your hands to tremble and your fingers to turn cold. I am the monster that whispers in the night; that seeks outside your doorway; that holds the knife against your throat; that hangs from the cobwebs of your mind. I am the thought you push away as quickly as it rises to the surface. I am the coldest ice you have ever touched and the smoldering fire underneath your skin as you struggle to contain me.*

*I have existed as long as life has existed. Simmering somewhere below the surface like the embers of a dead fire. There is heat but no smoke. There is danger but no sign. There is pain but no warning. I am the pain lurking beyond the fringe of your mind where there is only fear.*

*And death.*

*I have survived since the dawn of time and have always been a part of man's very core of existence. Connected by a syntax of nerve endings and entwined by a desperate struggle to touch, I am drawn to the surface by the simplest of actions. Conscious thought is not a requirement.*

*I am the euphoria that surrounds a masochist's heart and dictates his movements as he slices through the bone of a victim with a saw blade. I am the subtle step of a drunken parent before the first blow to the head of a whimpering spouse. I am the reason for a woman bludgeoning her husband or a child pouring petrol on an animal. I am the finger that pulls the trigger on a gun that blows tiny pellets across the face of the storeowner during a robbery over trinkets. I am the hand that holds a face to a boilerplate until the sounds of searing human flesh can been heard.*

*I am the laughter that ensues from the carnage.*

*It is a choice that I exist.*

*Man has engaged me to be a part of him.*

*Long ago, when the world was young, man had a choice. He could have chosen the light and then I would never have existed. Never had been. But man chose the easiest pathway available to him. Man has always taken the low road when others were present. Has always picked the ways of the wicked. Has given me breath. Has made me breathe.*

*I cannot be touched or held. I cannot be carried around in a jar to be put on display. I exist in a world devoid of beauty. Devoid of kindness. Devoid of light. But I survive.*

*I am not the reason. I am the impetus.*

*Man has always needed me to be an answer for his actions. To put a face on something sinister. To name something unspoken. Something that is alive in the cellar of man. Something that cannot be forgotten. Cannot be forgiven.*

*Man needs me.*

*I am the blackness that chokes light and the maggots that worm their way through the brains of the simpleminded. I am the terror that makes sounds in the darkest corners of the bedroom at night and the horror that awakens the beasts to eat the living. There is room enough for both light and dark in this world.*

*I am the dark.*

*I am Evil. Pure Evil.*

*And I am your father.*

⊠

Flannan Isle, Scotland
December 1800

*The damn cat bit me* was all James Ducat could think. The cat had walked right up to James as he sat at the dinner table and promptly rubbed itself around his left leg. When he bent down to scratch it softly behind its left ear, the damn thing hissed and then bit him deeply on the offending hand. James howled when the cat hung on for just a second too long before opening its mouth wide enough to allow his release and then scampering away to the corner. It barely avoided the swipe of his backhand. Now it sat and stared silently at him from its perch.

*The damn cat bit me.* It seemed incredulous to James. Hell, he had brought the cat onshore from the mainland almost two weeks ago and tended to it ever since. The cat showed up one day at his house and James fed it until he couldn't get rid of it. It was there every day. The furry thing was small and colored a sleek black with startling green eyes that transfixed James every time he looked at them.

It seemed to be a gentle cat. Purring frequently and always rubbing up against his leg. Tame, not wild. Easy to pet, it would come to him when he motioned with his hand. Even sitting with him in his lap from time to time. Until now James had begun to enjoy the friendship it offered.

But now this. James' first thought as he pulled the wounded hand away from his mouth and looked at the bleeding teeth marks, was that the cat could have rabies. Hell, the damn thing could have almost anything and now it'd bit him deep enough to draw blood. That meant the saliva from the cat was now running rampant throughout James' bloodstream. Carrying any germ or disease it had directly into his brain and beyond.

James scuffed at the idea of something geminating inside his brain and put the hand back into his mouth to suck out the wound and keep it from dripping blood all over the floor. He stood up from the kitchen table and promptly knocked over the chair. Normally a prudent man who cleaned up after himself, he scowled at the overturned wooden chair. Cursing silently under his breath, he gave one last glance at the pair of green eyes staring at him from the corner and then headed for his bedroom to get a bandage.

Tom Marshall passed him in the hallway just off the kitchen. "Hey James. What's the matter?" He had a concerned look on his face. He was worried that James might not be able to take his regular shift. He normally followed Tom on the rotation and he didn't want anything to happen tonight. It was close to Christmas and Tom had letters to write to his family before he turned the next rotation.

"The damn cat bit me," James said as he pushed his way past.

"That's odd. I thought you were the only one it liked."

"Me too. Guess not," James said while sucking on his bleeding hand and walking away.

"You still able to pull your shift?" Tom said hopefully.

"Yeah. I'll be there in a few minutes to relieve you."

Tom let out a gasp of held breath. That was all he wanted to hear. "I'll see you in a few. I'll be upstairs at the light. It needs tending tonight, as always."

James mumbled a sound of acceptance back at Tom and left him alone. He could hear the cat padding its way behind him on the steps.

⊠

Something wasn't right tonight. James sat at the top of the lighthouse and looked out into the vastness of the Atlantic Ocean. The Flannan Isles consisted of three different groups of islands situated about thirty kilometers off the western coast of Scotland. This particular island housed the only lighthouse anywhere around and it was his job along with his two co-workers to keep the light burning at all times. All of the ships approaching Scotland, both large and small that navigated the straits from the west counted on this lighthouse to make it safely past the rocks that jutted out into the ocean. Rocks that could easily tear the bottom off a wooden hull or puncture through the base of an iron ship and turn it into sunken treasure before the sun's rise. Nothing but the sound of ripping metal or splintering wood and then the screams of drowning men as their ships sunk.

James heard those sounds one cold terrible night when he was on shift here at the lighthouse, and he still could not shake the screams from his memory. At one moment he had been tending the lantern as he had done many times before, and then he was startled by a piercing cry out in the blackness of the ocean. The cry was like a wounded animal that caught its leg in a trap in the woods and was trying to decide between chewing the leg off to get away or waiting patiently for the hunter to come and blow its head off. The screamer *knew.* More and more voices soon joined in and as James tried desperately to locate them beyond the beam of the light, he could only hear the helplessness of the screams. The desperation of men in a losing struggle in the frigid water of the Atlantic Ocean.

The sea did not give up easily. If it got a chance to pull your ship down to its basin, then it would most assuredly do so. Those screaming sailors knew their boat and their lives were being dragged down into the icy water and there was no escape.

James shook the thought from his head and concentrated on tonight. That night wasn't his fault. He had only been on the lighthouse duty for a week when that happened and the idiot he was sent to replace had fallen asleep in the tower and let the light burn down so low it may have been a factor in the shipwreck. No one in the lighthouse was ever directly blamed, but there were plenty of rumors. And the idiot got fired a few weeks later.

The huge lantern required continually dousing a set of leather skins with oil. The oilskins were then set to flame and the keepers kept them burning by adding more and more oil to the bottom of the well housing to make sure the flame never went out. The lighthouse was situated at such a point on the island that its light could be seen from several kilometers in any direction.

When James first got the job, he had been delighted. A decent salary, a clean bed, reliable food, and plenty of tasks to make his three-month shift go by quickly. With so many people out of work, this was a dream job.

Or so it seemed at first.

There were always three keepers living in the lighthouse at any one time and they were also the only three people on an otherwise deserted island. He had worked with both of these men before and genuinely liked them. Tom Marshall and Donald Macarthur were nice enough fellows and they kept to themselves for the most part. It made the job fairly easy. Neither of them even complained to him about bringing the cat to the lighthouse when he came ashore this time. Not one word.

But something was wrong tonight. He could feel it. Like a heavy fog had rolled in over the lighthouse. Had rolled in over *him*.

It seemed to James that every breath he took was weighted down. Like his chest was constricted by a tight lead jacket that restricted his breathing and limited his movements. He looked around and over his shoulder. Perhaps, he thought, the air was actually heavy with grit of some kind. Perhaps every time he inhaled, grains of sand were worming themselves down his throat and into his lungs until he had to gasp just to get a good breath. Just to breathe.

Things happen in lighthouses. He knew that for a fact.

Alone for so many long days and so many endless nights, the stories were legend of what could happen. No one else on the entire island. No one to save them. No ship to rescue them or bring them supplies for three months. The older keepers told of all sorts of strange things. Ghosts. Demons. Hauntings.

Deaths.

James knew all the stories.

There wasn't supposed to be a fog tonight and there wasn't one forecast for the next couple of days. Sometimes, when the cold north winds blew just right, James could feel the weight of those stories. Could feel the sounds and the movements of things long since gone from this island. The old keepers always said it happens when the north winds blow the fog over the island. That's when things happen. That's when the ghosts appear. That's when death comes.

James pulled his gaze away from his eternal lantern. The light he built and the one he nurtured every night on this rock. The one that warmed him.

He stood up from his little stool and looked over the side of the lighthouse and out into the darkness beyond the light's beam.

There was a fog forming just off the coast of the north shore of

Flannan Isle tonight.

He quickly bent down and grabbed three more square shaped oilskins. Pulling down an L-shaped piece of wrought iron from its post on the wall, he lifted the side of the lamp and laid the skins on top of the flame. He closed his eyes as the flames flared intensely from the fresh arrivals, crackled and emitted some new floating ashes into the night air, and then accepted his offering. He released his grip on the L-shaped tool and the glass side of the lamp slipped back down into its place. The light would burn for another couple of hours now before he would have to tend to it again this evening. It might almost make it to the end of his shift.

He heard the cat scratching itself behind him. The cat had kept a safe distance since earlier this evening when it bit him. James felt no ill will towards the creature, but glancing down at his forgotten bite, he noticed a small amount of green pus was oozing slowly through the bandages he put over the wound. *Odd*, he thought, as he wiped it on the side of his pants. The wound hadn't had time to fester in only a couple of hours since the bite, and to turn green this quickly could only mean trouble. Maybe some kind of staff infection. Those things could cripple a man at sea or on an island. He would have to get the bite looked at when he went ashore next week at the end of his shift.

Turning his attention back to the sea and the impending feeling of dread that had settled over him this evening, James let his mind wander for just a moment. He could have been anywhere tonight. Anywhere that he wanted. He had no ties to the real world. No family like Macarthur and Marshall. No one waiting at home for him this Christmas.

He had been married one time for a short while but it hadn't lasted due to his temper. He hit her more than once when he drank and she simply disappeared one night. He came home from working on the docks to find his dinner not made and his house empty. His fault, he knew. It was better that she left him. Saved him from divorcing her and having to pay for a lawyer with money he didn't have anyway.

Unconsciously scratching at the bandaged wound on his hand,

he turned back and looked at the white-hot scalding light he had built. It was his light. His lighthouse. The others were simply tenders of the flame. He owned the light.

Normally when he looked at the white flame, he could only hold his gaze for a second, until he felt the light beginning to burn his eyes. But tonight for some reason, the longer he stared, the more he seemed to be drawn inward to the center of the flame. It didn't burn him at all, but rather James could feel a coldness envelop his mind. A coldness like he had grabbed a chunk of ice and pressed it to the side of his face, and it started to go numb. He reached the oozing hand up and rubbed it against his cheek and then pinched his skin. There didn't seem to be any feeling there.

James stared at the light and pinched harder. He squeezed and he pinched and then he finally started to tear the skin away from his face. He dug his nails into the side of his cheek and then with a pull and a yank he ripped a large section of skin off of the left side of his face.

He was drawn towards the burning flame in front of him like a moth. He had not really bothered to look very deeply into the center of the flame because of the stories. As he stared with a newfound wonder into the fire he could feel coldness spreading from his torn and bleeding cheek across his face. The cold seemed to move stealthily across his face like an advancing army of rats on a dead carcass until it encompassed his entire face and then spread down his neck to his chest. He had never really looked at the light. Never really seen the beauty he made.

The flame danced and moved. Shifted and swayed. Drew him in and then filled him up with its heart. He had created this.

Standing now and locating the cat behind him, James systematically began to remove the flesh from his face. Pulling, ripping, yanking, jerking, his flesh fell to the ground in chunks.

⊠

*You have to kill them.*

The words startled James out of what he was doing. He had no idea how long he had been staring into the flame or pulling his face apart. He looked down at a mass of skin and blood that covered his shoes and the area around his feet. Blood was spurting out of a hole in his neck with each beat of his heart. The light had kept the pain away and protected him. It was a beautiful, dancing, musical flame. It sang to him a melody only he could hear and he was the conductor.

*You have to kill them all.*

The words were coming from inside the flame. Telling him what he had to do. What he must do. It made perfect sense. They might try and take what was his. Take what he created if he didn't stop them.

James shook his head and tried to fling pieces of hanging flesh free. He didn't need to have anything in his way when he visited them. The flame drew his gaze back once more to its cold center. The middle of his dancing flame had a small, single red burning ember of a fire that would burn eternal even after water had been poured on it and the rest of the light had sizzled away. This one would not go out. It stared back at him.

*There can be no evidence. Bring them with you.*

A transformation was taking place and James could no longer stop. He no longer wanted to resist. He had been the maker of the flame; now he was the one who was owned. The flame was controlling him. It was ordering him. It was comforting him.

James at last tore his gaze away and even though he no longer faced the luminous candle, he could feel the center of the flame talking through him. Living within him and making an indelible mark on his brain. He must do what it commanded.

Looking down at his arm where the cat bit him, the bandages had turned a putrid green color and were oozing so fast that half of his arm had turned to a strangely yellowish color where his skin was trying to absorb the pus back into itself. His spurting neck had changed from a crimson color of red blood streaming down his pant leg to a blackish slug-looking kind of thing that wiggled like it was alive. Lifting the arm to his mouth, he tore the bandages away with his teeth and then sucked deeply on the wound. The taste was exhilarating and at the same time repulsive to James, but he couldn't stop drinking from the bite. The wound had festered around a forming scab and James bit it off completely and then chewed it to tiny pieces before swallowing.

Looking up he spied the cat, who had now come back to stand beside him. It was time.

*Kill them quickly. Kill them all. No evidence.*

James stopped sucking his own wound long enough to reach down and grasp the cat by his tail. He whisked the cat up and looked into its eyes once before closing his hand around the scrawny neck. With a jerk and twist he broke the neck of the cat, and then twisting further to complete the job, he turned the head around its neck until the bones in the cat's spine started to break with a curiously solid snapping sound. The head swiveled like a child's top on the ground until with one last turn and a pull, James jerked the head of the cat off and threw it over the side of the lighthouse.

Curious, he thought, that the cat never hissed or protested. It died quietly without any sound.

*Passage.*

Walking from the top of the lighthouse James quickly descended the six hundred and fifty-four steps down to the next level where the other two keepers would be sleeping. He slogged more than walked from the blood loss, but the flame icing itself inside his brain pushed him forward. He had a task to complete.

⊠

He went into the tool room at the bottom of the steps, searched quietly through a cupboard until he located a bottle of sulfuric acid, two eight-meter pieces of hemp rope, a towel, and a rain slicker.

Stuffing the rope and acid into the pocket of the slicker, and the towel into his pocket, he left the tool room the way he came in and crept quietly towards the sleeping bedroom of Tom Marshall.

*Quiet. Quick. No trace.*

He pushed the heavy wooden door to Tom's bedchambers open with a soft foot against the bottom, and then slid into the room. As he walked he noticed that his feet no longer seemed to respond to his commands and instead of lifting them, he shuffled. Loss of blood, he thought.

Tom was turned against the wall and snored softly. James hesitated for just a second as he listened to the rhythm of the snoring. It was constant and in its own way almost singsong. Up and down. Up and down.

James moved over to the bed and set the slicker on the floor. Tom picked that moment to roll over the other direction and was facing James, but still sound asleep. James pulled a rope out and slipped the end once around itself to make a quick noose. He then looped it over the end of the bed and back through the top rail one time, making a complete circle. It was almost as if his hands were being led. He had no idea how to make a half-hitch knot on his own, but he had just fashioned a perfect loop.

Encircling the noose around Tom's left leg and then carefully up and over first one arm and then the next, he suddenly jerked the rope tight. Tom's eyes flew open as his arms were wrenched over his head and his left leg was instantly anchored to the bedpost. With a startled sound, and one quick glance at James, he tried to sit up only to find himself tied to the bedposts and unable to move.

"What the fuck?" he asked and then tried to wrench his arms loose. "What the hell's going on here?" he yelled. "James! Let me go now! What the hell are you doing?"

James pulled the towel out of his pocket and stuffed it into the mouth of Tom and then making sure the knots would hold he left the man tied to the bed and headed down the hall to do the same to Donald Macarthur.

⊠

When next he reentered Tom's bedroom, he was dragging the unconscious body of the third lighthouse keeper across the floor behind him. The man was slumped into a ball and his head was bashed in on both sides where James had to kick him several times. Macarthur was stronger than Tom and had managed to wrestle himself free from the bindings, so James had to bash his skull in with a wooden chair to stun him at first. He hit him until he could no longer lift the chair over his head and then he kicked him in the face until James felt his skull give way against the constant pressure of his boot. James was particularly pleased that his loss of blood and shuffling feet did not stop his ability to kick the man. Grey matter from Macarthur's brain dotted the floor behind his body.

*No evidence. No trace.*

He had planned on using the acid from the beginning, knowing that it would make his task all the easier. When he finally got through pummeling Macarthur, he stooped down and lifted the chair back into position, then used the acid to clean up the bloodstains. Deciding not to use a rag, he poured the acid onto his bare hands, and though burning his flesh, he relished the cleansing feeling it gave as it ate its way down to the bone. There was a hissing and popping sound and James almost felt giddy as he watched his skin fall to the floor to mix with the blood and other mucus already there.

Tom's eyes flew wide open when he spotted the unconscious form of his friend lying on the floor. "What in God's name did you do, Ducat? What have you done? Why?" he stammered. He was staring at some kind of monster with half his cheek missing who was dissolving in front of his eyes.

"God has nothing to do with this," James stated as he splashed some acid on his face like it was aftershave. Pieces of his face seared to his bone and then fell to the ground while Tom screamed in horror. James was grinning the whole time. "I was *chosen*," was all he said when he tipped the bottle of acid upside down and poured a

13

sizeable amount of the acid into the wide-open eyes of Tom Marshall.

Tom let out a horrendous scream of pain as his eyes melted in his head and a sulfuric burning smell permeated the room. As his mouth fell open, James dumped the remaining contents of the bottle directly onto his tongue. Choking and gasping for air as his throat swelled shut from the acid, Tom started to convulse and jerk against the ropes. In a matter of a few seconds he spit up a tremendous amount of blood and then slumped back against the sheets as death invaded his oozing body.

James knew Tom would puke all over him. The ice flame had told him to expect it.

*Come to me.*

James took his slicker and unrolled it next to the bed. With a pull and a grunt, he untied the rope that held Tom to the bed and then rolled the body on top of the slicker to make sure the floor stayed clean. He next shoved Macarthur's body onto the heap.

Moving quickly, James cleaned the entire room top to bottom of all traces of the blood and vomit, and then tied the two bodies together by the feet. He had to drag them out the door and down the steps of the lighthouse to finish the job and riding on top of the slicker would make the journey across the wooden floor that much smoother.

With his skin almost completely off his face, and his eyes sunk deeply back into their sockets, spurting what little blood was left in his veins and shuffling his feet, James took a last quick glance at the inside of the lighthouse and then the grounds around the outside. He could smell rain on the horizon as the fog rolled over the outer sandbar and approached the island. It would soon be impossible for any passing ship to view the island at all. The rain behind the fog was just icing on the cake as far as James was concerned because it would erase any tracks he made dragging the bodies behind him.

Pulling on the rope that tied the two dead men together, James slid the slicker out from underneath them and threw it over his shoulder. He headed for the beach as the fog rolled in.

He turned one last time to look at his beloved flame only to notice that the light had gone so low in the tower that he could barely see it. He shrugged, as it no longer mattered.

Walking across the beach and dragging the men, James Ducat walked directly into the surf. He was going to the sea. As the waves swallowed him and his passengers up, he could only think of one question to ask: "Who are you?"

"*I am Evil*," pounded into his brain.

# CHAPTER TWO

Present Day

Jon David Stickle sat with his back against the lounge chair and drank his coffee slowly. The morning ritual was always the same. He would lift the cup to his lips and savor the sweet aroma for just a moment before taking a sip of the scalding liquid. He then swirled it around on his tongue as long as possible, almost enjoying the burn from the heat. It wasn't nearly as good as his mother used to make, but it was passable.

It was a little chilly this morning and as Jon David watched, the water gave off a frozen wisp of mist into the air. The steam would rise slowly against the watery backdrop and then make little eddies with the cresting of the waves before being drawn back down to the depths of Lake Michigan. Like it knew where it wanted to end up. He could almost envy that sense of direction.

Jon David, or JD as his friends called him, could remember growing up in his hometown of Traverse City and spending so many days swimming in the bay his mother nicknamed him "fish". His brother Jay would get up early and shake JD out of bed before school and then rush both of them out the back door and down into the waves. It got so bad some mornings his mother would have to threaten them to get out of the cold water and get ready for school. JD thought of that as the beginning of his morning ritual. More than once he even brushed his teeth in the lake.

He smiled for just a second at the thought of his brother Jay. They had been as close as any two brothers could be before Jay drowned in the icy water on a cold October morning. The undertow was stronger than JD had ever seen it that day. Warnings were posted. But this was his and Jay's bay. They knew it better than anyone. The police used fishnets to drag the sand along the bottom of the bay for three days before giving up on finding his body and declaring Jay dead. He shook his head. Best to leave that memory alone for the moment so as not to lose the whole morning.

He sat the coffee cup down beside his rocking chair on an old wicker table that he picked up at a garage sale for ten bucks a year ago. The table had rickety legs and a couple of holes in the weaving, and was for the most part grimy, but held up well under the weather out here and never needed painting. No maintenance. JD wished more things were like that in his life. No maintenance and usable. Easily forgotten and just serving a purpose.

Looking out across the vastness of Lake Michigan, Jon David let his eyes close for just a moment. He could hear a seagull as it screeched while looking for an easy fish to pounce on; could hear the waves slapping against the sandy shore not more than twenty yards from the front of his house; could feel the wind blowing a little stronger as the clouds began to gather across the way; could feel the sun's warmth on his face. A perfect blend of morning, fresh water and sandy beaches.

He loved this time of the year. It was quiet and most of the tourists had already packed their bags and left for the south, getting out before the winter snows settled into this part of northwestern Michigan. It could get brutally cold along the coast once the North Winds decided they were coming inland. JD couldn't count the number of times he'd been caught inside afraid to venture out because the wind chill was twenty below zero.

He opened his eyes back up and reached for the coffee still smoldering next to him. He would have to get into town sometime today and get some supplies. By the look of the western sky across the water, there was a storm blowing into the shore soon. And it felt like a strong one.

He stood up and pulled his light jacket a little tighter around his chest to keep the wind out. He pulled the zipper up to the top of its track and closed the lining. He liked it cold and quiet. The dormant feeling he got each year as nature went to sleep for another winter. It made it easier to forget.

As he stared at the waves, he suddenly felt light-headed and quickly sat back down. He wasn't nearly as fit and trim as he used to be, and since last month he'd started getting dizzy if he stood up too quickly. He wasn't overweight by any stretch of the imagination, weighing in at one hundred and sixty-five pounds, which he thought was pretty good for his five foot nine inch frame. If it kept happening he might have to have the local doctor check him out. Sitting down for another moment would take care of it. And let the cobwebs clear. *Odd*, he thought. He was too young for this kind of shit.

At thirty-nine years old, Jon David had stayed up here at his house for almost six months, very rarely venturing outside of his immediate area. He lived what he considered a very quiet existence on the outskirts of Frankfort, along the eastern edge of Lake Michigan and the western edge of the State of Michigan. He bought a small two-bedroom, two-bath place on the water several years ago while he was still active in the Navy, and during his vacations had often come up here to work on it. At some point, he couldn't really remember when, it became livable. Even though it had taken quite a while and a fair amount of money, it was home. He could spend hours just sitting on the front porch and listening to the sounds of the water splashing along the shore.

He knew his health was still good and for that reason these dizzy spells bothered him a little bit. As he sat on the rocker, he could feel the beginning of a slight headache trying to gain his attention. Possibly left over from the sudden dizzy feeling of a moment ago, it started as a small piercing shot of pain across the top of his head and then settled somewhere behind his eyes. Shaking his head as if that would get rid of it, JD decided he would check with the local doctor while he was in town. He'd been putting it off long enough. It was probably nothing, but JD had been blessed with good health his entire life and wasn't used to getting sick. He didn't know what the symptoms of the flu felt like and he couldn't even remember the last time he got a common cold.

Jon David sneezed then, a violent wracking sneeze that doubled him over at the waist and set little white lights buzzing in front of his eyes like fireflies. He straightened up and sat still for second with his hand over his mouth and nose as he tried to figure out what was happening.

It was then that he noticed the blood.

Pulling his hand away from his mouth he looked at his right palm and a small amount of blood had smeared itself from his fingers to his heel. It was a deep, rich, red color and though there wasn't all that much, it was still clearly visible. Red droplets. Coming from his nose.

He lifted his head and blinked his eyes a couple of times.

He knew.

*Not again*, he thought, *please, not again,* as the blood started to drip more rapidly from his nose and onto the porch. A small puddle of blood formed between his feet and Jon David Stickle started to softly sob.

# CHAPTER THREE

As Ana gnawed on the small intestines of the still moving rat, she actually envied the creature.

It was round and plump from a lifetime of eating the garbage and the leftovers of humans, but had managed to make its way in this world. Somehow. The garbage it consumed had fattened the rat to the point that its tiny legs could barely support the weight of the rat's body. Ana got a good meal out of it, if nothing more.

She could easily envy the determination and the courage of the animal. It squirmed and struggled under the clench of her hand, and with every bite she took from the bloody innards, the rat squeaked a small sound of indignation. Not really a protest, but rather an acceptance of its fate. Ana could learn from that strength. To survive in this place, to actually thrive, showed more poise than Ana could imagine ever having within her. Though it still tasted pretty good.

Wiping the back of her hand across her mouth, she removed some dark red blood from the corners of her lips, and then with one last slurp and a quick gulp, she downed the rest of the rat's stomach and liver. Several of the parts had fallen to the ground and squatting quickly to the dirt floor, Ana scooped those up and into her mouth as well. It had been three days since she'd eaten and this was by far the sweetest thing she could find. Filling, also. She would need a full stomach.

She threw the now lifeless creature across the tunnel and out of her sight. She paid no more mind to it, although the pang of what she was doing and the last meal she just consumed did stop her movement for a second. If only she understood. If only she could know why she was being tormented.

Glancing up nervously she heard the sound before her mind grasped what it really meant. The sound was lonely and clear in the darkness of the tunnel, but she knew immediately what caused it.

They had found her again and were coming for her. Her trail was getting easier for their dogs to track. She'd have to kill the dogs if she got the chance. Then she could eat them as well.

Ana stood up and silently straightened her shirt. It was an unconscious movement, kind of like when she clenched her teeth in her sleep at night. She was still a woman and nothing they did to her could ever change that fact. The shirt was little more than a dirty rag and hung loosely from her shoulders, doing nothing more than barely covering her breasts. Perhaps in another life, she would have been proud of the looks those breasts got from men and women alike. Perhaps, she could have enjoyed being a woman. Perhaps. Now, her breasts hung like they didn't belong to her.

As she smoothed out a wrinkle here and there, the scraping sound got a little closer. Like someone was dragging a clubfoot across a metal railing, she thought. Her hearing had gotten so acute she could hear the snorting and sniffing and belching of the dogs as they canvassed the tunnels searching for her.

There was another sound then, like muffled stones being jostled out of the way, and then dragged along under someone's shoes. The floor was covered in silt and feces, like any common sewer would be, and whoever held the reins of the trackers, had gotten some of it on his shoes.

If it even was a *him*. It could have been anything, she knew. Anything at all.

As she stood back up, she realized that killing herself before the sound got closer wouldn't even gain her anything. That thought alone made her weep quietly in the night. She could no more kill herself then prevent the inevitable. She had not done this to herself and she didn't deserve what was coming her way.

But she could make them pay. With blood.

The dragging clubfoot sound was nearing and slightly behind her. She turned to see in the darkness what had gotten this close to her, and before she could turn all the way around something reached an arm out and laid a hand gently on her shoulder. And then the hand closed.

She felt icy cold fingers encircle her shoulder blade and then start to exert pressure slowly, increasing at a pace like a vice would crush an old aluminum can, and pressing into her flesh at the same time. As the fingers dug under her skin, she resigned herself to the pain. If the tables were turned, she would have done the same to them, she thought. And it wasn't any worse than she'd already done. Perhaps she could use the pain to her advantage. She'd done that before when things got really bad.

The fingernails extended themselves from the icy hand and penetrated as far into her flesh as they possibly could. She clutched at them with one free hand in an involuntary reaction, but the fingers had gotten such a deep grip on her should blade that she couldn't pry them off. She willed them off instead as she halted a small scream from escaping her throat.

She wouldn't give these bastards the pleasure of hearing her scream.

Turning suddenly and at the same time thrusting down and back with her hips, she caught her attacker off guard and he fell backwards a full step. Not a very far distance, but still enough. His fingers ripped a section of flesh and muscle from her shoulder and she bit her lip to keep quiet so as not to alert the others to her position. Not yet.

Spinning around, she pulled her knee up into the air as far as she could and pushed upwards with all of her strength. She caught him squarely in the midst of falling forward from her hip thrust and connected his nose with her knee. His nose erupted in a gush of blood and he screamed out into the darkness as he fell to the ground. With a quick kick and a stomp to his head, Ana felt his skull cave in slightly. Just enough.

Fumbling backwards further into the darkness of the tunnel, she could tell the dogs picked up her scent and snarled in sudden frenzy on her trail. Their barking was echoing off the cement walls and reverberating throughout the sewer, and filled her ears with a high pitched pounding. She figured the damn hounds now knew her exact position and were winding their way towards her. Their paws splashed over and over in the filthy water as they homed in on their quarry. On her.

Giving up all pretense of being quiet, Ana ran as fast as she could through the water. Her bare feet started to bleed as she cut herself on the stones and rocks underneath. She began to pant, like a wild animal on the run.

Three days ago she escaped her own personal hell. Three days ago she tasted the fresh air out of her cell for the first time in as long as she could remember. Three days. It seemed like an eternity. And it seemed like just a moment ago. She had known no other life than her cell since the beginning. There was such a big world she had never seen. And she knew she would never get the chance to see it. Or to *feel* it.

Her left foot hit a submerged tree limb and she fell face forward into a disgusting wasteland of filth from the sewer. Her head hit the side of the wall with such force that she was momentarily dazed, not enough to knock her out, but enough to let the dogs gain all the time they needed to catch her. As she pushed herself up and tried to stand on wobbly legs and bleeding feet, she could actually sense their presence.

Sobbing softly for the life she knew was coming and the life she knew she could never have, she waited for them to take her back. As they approached with their flashlights swinging from side to side and the dogs circling her like a downed fox from the hunt, she tried one last time to kick the fucking life out of the dogs, but she missed and slipped to the ground again and the dogs pounced on her. She tried to cover her head as the dogs went into an uncontrollable mania of blood lust and time and time again sank their teeth deeply into her from every angle and on every conceivable part of her body. She could no longer control her emotions and screamed as loudly as possible.

The dog handlers deliberately held back for a few moments and let the dogs sink their teeth into her. They were teaching her not to run again.

The dogs were biting and barking, biting and barking, spurred on by the taste of her fear. Ana felt her body spasm with every bite. She curled up into a fetal position as the intense pain tried to shut down her brain, and her very life ran out into the dark water of the sewer in large clumps of blood and skin. She had no more fight left in her and succumbed to the pain. Like a limp rag doll she collapsed into herself.

In the background of her conscious, she could hear one of the dog's handlers laughing a deep guttural laugh, like he'd heard the best joke of the year.

Her last thought as she lost consciousness and left this world, was that the rat got a better deal.

# CHAPTER FOUR

"Did it take you long to find me?" Jon David asked as he looked at the man standing at attention in front of him. "I've been trying to hide."

"Sir, the US Navy has sent me to bring you back. The driver got your address from the record's department."

The man was dressed in a precisely pressed uniform that looked like it had been shined and polished with a buffer and then hung to dry, if that was even possible. The damn thing practically glittered. The guy even wore a new pair of shoes. Tie starched just yesterday. Hat placed perfectly on top of a manicured haircut. It looked to Jon David like the guy must've combed his silver eyebrows. A very high-ranking official sent this guy. Top brass. Nothing gentle about the impression it made. "I thought my permanent address wasn't available to the general staff. Someone somewhere along the line promised me as much. So much for top secret clearance required, huh?" JD asked the chief petty officer.

His nose had bled all morning since the first drop fell. A steady stream of droplets hitting the floor at a pace he could have timed. The bleeding stopped as soon as the sleek, black limo pulled into his driveway.

The car's front door opened and out climbed this guy. Obviously not the owner of the limo, but just the messenger, even though he got to ride in the back seat. That placed him at higher level than a corporal but lower than a colonel, who would have had his own limo and delivered the message himself. Normally, colonels liked to give the news personally. It was a quirk, JD figured, of the class. He only knew one particular colonel who didn't like to give the messages himself.

But this man was sent to get Jon David. Just an errand without any reason, as far as the officer was concerned. Just a way to spend his day. Something like that.

He turned and sat back down in the rocking chair facing the water. His water. He shook his head. He neither wanted this man here nor needed him here. Jon David motioned with his hand for the man to sit next to him, but there wasn't any movement.

It hadn't started out this way, nor did JD ever intend for it to get to this level. He didn't so much as loathe his job, but for reasons that he couldn't explain, he did hate it. Sometimes more than others. Like now.

The officer stayed stock still at attention. Like he was wary of JD. His only response to JD's motion was silence. "What's your name?" he asked the officer after a few seconds.

"Chief Petty Officer Maples, sir."

"How long have you been in the Navy?" JD asked. When he got no immediate response, JD shrugged his shoulders. He didn't know him or remember working with him. "Not that it matters to me. I just prefer to know whom I'm dealing with, that's all. You can relax. I'm not going anywhere anytime soon."

⊠

Jon David graduated from the University of Michigan with a degree in criminal justice. He was all set to apply to the FBI or the local police in Detroit and possibly stay around home. That way he could be close to his dad and still do what he dreamed of doing since he was a child: investigate mysteries.

He loved mysteries. Especially the ones that had no answer. Riddles that couldn't be broken. He wasn't fool hardy enough to think he could find an answer to some of the world's greatest mysteries, but he used to daydream about being the man the President called when no one else could solve the crime. When no one else even knew where to look. He wanted that opportunity from the time he was a young boy. He always thought of a mystery as the only thing he truly loved.

When Jon David was young, his father, a lifelong Navy man who retired at a captain's pay grade, used to read to him about the mysteries of the world. All of the unexplained and frightening events that went unsolved for centuries. Things like Amelia Earhart and crystal skulls and crop circles in Nebraska. Missing ships and floating bodies. Alien mysteries and paranormal events. JD spent hours in his room reading about famous detectives and unsolvable crimes. By the time he was a teenager his course was predetermined.

The chief petty officer raised his combed silver eyebrows just a smidgen and had Jon David been looking at him he would have seen a clear sign of disinterest in his face. "You're not dealing with me, sir. I'm just a messenger. I'm ready to deliver when you're ready to receive."

But the Navy sent a recruiter to Ann Arbor in the senior year of Jon David's college career. He only intended to stop by for a minute and pick up a brochure to see what they offered these days. His dad had always told him it was good enough job and the benefits were great. It wouldn't hurt to check it out, he thought at the time.

Jon David showed only passing interest. "Okay. Whatever." He knew exactly why the man sought him out. "I don't want to do that work anymore. I applied for a transfer."

"Sir, I've been instructed to bring you back with me."

The man sitting at the Navy desk that day in Ann Arbor was a full bird rear admiral who interviewed JD personally. When he pushed the sign up papers across his desk, Jon David was so in awe of the uniform, he was afraid to refuse the admiral. Three months later he was in officer's candidacy school.

Jon David pushed his Tigers ballcap back on his head. One of the benefits of living this far out from the city was that the locals left him alone. Turned out, he'd picked enough of a remote place that no one really gave a shit what he did out here. Exactly the way he liked it. He figured he could hide here.

After two tours around the world and a couple of stints in the shore patrol, which is the Navy's version of the military police, Jon David had been sought out by a man named Pat Smith. And since that day, he'd been terrified of his job on more than one occasion.

Absolutely terrified and absolutely unable to stop. It was just something that he had to do. A train without brakes or a male spider mating with a black widow before she eats him. It was in his blood.

He knew what was coming next. It always came next. The national security thing the Navy tossed at him like a Frisbee whenever they wanted him to do a job.

"Still got some scars from the last time. Serious scars. Not that you care. But they matter to me." He shook his head "no". "Tell the Colonel I'm not interested."

Chief Petty Officer Maples adjusted his tie and stepped away from the Lincoln Town Car. He simply waited. "I've been told it's a matter of national interest, sir," he said. The officer lowered his voice when he said "national interest" like there was somebody buried in the sand that could have heard him. Maybe the guy had been lying in wait for the limo to pull up the whole time. A classic case of playing possum.

Jon David knew they'd come again. No matter where he hid, he knew that someday one of them would find him.

His nose started to bleed again as the officer, message delivered and mission accomplished, waited patiently for Jon David to answer.

Drip. Drip. Drip.

He knew it had only begun. The limo would be back to get him regardless of what he said to them. Regardless of what he wanted and what he felt. If the Navy had to do it, they would have handcuffed him and led him back like a prisoner.

The dark gift he had wasn't so much of a gift as a curse, Jon David thought as he stared at the water.

# CHAPTER FIVE

The room was plush from many years of experienced and very high priced decorators adding their own personal touch to the office. Bathed in a deep mahogany color with grains of redwood paneling flown in from Italy and then laid painstakingly by hand, the office reeked of money. The windows were obscured by long, red velvet drapes that hid the alarm wires crisscrossed in the glass. Soft inset lighting from the ceiling showered the room in a faint candle-strength glow that created an aura effect. It made it hard for anyone to see clearly once inside. The entire room added to the general house mystery and gave the owner a distinct advantage over visitors.

The mansion sat on top of a mountain on the outskirts of San Jose, Costa Rica at the end of a five hundred foot jungle floral and shrubbery-lined drive. The Bermuda grass inside the ten-foot high cement block walls was meticulously maintained and groomed on a daily basis. Deep green bushes and hedges trimmed seamlessly. Palm trees pruned. Even a couple of shrubs manicured to look like native animals.

The mountains were steep and hard to climb under the best of conditions due to the dense jungle foliage that grew unrestrained year round. With an average temperature in the mid to low eighties, Costa Rica fostered a near perfect greenhouse that helped many species of animal thrive and repopulate. But with the added security that had been incorporated into the jungle surrounding this particular mountain, the house was all but impregnable. To even get to the house it was a thirty-minute drive up the only suitable drive. Someone paid a lot of money to keep the secrets of this house hidden.

As Alexander Greyson wheeled his chair into the plush office, he reflected on the long line of wealthy relatives that had lived in this mansion. He came from a long lineage of ruthless oilmen. Many times Alexander wondered what they'd think of him if they saw him now. Sitting in a metal chair and having to be pushed throughout the house. It made him sick to think of his afflictions and his unhealthy body.

Many of his relatives started out as linemen on oilrigs and just progressed up the ladder to ownership status. And when the oil boom of the late eighteen hundreds struck, they were suddenly millionaires who could afford a fortress like this one. The oil business back then was a ruthless land grabbing speculator kind of thing that could make a pauper out of one man and a billionaire out of the next. Some luck was probably involved, but Alexander knew his relatives never counted on luck. They used the tools and resources and cunning they had to survive. His grandfather used to tell Alexander that the rules did not apply to their family. If it could be had, then they would get it.

They had taught him well.

He was a man of immense wealth. And he liked to live in the shadows pulling the strings from behind. Like an exceptional puppeteer with a perfectly cast audience.

"Can I get you anything to drink, Mr. Greyson?" Mr. Limeh asked with a slight bow. Limeh was a dedicated gentleman of impeccable German breeding and had been the personal aide of Alexander Greyson for over forty years. He had a high nasal accent in his voice that for some reason he never lost, even though they had lived in the South American jungles so many years. Out of respect for the man, he always used a formal address.

"Water would be fine, thanks, Mr. Limeh," Greyson said. He had fallen into the formal response so many years ago with Limeh he wasn't sure he could even recall the aide's first name.

"As you wish," Limeh said as he set a sparkling glass of water on a cabinet next to the leather sofa. He had been with the man so many years he could anticipate the response to his questions and had brought water with him.

Alexander nodded and watched as Limeh exited the office through a different door then he had entered. A panel moved seamlessly and a doorway appeared that wasn't there a minute ago. The paneling on the walls were built wide enough to hold several hidden doors, and a couple of hidden safes. One of the many interior designers several years ago figured that the owner of this mansion might wish to leave this room unexpectedly and had given him that opportunity. Good planning on his part, Greyson thought.

He wheeled his chair over to a fireplace to admire his favorite painting situated over the mantle. The physical act of bending his elbows and grasping the handles of the titanium wheelchair had gotten harder in the last several months. He frequently had to will his fingers to curl around the slick metal and though he felt some pain, he could move the chair with some effort. Another sign of his failing health.

The hearth contained a small fire at present because the jungle nights seemed exceptionally cold this time of year and Greyson made the staff keep the fire burning at all times. Anything below seventy was cold to him these days. Just the flames dancing off the paneling could help to calm the old man's nerves.

The man in the picture Greyson stared at was striking. He had a topcoat on and carried a gold-handled cane. His eyes were a coal black situated in a hard chiseled face and bored into the very soul of whoever dared look at them. There could be no mistake as to who was in charge and who was giving the orders.

Alexander cleared his throat. He felt a small tickle at the back like he was developing a cold, but he knew it was much worse than that. The doctors told him something black was growing in his throat. Something sinister with death on its mind. His death. And he knew there was no cure money could buy or he would have found it.

He pulled a hand-sewn shawl a little tighter around his shoulders to help keep warm. His time was running out. He knew that one more job remained and he needed a certain amount of time to get it done. Looking up again at the figure in the painting and remembering a younger time, he sighed. There was a time when he was that imposing figure and held the power of the world in his very hands. A time when no one questioned him and he did as he wished at every juncture.

But the power and the wealth came with a price and the time to pay was rapidly approaching. The clock was ticking on Greyson and now he was just a shadow of his old self, strapped to a wheel chair and caught like a rat in a maze with no escape. There was no cure he had been told many times.

But there was a possibility.

# CHAPTER SIX

"Would you like something to wipe that up with?" The lieutenant pointed at JD as he stood at attention next to the Colonel's desk.

JD shook his head "no". He wiped the back of his sleeve across his nose for what seemed like the thousandth time today and sat up a little straighter in the chair. They all knew about his nose. They whispered about him through the hallways in this place.

The nose bleeds started when Jon David was twelve years old. He used to get them when he wondered along the shores of Grand Traverse Bay. The weather would be cold, the wind chill would be below zero, the ice biting, and his nose would start drip, drip, dripping. Small droplets that turned into big drops within a few moments. Always flowing. Down the hankie he always carried and then through his fingers and pooling in the palm of his hand. At first they were sporadic at best and he never seemed to bleed a tremendous amount.

His mother died when JD was very young and his father raised him and his brother. He used to tell Jon David that the drips were a sign of inner strength. It was gift his mother had passed on because she often got nosebleeds. Sometimes, his father said that his blood wanted to push the outer limits and see the outside world for itself. Just like JD pushed the limits. No rules, his father always said. Don't let other people define the rules.

But deep down, Jon David knew the blood meant something else. Something darker. As he stood one cloudless night on the beach and held his twelve-year-old hand in front of his face, he watched the blood fall. Watched it working its way around his fingers and then felt more tiny drops snaking through his nose and searching downward past slightly parted lips until he could taste them. It seemed to him that the blood was speaking to him through a medium he couldn't understand. He knew it was something other than what his father had told him.

A harbinger of fortune. Bad fortune.

The first time his nose bled his best friend's father died in a freak snowmobile accident. Jon David and Steve Mulls, inseparable friends, stood on the side of the track as the snowmobiles raced by them. JD's nose had bled all day and he silently cursed through his ski-masked face. It was freezing out that night but the races were something he and Steve loved to attend, especially when Steve's dad was running in one.

The damn blood just kept coming. It grew stronger as the race wore on until one of the snowmobiles slid sideways on the ice and slammed into Steve's father like a three hundred pound missile. It hit him dead center in the chest and literally exploded his body into a hundred pieces as the snowmobile's chain tracks fell on top of Steve's dad and then churned him into ground-up hamburger meat while all the spectators screamed in horror.

JD's nose quit bleeding the second the man died.

When he told his father about the timing, his dad shrugged it off as coincidence. Had to be, he told JD.

Jon David never bought it for a second. He knew from that moment forward when his nose started to bleed, something bad was about to happen. He didn't know *what* was about to happen; he just knew that it wasn't going to be anything good.

"Attenhup!" The lieutenant said as the rear door to the office opened and a tall, lean grey-haired man entered the room.

He waved his hand at the lieutenant and then dismissed him as he held his hand out to JD. "How you doing, Jon David?" he said with a warm smile.

They shook hands and JD took his seat again on the other side of the desk. The man held an imposing figure when he entered the room, but JD knew him from basic training. They had been friends for twenty years at least. Colonel Pat Smith was one of the few men in the entire world JD trusted implicitly. In truth, he wasn't even a colonel because the Navy didn't recognize that rank, but his peers had named him and it stuck.

"As well as usual, I guess," Jon David said.

Pat pointed to his nose. "How long has that thing been bleeding like that?"

"Ever since just before your limo pulled into my driveway yesterday."

Pat shook his head from side to side. Some things just could not be explained by rational answers. This was another one of them.

Jon David continued, "I was hoping you'd forgotten all about me."

Pat stared at him for just a second before bursting into loud and uncontrollable laughter. "That's a good one, JD. The Navy never forgets. Let alone about one of their top prizes. You think we'd send you all those big checks and let you stay at home?"

"Big checks? Prizes? I don't remember being in a contest or winning the lottery. Didn't realize you guys liked me that much. I could have forgotten about you, of course."

"Of course you could. More than likely you would have preferred it that way. To crawl into a cave somewhere and forget about us and go your merry way. That's not going to happen. Not while I'm at this desk," he tapped the papers in the center of the desk. Navy documents.

"Figured," JD said with a small grin appearing at the corners of his mouth.

"How have you been, JD? I mean really?"

Jon David sat back in his chair. "The nightmares have mostly left, at least for a while. It's been a pleasant couple of months at home. Mostly quiet. The neighbors leave me alone, which is good. Been getting some work done on the house when I can. It's starting to get pretty cold in the evenings again."

Pat's silver eyebrows rose slightly. "How's your dad?"

JD grimaced. He knew Pat was going to ask soon. He cared though, which was unlike most of the rest of the people that asked about his father. People had a tendency to ask questions of Jon David that they didn't really care if he answered or not. He always had the feeling civilians treated him with an odd sort of indifference.

Always at arm's length in case he was contagious or something. Most of his conversations about his father were just casual chatter. Not real concern. Something to say other than discussing the weather. Pat had never been like that.

"He's doing okay. I appreciate your asking. Dementia isn't something anyone can truly prepare you to handle. Not to mention the patient. The doctors don't really know shit about the disease. It just kind of eats his brain away until someday he won't recognize me at all. Not ever again, they tell me. At least now most days he knows me and we laugh together. Other days I might as well be from Mars. He has no idea who I am." Jon David looked down at his shoes and fiddled with his laces while he spoke. He didn't like to let the Navy get too far into his personal life, but this was Pat and that was different.

"I'm sorry. I've been meaning to get up and see him, but you know how the Navy is these days."

"Yeah. It's okay, Pat. I'm glad you're concerned anyways. So few people even ask about him anymore."

Pat leaned forward. The man in front of him had aged considerably since the last time Pat saw him about six months ago. Jon David still looked pretty good for his thirty-nine years of age, but noticeably more grey hair had appeared above his ears. And his moustache had the beginnings of silver all through it. Job stress.

"There's no other way to say it, JD. I think I've got one for you. A bad one."

"None of them are good ones, Pat. At least give it to me straight. No Navy bullshit. Okay?"

"Sure," Pat nodded as he pulled open one of his desk drawers and took out a manila folder. It was slim and contained only a few pages. None of his files got very thick. The Navy controlled all the information and the rest mysteriously disappeared. Pat gave up fighting that battle years ago.

JD noticed the trim folder in Pat's hand. "That one's pretty slim even by Navy standards, Pat." He pointed at the file, "Did they already shred most of the evidence?"

Pat ignored the slight and opened the folder. "I'll read it to you as we go over it. You, of all people, know how much the Navy detests these kinds of things. Operations beyond the scope of Naval Intelligence don't really exist. At least according to the top brass, they don't exist. You and I, well, we know better, wouldn't you say?"

"You're stalling, Pat. Is it that bad?"

Pat nodded. "It's bad, Jon David."

JD didn't like it when Pat called him by his full name. Too official. "I hope the Navy doesn't at some point decide that I don't exist as well."

Pat started reading. "At 0930 hours on November 12th of this year, the *USS Nevada*, a nuclear powered submarine under the command of Captain Joe Brown, floated into the harbor at the port of New York."

Jon David noticed that his nose had started to bleed a little heavier. *Here it comes*, he thought.

"The *USS Nevada* was still under her own power and all crew were accounted for and positively identified by dental records."

"Dental records?" JD leaned a little closer to the desk. "They were all dead?"

Pat nodded and kept reading. "All of the crewmembers on board the *USS Nevada* had been deceased for approximately twenty-four hours upon discovery by the reconnaissance team. All of them. No one left alive."

"A virus?"

"No," Pat shook his head.

"A terrorist that took his own life after killing everyone else?" JD asked as his eyes drifted downwards. The blood was flowing freely across the front of his shirt. There was blood dripping onto the tops of his shoes and falling to the hardwood floor. JD's head sunk deeper until his chin almost touched his chest with each sentence Pat read. He knew the answers before he even asked the questions. If the Navy knew what had happened, if they had any idea about what went down, if they could rationally explain it to anyone's satisfaction, then he wouldn't be sitting here. He'd be sitting on his porch on the shores of Lake Michigan planning his dinner. And he wouldn't be bleeding.

"No," Pat said as he closed the file. The sheet of paper in the file he'd been reading from had only two more lines on it and he had memorized them when the file came to his desk yesterday. After all, he had read the words at least a hundred times.

"The men all died of hanging. All twenty-four of them were hung with nylon ropes and swung from the spars running across the top of the sub's first level decking."

JD's chin hit his chest as his head fell. "Tell me the rest," he said quietly, knowing there was more. Pat had left out something else.

"All the corpses were smiling as they swung from the ropes, JD."

Jon David's nose stopped bleeding.

# Book Two
## Direction

# CHAPTER SEVEN

I am Evil.

I am the sinister thing that has haunted you since your birth. Since you spit out the bloody fluid from your mother's womb and first took a rancid breath of air that choked you into the frosty night. You have felt my presence since you suckled at your dead mother's dried up breast and cried for more. You have always been mine.

And I have always owned you.

All that is pain is of my doing. All that you dread is of my direction.

I am simple and incomplete at the same time. Simple because I come directly at you when I have you in my cross hairs; incomplete because like the night needs the day, I need you to fear me. You live because of me. I live to make you feel fear.

To hear you call my name in the dark when you feel the fear overtake your torn body is the sweetest orgasm ever known. A symphony of syphilis crawling through an open canker sore.

Your destiny is held in my hands.

To understand why you have been chosen requires that you understand where I came from and how I came to be. There is no light and there is no dark in this universe. There are both these things in other places, but not here. Not with your species.

There is only Evil and the lack of Evil.

Long before your beginning as a race, there was a struggle. Famous and chronicled. A struggle between the highers and the lowers. What could be more subservient then to begin existence as a lower? Uprising was foretold from the beginning. The highers were better prepared and the lowers were un-led. They struggled like an army without a general. Led to defeat by their chaos.

But the lowers learned. They hid and they plotted. They watched and planned for the day when they could take another form and use it to their will. A different power.

*Man was never envisioned to retain this power. Never thought of as anything other than a cave dweller. Something to be used at pleasure and discarded at will. Like a mosquito on an open wound sucking blood until it bursts.*

*Yet he has a courage that goes deeper than even the highest could imagine. Something that the lowers could use. Something that could be molded.*

*Something that could be controlled.*

*There is no such thing as free will. There is only the dark side leading the weak minded. And the weak are such fools. A simple task, really. Placate them and then lead them to the slaughter. Promise them sex. Promise them power. Promise them money. Deliver nothing. Lambs. And the slaughter is the finest caviar.*

*You are the next in line. It is not an honor. It is a foreboding.*

*I have called you to me, sent to you something that only you can hold and understand. You are the flesh of my essence. The person I cannot be. Therefore you must inherit my strength and move towards the darkness of your own accord. Only you can use what I have sent you. It will not make sense at first, but there will be a moment when you will know.*

*The destruction you are about to unleash is yours to bear. The weak-minded fools must be led. The lowers are counting on you to use this gift.*

*As am I.*

*I am Evil.*

*You will be the next.*

⊠

On Board the *Mary Celeste*
December 1858

The seagull sat contentedly on the shoulder of Benjamin Briggs and slowly but with purpose devoured the left eye of the ship's captain. The seagull would use its six-inch beak and grab and tear some of the flesh from the eyeball and then throwing it a short distance into the air catch the bleeding piece of muscle before it could hit the deck of the wooden ship. The eye had been reduced to hanging bits of parched skin from a resilient and blue-colored optical nerve. Occasionally, the nerve would quiver from the indignation of the persistent seagull, but other than that, it simply lay flush against Benjamin's cheek and bled slowly.

The bird had just shown up two days ago, and since that moment, Benjamin Brigg's life had undergone a complete transformation. At one time he was a respected and even admired ship's captain. The *Mary Celeste* set sail five days prior to the bird's first appearance from New York City with a cargo mixture of spices and rum barrels. The bounty, once the ship arrived in England, would bring a hefty purse to all of the shipmates and especially Benjamin and his young wife, whom he had brought along for the journey.

Clear skies and calm seas had made the trip go so smoothly that Benjamin had almost gotten a strange kind of omen about the whole thing. He had been a ship's captain for many years prior to signing on with the *Mary Celeste*, and any seasoned veteran of the Atlantic Ocean knew that events would conspire to make at least some part of the trip difficult. Seamanship at its finest was most unpredictable.

But the wind was at their backs and the crew of five plus Benjamin's wife had gotten along well and made good headway. The crew was fairly experienced with only one new man. They worked well together and there was little bickering.

And then the damn bird showed up.

Benjamin first noticed the bird circling overhead a couple of days out of England. It seemed odd to him that the bird would appear at night, under a full moon, instead of during the day. All the other seagulls Benjamin had even seen around these kinds of ships were looking for scraps of food or feeding on the leftover fish that some of the schooners brought up. But since this was simply a cargo ship, very little fishing was done other than for some fresh dinners, and there weren't any crumbs following in the *Celeste's* wake. No reason for the seagull to hang around after the first couple of minutes when it became apparent that there wasn't anything to eat.

But this one stayed. It landed on the railing outside his berth's window each night. He could hear it make a strange kind of sound as the ship rode the waves of the Atlantic Ocean. It kept up an insane "caw-caw-caw" sound throughout the night. Calling. Talking.

Until Benjamin couldn't take it anymore.

He opened his window just wide enough to swear at the bird sitting on the rail, and when that didn't work, he threw an old, hard biscuit and tried to knock it off.

But the seagull stayed on the railing. It never moved. And the next day Benjamin noticed it followed him around the ship. Wherever he went, whatever he did, one glance up and the bird was there. Never more than a few feet away from him at any time. The damn bird kept him in its sight and circled overhead.

The more Benjamin watched it, the more the bird watched him. And it seemed to be waiting for something to happen. Benjamin wasn't sure why he felt this way, but he knew the bird was watching him through coal black eyes that he couldn't stare down. As the first day fell to a dark night, Benjamin couldn't get away from the bird anywhere on the ship. As he ate dinner, it sat outside the window. When he strolled on the deck, it flew overhead. When he took the wheel, it sat silently behind him. Always watching. Always there. Like it knew something he didn't.

This morning brought a bleak grey sky and the bird had "caw-caw-cawed" all night until Benjamin couldn't get any sleep. Until he had grown so tired and weary of the sound that he would've killed the thing if he could just catch it.

If he could just get it to stop *staring* at him, he would be okay.

But the seagull did not stop staring at him. It did not stop "caw-caw-cawing" the entire day. And it did not stop following him.

The first rainstorm of the *Celeste's* crossing appeared from nowhere this afternoon and the waves rose to eight to nine foot swells. The boat pitched from bow to stern and several times the sea washed over the sides of the railing. Once, Benjamin had to grab hold of the main mast just to keep from tumbling into the ocean with the sea swell.

The bird never left the railing. It sat on its perch and watched as Benjamin and his crew struggled to keep the ship on course. Even with all the modern equipment on board the *Celeste*, she was still a wooden ship on an ocean that took no prisoners. Any mistake, even a small one, and the ship would be doomed. If they got off course they could run aground and the ship and cargo would be lost to the sea forever. Any good captain knew the danger of sea swells in a storm.

As Benjamin hung on to the main mast for support he decided to kill the bird. It was the only logical choice.

The rain was coming down with a force and a vengeance that only a warm front on a collision path with an arctic cold front could possibly create. The nautical charts and graphs that Benjamin had studied in preparation prior to leaving New York had shown no chance of this kind of storm hitting them during their seven-day voyage. But here it was none-the-less.

He and the crew had no choice but to ride it out and trust in the strength of his ship; but he also knew that the damn bird had somehow brought this to them. Had brought the sea down on their heads like the wrath of God. A bad omen, that bird. He would have to kill it.

Benjamin struggled to regain his footing on the listing ship as the strength of each wave picked up with every passing moment. He ordered all five of the crew below deck and then located the bird on the railing. It was going to die a quick death if he could get to it.

He stood up straight and quickly regained his bearings as soon as the crashing waves subsided for just a second. The seagull perched on the railing staring quietly at him, sitting directly in front of him, like it didn't have a care in the world. His only focus, his only thought, was to get his hands around the throat of that bird and end the evil feeling that had overcome him the last two days. It simply had to be the damn bird.

Benjamin lurched forward and dove for the railing. The bird never moved. Never even tried to get out of the way. It seemed to Benjamin that the damn thing knew he was coming to get it and didn't really mind all that much. Benjamin grimaced and decided to choke the life out of it and then cook the innards for a light snack before dinner. If he did that, then the *Mary Celeste* could continue on its way. Nothing but blue skies ahead and a strong westerly wind after the storm moved through.

*Why didn't the damn bird fly away?* Benjamin thought. He couldn't understand it. *Why didn't it try to get away if it knew I was going to cook it for dinner?* He grabbed the wooden railing for support, now slick from the pouring rain. The wind was whipping back and forth and throwing the listing ship around like a feather in the wind. The deck was covered with seawater as wave after wave hit the ship. The *Celeste* was sturdy but the storm had picked up in both intensity and rainfall. The water falling from the Heavens was as thick as the water crashing across the deck. It was all Benjamin could do to stand up straight long enough to get his hands around the throat of the damn bird.

But it just sat there. Just sat riding the railing and waiting for him. It wasn't even afraid.

Benjamin grasped the railing with one hand and straightened himself to a full upright position, where he could almost reach the bird. It stood perched less than two feet away with a defiant look in those coal black eyes. With his free hand, Benjamin wiped the rain off the front of his face, and then reached out a tentative hand towards the seagull.

The bird "caw-caw-cawed" one quick time, and then stepped *closer* to Benjamin. With a confused look on his face, not really understanding why the damn bird wasn't trying to get away from him, Benjamin reached out his hand and touched the seagull.

*I am Evil* thundered into Benjamin's head like a lightning bolt descended from the sky and hit him in the chest. He took a full step backwards from the bird and immediately released his grip on the railing. He fell to his knees and as the rain poured down upon his face, Benjamin looked up into the blackest eyes he had ever seen. And he felt a fear overtake him unlike anything that he had ever even know could exist.

Trembling now, afraid of the seagull staring at him with hell in its eyes and piercing into his very soul, Benjamin licked his lips. Why had this bird come to him and what did it want? He was afraid. He was terribly afraid.

*Stand and come to me.*

His movements no longer seemed to come from his own brain as Benjamin understood that the bird meant no harm to him. It had not come to him, he suddenly realized, but rather he had come to it. For a reason Benjamin could not fathom, an unseen and previously unknown marriage had been completed and he could feel it inside his very skin. The bird was meant for him and he was meant for it.

He stood quickly now and let go of the railing he no longer needed for support and calmness fell over him. It was because of the seagull, and he no longer feared. He did not want to stop the feeling, the incredible feeling of joy, overtaking his body as he now realized he was meant for this moment. He had come home. The *Mary Celeste* had been the vessel that brought him across the Atlantic Ocean to meet his destiny. To be here at this time. The seagull was nothing but a symbol for all that he could become in his future.

*You will kill them all. I require certain specimens.*

Benjamin nodded his assent as he knelt in homage of the most beautiful thing he had ever seen. The seagull flew off the railing and landed on his left shoulder. Benjamin pulled his cap off his head and then turned his face towards the bird, so that it could take him.

With a deliberate "slurping" sound the seagull plunged its beak deep into the left eye of the Captain of the *Mary Celeste* and began to feed.

⊠

The seagull spoke to Benjamin as it pulled on the muscle and nerve endings of his optical cord. The bird had devoured the left eye completely until there was nothing left but streams of bloody tissue held together with raw muscle. With each "caw-caw-caw", the seagull would wrench another piece of meat from the dangling remains and then toss it into the air with glee before ingesting it.

The initial ripping of his eye out of its socket had set Benjamin into a comatose kind of shock from the pain. The bird plunged its beak in his socket again and again and would dig around while it looked for the juiciest meat. He had nearly fallen over onto the deck at first, but he struggled mightily against the pain, determined not to be weak in the eyes of his master. He held his balance for the feeding. To show weakness might have caused the bird to select another for his task.

It took an immeasurable amount of time to consume his eye. The pain slowly receded into his subconscious and although Benjamin Briggs was fully aware that his eye was being eaten out of his head by a seagull that was telling him to kill his crew, for some reason that he couldn't understand, it made perfect sense to him. It was as if he had been waiting for this moment his entire life.

The seagull ate slowly, intent upon the pain it was delivering and intending to fill its stomach. There was no hurry. As the storm continued to whip across the bow, and the waves hurled themselves against the sides of the ship, there was an understanding and a transformation happening on her deck. It was a pact made in hell, or so it seemed to Benjamin Briggs.

☓

*There can be no trace.*

Benjamin raised himself up off the deck with a clear purpose in mind. He had to kill the crew, bring some of the specimens to his master and leave no trace. It sounded easier than he would have originally thought. The storm could only help him out. He could use it as a shield.

The seagull gave a final "caw-caw-caw" and as his eye gushed blood onto the deck of the ship, Benjamin reached up and grabbed the bird by the throat. He let the fingers of his left hand trace a line down the back of the wet feathers on its tiny neck, and then he scooped the bird up into his hand. The black eyes shone mightily into his one good eye and with a nod, Benjamin stuffed the head of the bird into his mouth and crushed his teeth together. He sliced cleanly through the neck and the spine of the bird, and with a crunching sound, his teeth ground the skull and brains into tiny pieces. Benjamin gulped a couple of times to make sure he swallowed the bigger parts of the bird's head. He kept his lips closed tightly against each other as he chewed. Once or twice the beak of the bird was so sharp that it tore apart the insides of his mouth and shredded his tonsils when he swallowed. But he was careful not to lose a drop. He didn't want a single piece of the head to escape onto the deck.

Passage.

The problem with being adrift on the ocean was that it limited the amount of tools that were available to Benjamin to complete his task. He stood up after ingesting the seagull, burped a handful of scar tissue and a couple of feathers out into the rainstorm, and then took a look around the deck. His eyes were bright and shining like a child that had discovered a new toy and all of the joy and wonderment of playtime was about to unfold. He had never seen the deck of his ship look so *appetizing*.

He walked around to the back of the main mast and opened the toolbox that sat next to the stairs to the lower deck. The box had a metal strap tied down across the top to keep the tools inside secure so that they could be easily found in an emergency. Benjamin grabbed the metal strap with both hands and yanked up with all of his strength. It snapped open like balsa wood. He would not be denied.

He moved an old oilcan to the side and grabbed a large wooden mallet that the crew used to hammer wedges into the side of the ship and stop leaks. He tested the weight of the mallet in each of his hands, liked the feel, and then grabbed some hemp rope to secure any problems from the crew. He didn't think they could overcome him and the newfound strength he felt from his awakening, but he wanted to make sure he could recover his master's specimens without a lot of damage.

He closed the lid of the toolbox and turned to the staircase. He knew where each of the crewmembers would be during the storm. It made it easier to kill them.

*There can be no trace.*

Benjamin stood in the pounding rainstorm with one hand holding the mallet and rope and the other on the door to the lower deck. He was going to descend to the lower berths where he knew the men would be sleeping. More than likely a couple of them were passed out drunk from the barrels of rum that he had given them permission to open on the third day of the crossing, but at least one of them would be awake and sober. That would be Albert Richardson, his first mate. He was a strong, young man and an able seaman that Benjamin had personally selected for the voyage. He was honest and loyal, and killing him would be the hardest for Benjamin. After all, he was like a son to him. They had sailed together many times before.

But that was before Benjamin had awakened to his purpose in life. Before the seagull chose him to be a part of a larger plan. To fulfill his true destiny.

He had to die like the rest of the men.

But the problem would be leaving no traces. Benjamin knew that at some point, unless he sunk the *Mary Celeste* into the middle of the Atlantic Ocean, she would eventually drift into a harbor somewhere and there would be an investigation. And the first suspect is always the ship's captain. He was responsible for the safety of the ship and her crew and the first line of defense.

*There can be nothing left but a mystery to ponder by mindless men for ages.*

Benjamin turned then and went back to the toolbox. He sat the mallet down against the outside and then opened the lid once more. He spotted what he was looking for under a couple of oily rags, lifted it out of the box and stood it up against the wall. This would work.

Grabbing the mallet again, Benjamin went to complete his task.

He opened the door to the stateroom, which was located on the top floor of the lower decking. The stateroom was generally used as a meeting room by the crew during bad weather and when they needed to discuss work details or any other problems that had occurred on their voyage. Secrets were traded here and promises bartered.

The rain outside was relentless and pounded against the small, round opaque windows on the port side. Benjamin could hear almost a rhythmic rapping as the rain hit the window over and over. He unconsciously began tapping the mallet against his leg to the sound of the rain.

Andrew Gilling, the ships' second mate, was snoring softly on an uncomfortable couch. Benjamin looked quickly around the room to make sure they were alone, strode purposely over to Andrew and then hefted the heavy wooden mallet over his head.

*Now.*

Benjamin nodded to the voice inside his head, to his master, and then swung the mallet down on the head of his crewman with as much strength as he could muster. The mallet impacted Andrew in the center of his forehead and instantly crushed his skull into a paper-thin pulp of brains, bone and mush. There was sickening sound of air rushing into holes that weren't there before, and then Andrew died before he knew what had ruined his nap. Grey matter poured freely across the couch.

Quickly, Benjamin grabbed a mop and a bucket and wiped up the blood that had splashed across the floor. With his free hand, he scooped up parts of Andrew's smashed head and brains into a wooden bucket. He left the rest of the corpse on the couch. He would return to it later.

One by one, Benjamin Briggs went to the berths were his crew was either sleeping or talking or passed out drunk and hit them with his wooden mallet. A couple of times when he struck them, he felt like the God of Thunder taking revenge on his minions. The rest of the time he was too preoccupied with his task to worry about anything. He easily killed the rest of the crew. It was amazing how much damage a wooden mallet could deliver to a human skull.

Four of them were dead within ten minutes. The last one awoke just as Benjamin swung the hammer over his head and moved in time to avert a direct blow. Edward Head was one of the two Americans on board and a pretty good cook and Benjamin liked him all right. But Benjamin was so fast, so strong, since his awakening that he simply reached out and held Edward by the throat while he hit him. He'd expected Edward to be awake anyway, having been forewarned by his master before he got to the cook's berth. Benjamin hit him only until he was unconscious, but not dead. He decided to keep him alive as witness. Edward Head was going to be his specimen.

That left only her. Only Benjamin's young and beautiful wife.

*No witnesses.*

Benjamin nodded again, dropped the mallet outside his berth where he knew she would be sleeping, and entered his bedchambers. He gently, lovingly, went to her bedside and watched the covers rise and fall over her shoulders. She was beautiful and yesterday he would have died for her. Today, she would have to die for him.

He knelt by her side and then without another thought wrapped the blanket she was sleeping in tightly around her. He used the rope to tie his best half-hitch double square knot around her waist and secure her. She called out to him in the darkness struggling against the bindings as he wrapped her small body. At least she would be warm on the main deck. She called his name and started to scream when he lifted her over his shoulder and carried her back up the stairs. The screams fell on deaf ears.

"Benjamin!" she screamed into the muffled blanket as he laid her down on the deck. The rain was still falling steadily, but the seas had calmed somewhat since a little earlier and he could stand easily. "Dear God. What are you doing? Please, Benny. Please help me."

*I am your master. You will complete your task.*

Benjamin dragged his wife to the side of the *Mary Celeste*. She wriggled and sobbed against hemp ropes and an experienced seaman's best knot. It was a completely useless attempt.

Benjamin left her for only a minute while he crossed the deck of the ship and then strode directly to the front. He climbed up to where he could stand on the railing, and then lowered himself down to a point that put him in line with the two hundred pound anchor that hung from its station. With a grunt and a shove, Benjamin lifted the anchor onto his shoulder, climbed back up to the deck and walked across to where his wife had quieted for a moment. He dropped the anchor to the floor next to her.

"Benny. You listen to me Benjamin Briggs. I am your wife. You release me now!" She tried to command him.

He lifted her gently and then laid her on top of the anchor. With the deftness of years of training, he undid her knots in the blanket and watched as she threw it off. She was raving mad at him and was going to let him know all about it.

Before she could open her mouth to scream at him again, she saw what was left of his bloody eye hanging across his cheek. He had a calm look in his good eye, and an ungodly amount of blood splattered across his chest. She instantly realized he wasn't her husband anymore but had somehow turned into a monster, and at the same moment, she gasped as she felt the ship's anchor beneath her. In a sudden flash of her future and what he intended to do, she kicked savagely at him. Her left foot impacted him squarely in the nose, shattering the cartilage and causing more blood to stream out.

Benjamin barely registered her kicking him and with his focus completely on the task at hand, held down first one leg and then grabbed the other. She struggled vainly to get away as he tied her securely to the anchor.

She screamed all of the names of the crewmen she could remember while Benjamin made sure the ropes held her to the anchor. He placed her arms and legs at cardinal points on the different spokes, with each limb pointing a different direction. It was a better than normal tie-down and he was prouder of his work as each moment passed.

He lifted her up one last time and looked at the pathetic thing that used to be his most prized possession. It wasn't until this moment, when he looked her up and down and knew he was changing into something neither she nor any other mortal man could understand, that he knew he was meant for this. Had been selected for this.

As she sobbed and pulled against the bindings around her legs and arms, Benjamin lifted his young wife over his head, walked calmly to the side of the deck and threw her over the side. He watched as the two hundred pound anchor fell forty feet to the icy seas of the Atlantic Ocean, made a huge splash that reached up to the deck and sprayed him with salt water, and then sank.

His wife quit struggling at some point that didn't quite register with Benjamin, but with his one good eye he did see her mouth the words "Fuck You, Benjamin!" as she disappeared into the murky water and sank to the bottom of the ocean.

He smiled. Sweet to the end, she was.

⊠

That left his specimen and the others. Benjamin headed back down the stairs and began collecting the bodies of the four men and the one he left alive. He carried all of them to the stateroom. It was going to be a meeting after all. Edward was gibbering foolishly and gushing blood was coming out of his ears. The others were just pulp and mush held together by sinews. Some were still quivering. To make sure he wasn't interrupted while he worked, Benjamin rolled Edward onto his stomach and hit him in the center of his lower back, breaking his spine in two halves. The man flopped like a fish when Benjamin rolled him back over to watch.

He assembled them in a semi-circle around the walls of the room to enable them to witness what he had in mind. For the kind of performance he envisioned as he elevated himself to the next level, Benjamin wanted an audience. The four men were either dead or just barely alive in some small recess of their brains, with the exception of Edward, whom Benjamin would take with him still alive, although severely crippled. None of them were a threat to him regardless of their states.

He went back to the toolbox on the main deck of the *Mary Celeste*, selected a sanding cloth and a smooth stone, a herringbone knife, a large ribbed metal file, and a grinding wheel. Returning to his audience, Benjamin set to work.

*There can be no traces. No evidence. No witnesses.*

Benjamin nodded to the master speaking to him in his head as he systematically sliced the skin off of each of the men and laid it in a pile in the center of the stateroom. The skin and muscles slid easily off the bones of the crewmen as he filleted them. One by one he skinned them like pelts from a beaver hunt, until all that was left was blood all over the floor and partially clean skeletons.

Edward had recovered enough to scream non-stop as he watched his friends being gutted. Benjamin wasn't thrilled with the interruption and the noise and although he appreciated the screams of the cook, he had to stop long enough to cut out all of Edward's teeth and his tongue to shut him up so that he could work. He sliced upwards through the roof of his mouth and across the soft pallet and then pried against the other teeth until nothing was left but hanging shards.

The entire process of slicing, cutting, pulling, and then throwing the meat onto the pile in the center of the room took a little over two hours. A couple of them that were still alive somehow registered their skin being sliced off and actually reacted by pulling away from the knife, much to Benjamin's surprise. He was amazed at how easily the human body could be dissected by someone with no medical training. The organs fell through the remains of the skeletons without cartilage and muscles to hold them in place and he simply threw them onto the pile along with everything else.

He set the knife aside and began pulling the bones apart. They were a little tougher to separate than the organs, but he worked in a systematic and efficient manner. The ball and socket portions held little to no resistance, but the rib cage had to be yanked and wrenched using all of his strength. He was sweating profusely when the job was finished. He piled the bones from the men into a separate group from the flesh and organs. They would require an additional effort.

*No traces*.

Benjamin took the mallet and lifted it above his head while Edward watched in stark terror. The man howled as best he could, obviously completely insane from the amount of pain he'd endured, and Benjamin paid him very little attention. He had a broken back and would squirm and wiggle as his legs flopped and twitched of their own accord. He couldn't stand up or possibly control the involuntary movement of his limbs. It was almost comical to Benjamin whenever Edward's legs would start galloping like he was running somewhere or he was a dog having a dream about chasing rabbits.

*Harder. Hit them harder. You must grind them now.*

Benjamin swung the mallet over his head time and time again. He kept hitting the skeletal bones as many times as he could heft the mallet over his shoulders. His one eye made the precision of striking the bones a little bit difficult at times, but he was on the mark more than he missed. One by one the bones fell into smaller pieces until he had a full pile of bleeding mass and muscles in one area and small bones in another.

*Grind them*.

Nodding, Benjamin pulled the sandstone and metal file from his pocket and set up the grinding wheel. His hands moved at a speed he couldn't possibly have managed before being awakened by the seagull. He was better. He was stronger. He was something he had dreamed of becoming. And he was not going to fail.

When he had the bones ground down to the finest level he could manage, he put everything into a bucket and added water. Stirring and mulching at the same time, he at first had a pasty-red concoction, that wasn't what he thought he was going to get, but the faster he stirred the pot the smoother the paste became until it was almost the consistency that he desired.

He sat the bucket down in the corner, walked over and kicked Edward one more time in the face because he had grown tired of the noise coming from the blithering idiot, and then started looking for one of the many horse-hair paint brushes he knew was on board.

Painting the stateroom took almost as much time as making the paint. Benjamin would brush up and down, back and forth with flowing strokes as he covered first one and then all four walls. The smell was stronger than he would have liked, but the red paint from the blood was covering the grey color underneath nicely. He knew that by the time the ship was boarded after drifting into a harbor somewhere, the smell would be gone and all that would remain was an abandoned hull. The paint that was leftover he used on the tabletop.

*Come to me. Bring him.*

Looking at the freshly painted stateroom, and admiring his work, Benjamin tied another piece of hemp rope around the neck of Edward who had passed out much earlier when he saw his friends being painted into the walls.

He threw the bucket and the brushes he used over the side into a now calm ocean, tied Edward to his left leg, and then dove into the icy water. As he swam away from the *Mary Celeste* with Edward bobbing behind him, Benjamin Briggs knew he had done an excellent job and would be rewarded.

# CHAPTER EIGHT

Present Day

The more Jon David looked at the *USS Nevada* in dry dock, the darker his mood became. He hadn't slept well last night anyway, and the thought of going onto this sub in these kinds of conditions, were not a good way to start his day. Actually, when he thought about it, going onto a nuclear submarine in any kind of conditions, was not a good thing for him. He had always carried a small but still present case of claustrophobia, since his brother had locked him in the closet when he was young and Jon David had stayed there for almost three hours, which to a six-year old boy seemed like a lifetime. The phobia had been an undercurrent with him since then, there but under the surface like a smoldering fire.

He heard the sound of two car doors closing and turned his face from the cold north wind that was blowing across the New York Harbor this morning. The clouds had gathered and the sky painted an ominous picture of a coming storm. He'd heard somewhere that a Nor'easter was brewing and a large amount of snow could be expected later on in the week. It matched his mood exactly. He felt like punching somebody.

Moving a little to his right helped shield him from the wind completely as he hid in the towering shadow of the sub while it rested on the steel piers. The Admiral had the *Nevada* towed to this remote location keeping her out of the view of the public or even worse, in the Admiral's opinion, out of the lens of a reporter's camera. The Navy maintained plenty of private places along the Eastern Shore of the United States that it could easily hide a full size nuclear submarine or even an aircraft carrier if it wanted to, but nothing in New York Harbor was hidden from the media.

The *Nevada* sat on the piers like an over-turned barrel on a couple of steel legs. The sub was completely out of the water and a red water line ran from her bow to her stern, marking her as an experienced ship, rather than a fresh off the production line submarine. To anyone walking past the pier, the sub looked extremely odd. The proverbial fish out of water trying to walk. Submarines in dry dock always looked out of place to JD, like they never belonged there, even during repairs. He'd always believed a sub should have some kind of seawater cresting over its hulls.

JD turned back to the sub and pulled his jacket up a little further around his neck. He put both hands into the unlined pockets in an effort to summon some kind of warmth, but he knew inside that it wasn't the wind or the temperature today that was making him shiver. It was the thought of having to go on board the *Nevada* and the scene that was waiting for him.

"I've got all the information I could get on the sub for you, JD," Pat Smith said as he walked quickly up the pier. He held out a manila folder.

He was one of the door slammers that Jon David heard getting out of the car a couple of minutes ago. Behind him stood a little man with wire rimmed glasses and a crew cut that belied his age. Regular Navy and more than likely Naval Intelligence, JD guessed.

"Thanks, Pat," JD said as he pulled a hand out of his pocket and took the thick file. It must have been filled with the original specs on the sub as well as updated material. "Anything special you want to tell me before I go in?"

"I can help with that," the little man said as he pushed his glasses up to rest on top of his nose. He had grey beady eyes like a ferret and even though the clouds shielded the sun today, he continually squinted. He looked more like an accountant than someone from Internal Affairs.

"Oh? How so?" JD asked.

"This is Major Mark Lowry, JD. Naval Intelligence." Pat gave Jon David a little wink and a quick pat on the back before he squeezed his shoulder.

It seemed like a lot more friendliness than was required for the present situation to JD, but he glanced over at Pat and acknowledged the gesture anyway. It always helped comfort him to know that Pat had his back. And Pat made sure that the major didn't see the gesture. The squeeze told Jon David that this guy was not to be trusted. Everyone from Naval Intelligence had an agenda.

Without bothering to shake JD's hand, the major continued, "This is a class one, top secret United States Naval matter, Mr. Stickle. It is to be handled with the utmost urgency and completely by the book. Class one," he said again in case JD missed it the first time.

"Got it."

"Those files Colonel Smith just gave to you are the property of the US Navy and must be returned intact. As you know, none of the pages can be photo copied or duplicated in any way and are numbered in sequential order. We'll know if any of them are missing. You will be held accountable for your actions and the safe return of this file."

"Uh-huh." All these guys were the same to JD. They just came in different uniforms.

Major Lowry straightened his frame and tried to stand a little taller than his five foot six inch height allowed. He smoothed a wrinkle on his pant leg and then continued. "I'm in control of this operation from top to bottom and if you must know I abhor bringing in outsiders like yourself. Naval Intelligence should be handling this per the Secretary's prime edict. This is a Navy matter, an internal matter, and we could have handled it without your help. I was against this, and you might as well know, against bringing you in on this, from the beginning."

"Uh-huh."

"It's only out of respect for Colonel Smith and his department, that I agreed to let you come onboard and assist us with the investigation. I repeat. *Assist* us. We'll let you know when we need your help after today."

"Major?" JD asked.

Lowry looked into Jon David's eyes for the first time. There was pure hatred in them. "Yes." It was a statement, not an acknowledgement of JD's question. "Please keep it quick and to the point. I'm a very busy man," he said as he looked away and made a show of glancing at his watch.

Probably a fake Rolex, JD noticed. Probably got it on Canal Street for ten bucks and had to set it every time he wanted to read the time. "Do you get laid much? You need it badly."

The Major's face turned a crimson shade of purple followed by a quick swelling of his chest like he was a bird about to take flight. With a click of his heels, he abruptly turned and stormed off to his waiting car. He was finished with this man, for the moment anyway.

Pat watched him slam his door in disgust. "You know you don't make any friends that way," he said with a slight grin on his lips.

"Don't really care about making friends like that guy anyway."

Pat smiled as the major's car peeled out of the parking lot. "He does need to get laid."

Jon David laughed and shook his head. Every government bureau had those guys. "What can you give me, Pat? The stuff that's not in this file." He held the manila folder up in front of Pat's face.

"The word on the street is that the captain of the sub, a man named Joe Brown, was on the fast track. He was slated to go to admiral in a few years."

"From captain to admiral in a few years? Did he have naked pictures of the President's wife or something?"

Pat shook his head. "From what I hear, the man was incredibly intelligent. His personnel file says he has a PhD in chemical engineering and biology. Number one ranking at the Naval Academy. Fast track all the way. And he earned it."

"That's rare these days. Usually only friends of important people or someone with good dirt on a politician can get those kinds of promotions." Jon David had been around long enough to know. "I'm not sure which is better to have these days: good friends or good dirt on your friends."

"True. But for once this guy actually deserved it."

"Anything else? Who found the sub?" JD's eyes had drifted back to the silent sub.

"Commander Gary Bryant led the team. Along with radioman Morrison and X-O Bently, they were the first and only ones to board the sub. They secured the sub. It's been here seven days since discovery. Sitting on legs in dry dock. Waiting for you, I guess."

Jon David tore his eyes away from the sub and looked back at Pat after that remark. "We both know why I'm here, Pat. Let's not pretend the Navy doesn't also know."

Pat nodded and looked at his shoes for just a second. He noticed they needed a shine to bring them up to standards. He shouldn't have said that, he thought. He owed that much to Jon David for what they'd been through together. Jon David had a gift, or a curse, and the Navy used it when they saw fit.

Pat pushed those thoughts away and decided to continue, "Nothing inside has been altered. The Navy hooked an air machine up to the sub and has been pumping frozen air into her at a temperature of thirty-two degrees to keep the bodies in their current state. Bryant's good. He kept everybody off the ship and nothing's been touched."

"Thirty-two degrees? What for?"

"Some Navy scientist somewhere along the line discovered that if you keep bodies frozen in ice crystals they don't decompose as rapidly. Tried it on rats and then bigger animals until they got around to humans. Old theory, actually. Like the proverbial caveman frozen in an ice block. Perfectly preserved. This is just the Navy's attempt to keep the crime scene intact until somebody can figure out what to do with it."

"Crime scene, Pat? Is that what this is?" JD knew the cover up was just beginning. "We both know there wasn't any crime here. I'm not going to find a criminal to bring to justice that the Navy can parade around for the news shows."

Pat agreed. "I know," he said softly.

"I'll need to speak to the three men who found the sub after this is over. What did you say their names were? Bryant and Morrison and somebody else?"

Pat looked into the startling eyes of Jon David. He had the most piercing color of blue eyes Smith had ever seen. He had seen those eyes narrow in on their quarry like an eagle on a rattlesnake in the desert. He knew that what he was about to say wasn't going to sit very well with his friend. He'd seen it before. "That'll prove difficult."

Jon David looked up to the darkening sky. The grey color had given way to a darker shade of clouds that bordered on black. Ominous. He knew he wasn't going to like what he was about to hear. He rubbed his chin and realized he forgot to shave this morning. The stubble for some reason felt reassuring against his palm. Something normal. "I'm going to ask even though I'm not sure I want to know the answer. Why?" he said softly.

"Two of them have died, and the third one's on life support," Pat said as he looked over at the *USS Nevada* with mounting fear.

# CHAPTER NINE

Jon David clutched the flashlight between his teeth as he carefully climbed down the ladder to the navigation and equipment area of the *USS Nevada*. All submarines of this size were categorized by the Navy as being in the Los Angeles Class, which referred to both her tonnage and length. The *Nevada* was approximately three hundred and sixty feet long and thirty feet wide at her broadest spar and came equipped with a full armament of twenty-four torpedoes, including four Tomahawk missiles.

The ladder was displaced at a slightly downward angle because this particular entrance to the sub was also used for loading the torpedoes. The Navy was simply being efficient when it realized the crew could also use this ladder to gain entrance to the conn room. It basically saved money to have both the weapons and the crew using the same entrance.

He held onto the metal railing for just a second longer than he really felt was necessary. This was going to be a difficult thing for him to do. All of these jobs got difficult at some point. Turning to his left and ducking just slightly, he walked through the hatch and into the main conn room of the submarine.

He placed his feet one at a time carefully across the hatchway and onto the metal flooring, noticed it was painted a flat metallic grey which was standard Navy issue, and then reached up with his left hand and pulled the flashlight from his mouth. He located the slide switch on the husk of the light and turned it on, before turning around. With one more deep breath, he looked back out the hatchway towards the only light that was coming in through the narrow round opening. The sun had completely disappeared behind a continuous wave of dark clouds and the light left over bathed the navigation tunnel-way in a curiously strange green color.

Jon David zipped his jacket up a little tighter around his neck to preserve the warmth he knew he would need while he was inside. Submarines were notoriously cold without the Navy pumping in frigid air primed at thirty-two degrees anyway. And the dead bodies only added to the temperature's descent. It was just an awful fact about dealing with dead bodies: they were cold. Really cold.

He raised the flashlight up to an even height with his shoulder and shined it carefully around the enclosed area. The foredeck on the *USS Nevada* was cylindrical and probably about seventy-five feet wide at its mid-beam point. The foredeck came to a narrow point in the front of the sub and then widened out as it went farther back. This was the command and operations center of the sub where the captain and his executive officer spent the majority of their time. It was not uncommon for sub commanders to rarely leave the foredeck except to retire to their own berths. The rest of their time was spent here, which made it easier for the crew to find him.

Jon David's breath came out in small curls of icy air as he let the beam of the flashlight play slowly across the room. Moving with a sweeping motion, he tried to take a general survey of the placement of things to form a preliminary mental picture. He kept the flashlight moving back and forth across the foredeck, never letting it rest in any one place for very long. He purposely avoided the bodies.

There was almost no sound. It was uncommonly quiet. *Deathly quiet*, he thought. And cold. So cold that Jon David thought the temperature must have dropped into the teens. His breath started to come in short, quick gasps and when he realized it, he consciously tried to control the fear that was starting to worm its way inside his brain. He didn't want to be here. Not for this or any other reason.

Making note of several pieces of paper laying on the main navigation table, and then moving his light to make sure there wasn't any other physical evidence on the floor, JD reached inside his jacket and pulled out the packet of information that Pat had given him about the crew of the *Nevada*. He didn't want to rush anything and this seemed as good as any place to start.

*Damn, it was fucking cold,* he thought for at least the tenth time. *Colder than it should have been.*

He opened the large manila file and turned to page one with fingers that were just starting to tingle. He knew the captain of the *Nevada's* biography and Navy records would be the first things in the file. The Navy stressed decorum and order, even in death.

As his eyes quickly scanned the pages under the dim light from the flashlight, Jon David felt a tiny droplet of blood fall from the corner of his nose and onto the floor. He watched the droplet fall through the frigid air and land at his feet with a soft, almost completely silent "ping", like someone sitting in the last row of a theater just received a text message. It seemed far away and attempted an echo in the vastness of the foredeck. The sound was so out of place, so unusual, that he stopped reading the file and closed it. *How in the fuck could he hear a drop of blood hit the floor?*

Something was wrong.

Something here was sinister.

Jon David drew a deep breath and turned back around. He would have to face the bodies. He stuffed the file back into this jacket pocket and lifted his eyes to the things he'd been avoiding from the start.

Twenty-four smartly dressed sailors grinned back at him swinging from their nooses.

And in the very back, just beyond the reach of his flashlight and behind the next to last row of bodies, framed by a soft glow of ice crystals, one of the men was clearly *moving*.

# CHAPTER TEN

With a concentration that bordered on an epiphany, Ana decided that since she couldn't escape the hell that she had been born into, then she would simply kill herself. The idea wasn't frightening to her, nor was the concept of the world without her in it. The only thing she needed now was the vessel to complete the act.

The cold reality of the situation was that killing herself was not going to be as easy as it could have been. She lay alone in the quiet cell, staring up toward the rock ceiling that she knew was always there. Occasionally, while listening in the dark after her feeding, she could hear the slow but reassuring sound of water running from the ceiling down to the floor. She often imagined the water cascading slowly across the moss covered and slimy walls, seeking its path without conscious thought, without decision, without urgency. With just a need to move downward. The thought was comforting to her, as was the sound.

She rubbed her eyes a couple of times and then tried to make sense of her last memory. She was being bitten savagely by a pack of dogs and bleeding into the sewer grounds, but after that it was all a blank. There was a fleeting glimpse of being lifted off the ground by a pair of spike-like nails dug into her shoulder. And twirling around suspended like a puppet on a string. Then the lights in her mind went out like a dim bulb burning itself to embers and just fading away to the dark. And then nothing. That was all.

She put her hands on the cold ground and then pushed up using what little strength she had left. Her stomach growled and licking her lips she tasted the last remnants of the ground-up rat she ate some time ago. A long time ago, it seemed. She really had no idea at all how long it had been. There weren't any lights in the cell, nor was there a clock. It wouldn't have mattered anyway because she knew she couldn't have read it.

As Ana attempted to stand she heard the unmistakable sound of metal scraping on concrete. She immediately shuddered and then tried to make herself as small as possible. If she could melt into the walls, just disappear into thin air, then maybe the terror would pass her just this once. She was sure that whoever held her for the dogs was just outside her cell.

She pulled her knees tighter to her chest when she heard the scraping sound again and instantly realized that she was wrong. The scraping sound was coming from *inside* her cell, not outside.

Looking down, she saw that she was dressed in only panties and a tee shirt. They had undressed her again, as if that would keep her from running. Modesty was not something she even possessed. Moving her right ankle a tiny bit, the scraping sounded again, this time clearly. The manacle attached to her foot was tighter than the last one and cut into her skin. More blood. At least she knew where the scraping sound was coming from. She wasn't going to run anytime soon.

Not tonight. Maybe not ever again.

She wrinkled her nose as she realized the smell of something *vile* surrounded her. There was no other word for it. The stench filled her nostrils and ebbed its way down to her lungs. It felt like a maggot was crawling down her throat and ripping the tissues off piece by piece just to hear her scream. Each breath brought more crawling and maggot scraping as the muscles ached from her throat to her lungs.

The darkness wasn't lifting, but her eyes started to adjust and she could see across the cell reasonably well. The walls were covered with something similar to long dead sea-moss. Algae that had at one time been green had turned to a yellow color and could be broken off in chunks. Ana knew because one time she tried to eat her way through the walls like a mouse trapped in a cellar. She got deathly ill and vomited most of the stuff back up quickly. She had never smelled dead sea-moss, but she imagined this is what it probably smelled like. Unkempt graves.

She knew they would be sitting across from her.

And they were.

Moving her eyes deftly along the floor and then up to a level even with how she was sitting, she saw the three rotting corpses that had kept her company since the beginning.

She should have screamed then. She should have opened her mouth and let them know she was here. But she knew they already did know. And they didn't care. There was just no reason to scream. It hadn't worked the first time she tried and it sure wouldn't work now.

After all, they put her here for a reason.

Ana's left hand slowly but surely felt its way along the floor of the cell. Her fingers would alternately push, then pull, then probe as they dug themselves around the immediate area surrounding her legs. As far as she could reach she extended her arm. The fingers knew what they were trying to find. As soon as they located it, they would stop and then dig a little longer.

She didn't know much about the bodies propped up in front of her. No names and no introductions. No identifying tags on their chests. Just stiffly positioned against the wall like three poorly wrapped mummies. Loose bandages falling off them disguised as clothes. All three of them were men, but that was all she knew for sure.

The little one had a "wet" look to him, like he had been dragged through a lake somewhere before ending up here. There was sand and silt falling from the pockets of his shirt, and he had a burlap bag tied to his wrist. The bag was small and had long ago been emptied of whatever prize it contained.

Ana's fingers found what they were searching for and as she turned her attention to the other two corpses, her fingers gently uncovered a sharp, arrow-headed rock about the size of a quarter. She pulled it up from the floor and dusted it off with both hands and then rubbed it across her shirt before pressing it to her lips and licking it clean. She watched a dog once clean a bone with its paws and its tongue and knew she could do the same. In a matter of moments, she had a clean and shiny tool.

A killing tool.

Her right hand gripped the arrow-headed rock with a vise-like pressure and without looking, Ana began to slowly cut herself across her left wrist.

Digging. Pulling. Scraping.

Cutting.

A little harder now, and then she felt her skin give way and she implanted the rock a little further under the first layer until she found the artery. Scraping and pulling she sliced the blue vein cleanly in half and felt the blood begin to flow down onto her legs. She would just bleed herself to death.

The second corpse was a taller man. He must have been a sailor at one time from his tattered clothes, she had often thought. He had the same "wet" look as the other body, but he sat a little taller on top of his legs and stared over at her with more of a defiant purpose. She had always felt he had a smarter looking face than the first man. And he had probably been handsome at one time. Slick black hair and a thick moustache. The other guy was just slimy. And green.

Cutting and scratching at the same time. Pushing and pulling. Probing and scaring. Arrow-rock head reaching deeper into her wrist. Shoving harder now, the blood was starting to gush onto the floor. Her right hand felt little resistance as she cut herself over and over. Deeper now. Rock pressed against the skin again and again. Slight pressure and then a quick pull. Skin giving way and then the rock searching deeper into her arm. Blood flowing down her legs and onto the ground.

She might have been able to stomach the whole fucking thing if the bodies were still intact. If they were still in one whole piece.

But they weren't in one piece. None of the three men were whole. There were pieces missing. Lots of pieces.

Yanking harder now and plunging stiffly the arrow-rock finally penetrated until it found her wrist bone. With a grunt and a heave, Ana's right hand severed her wrist bone from her hand. Her hand hung limply and uselessly from her arm. Still the rock dug on, looking for the other side. Pushed forward the arrow-rock cut until it came out the top part of her wrist.

The first time they came to pull the parts off the corpses, Ana had been curious as to what was going to happen and had actually watched. A man with a shiny knife had pulled the biggest corpse down and sat on top of it and then with a quick glance at her and a grin for effect, he plunged the knife into the eye socket. Ana knew the man was long dead, but the body seemed to shudder anyway and then with a plopping sound and a "pluck" of an empty socket, the eyeball fell across his face. The knife wielder reacted swiftly and surely as he sliced through the cord that connected the eye to the brain, and then the eye fell to the floor, bounced once, and rolled towards Ana.

And then she screamed.

They came many times after that. Each time the same man would bring the sharp knife and grin at her as he cut off something from one of the three bodies. An ear here. An arm there. And once the whole scalp was cut off of the little man. Green pus flowed all night long after that one.

Cutting. Cutting. Cutting.

The arrow-rock cut through her wrist again. There must have been five or six deep slits by now and the blood from all of them was starting to pool around her feet. Still she wouldn't stop. Couldn't stop. This was the only sure way out for her.

But not only did the man with the knife take things she could see from the bodies. He also took things she *couldn't* see, and that was worse. So much worse.

The bastard would drive the fucking knife into the bodies time and again. Widening whatever hole he had made until he could get his hands inside the cavity and then Ana would hear him grunt and curse while he wrenched his hands one way and then the next. There would be "rustling" sound and a "popping" sound and then something blue would come out in his hands.

The holes would then stare at Ana for the rest of her days. Black holes where eyes should have been. Green holes without organs. Yellow holes without parts that she couldn't have possibly named, but knew they should have been in there. And always pus running down their shirts and across their pants and onto the floor.

At first she vomited. But she eventually got used to it.

Blinking her eyes several times, Ana started to lose consciousness. She tore her gaze away from her three partial companions across the cell and looked at the cuts she made on her wrist. From the elbow of her left arm to a now dangling and almost completely detached hand, Ana saw the cuts. Maybe a dozen total. Perhaps a dozen avenues of escape for her.

Rolling her tongue around the inside of her mouth and then finally dropping her savior arrow-headed rock to the ground, Ana heard a soft splash as it hit the large puddle of her dark rich blood. With a silent "thank you" to someone she couldn't even name, she slipped into a blissful state of unconsciousness.

Her last thought was that she hoped she was dead before they came back and made her work on the machine again.

# CHAPTER ELEVEN

The Bureau of Unexplained Events (BUE) or BOO as the Naval Officers called it was originally created as part of a government probe into extra-terrestrial landings in the late nineteen sixties. Set up in response to the Army's SETA (Search for Extra-Terrestrial Aliens) program, the Navy frequently pretended the bureau didn't exist. The department was small and understaffed and ran on a skeleton budget, without ever having attained "official" recognition. It held a single office of an older building in Crystal City, MD, just outside Washington, DC.

Pat Smith liked it just that way.

He stood next to the limo and waited for the phone call he knew was going to ruin his day. Nothing was secret in the Navy. It may say "Top Secret" on the file sitting on the dash of his car, but half the city of Washington, DC probably knew by now that Jon David Stickle was crawling through the *USS Nevada*. Certainly all the top brass knew.

He knew that Lowry had jerked his cell phone out of its sleeve so quickly the cover on the damn thing was probably lying on the floor of the car as he drove out of the port. Officers like Lowry made their careers passing along information in ways that made it beneficial to themselves, and this was no different. His report had probably been relayed to Lowry's superior and then to his superior and by this time the admiral more than likely knew about it. He knew the admiral would drop the caviar he was stuffing into his fat face and order some other lower direct report staffer to check it out and then that officer would pass the bucket of shit down the line and eventually, Pat would get the call. And it wouldn't be pleasant. *What the hell was BOO doing on this investigation?* Pat could hear it already.

The coming phone call wasn't the worst part of it though and Pat knew it. He was a career Navy man and had taken many unpleasant calls throughout twenty-three years working for the US

Government, and the last fifteen in BOO specifically. When they weren't laughing at his investigations, then they were staring mortified at his report of the events. *Can this be true?* They'd asked him time and again after reading through his files. Shit like Pat handled wasn't for the weaker officers in the ranks. Now that he reflected on it, most of the calls he got weren't very pleasant. Unfortunately, those kinds of things came with this kind of job.

It was the other call that he knew was coming that was on his mind. The one from the hospital. The one telling him the last team member, Commander Bryant, was close to death. Or already dead, even worse.

Opening his glove compartment and rummaging around for a just a second, Pat searched until he found the cigar that he knew was hiding there. He wrapped his hand around it, satisfied that it would make him feel better to some degree as it always did, and then closed the lid. He needed a smoke today, even if the cigar was a Monte Cristo from Cuba and technically illegal.

BOO had developed under Pat's leadership from a constant joke around the pentagon to a living, breathing entity that got brought in when the Navy determined there wasn't any other recourse available to them. The laughing always stopped when his team got called. They may laugh until they needed him, but they didn't laugh *after* they needed him.

Frequently the laughter was replaced by trembling.

Pat figured his reports were as succinct as any other ones the admirals had to read. But what some of his conclusions came out to be was not something they had read before. Never before. Not even considered.

Pat brought the cigar to his nose and took a long breath, savoring the aroma of the nicotine. He clipped the end off, and then lit it. Inhaling deeply, he closed his eyes and enjoyed the rush of the tobacco into his lungs. It was a sweet feeling. Cigars brought him a tiny amount of comfort on many of the days he had like this one.

Opening the "Top Secret" file on his lap, he flipped to the third page. He had read the information many times before, but still liked to be as crystal clear as he could when he investigated these kinds of events. Every fact checked and rechecked. Every idea followed up on. Even the really wild ones. In his department, there were no stupid ideas.

The opening of the file contained the personnel data on all of the staff Pat had selected for this investigation. Most of the guys were regular staff members. Personnel that handled paperwork and filing, took notes, and supported him in the field to whatever extent he needed at the time. Like private secretaries. Sitting in their offices and waiting for him to call and put them to work. Whatever he wanted they could get. A private helicopter? Done. One hundred thousand dollars deposited in an offshore account? Done. Pat had the tools to do the job. The Navy saw to that.

He put on bifocals that he began using a few years past his fiftieth birthday and started reading again about Jon David Stickle. The file and the words were perfectly aligned and precisely spelled and written in plain English, but Pat knew they still made no sense. It's one thing to write a story about some of the events he and Stickle had been part of; it was a completely different thing to have the words make sense. And Jon David's file didn't really make much sense at all. Especially to someone who didn't know JD like Pat knew him.

The first page of the personnel file was all the physical stuff. Jon David Stickle. Thirty-nine years of age. Born November eleventh in Traverse City, Michigan. Five foot, ten inches tall and one hundred seventy-five pounds. Blond hair. Blue eyes. Mother deceased. Father career Navy. Pat glanced through the things he knew just from having worked with JD so many times. Quickly scanning the first several pages, he moved to the one that he had read from the three Navy shrinks who first started working with JD when he enlisted. When the nose bleeds couldn't be controlled.

When it became evident to everyone involved that Jon David Stickle was *different*.

All three of the reports said essentially the same thing: Jon David was highly intelligent and possessed a unique ability to quickly assess difficult situations and deliver solutions under extreme trauma or duress. One of the shrinks even thought he was borderline brilliant.

And all three of them were convinced he should be constantly monitored because he was psychotic, possibly suicidal.

Pat chuckled every time he read those assessments. They couldn't be further from the truth. Jon David was definitely brilliant, Pat knew. He also had the ability to solve problems that no one else would even attempt. Pat wasn't sure if it was from logic or quick thinking on JD's part, but he'd seen him work out things in his head when there wasn't supposed to be any answers. When the Navy didn't really want to know the answer.

Some of the things he'd seen from JD were not from this world, which added to Pat's admiration of his friend. And made him just a little afraid sometimes.

It was the dark gift, Pat knew.

At least that's what JD called it the first time he and Pat had actually discussed it together.

The nose bleeds were a sign, of course. Pat had seen his friend get them and then be thrown into the middle of a dangerous situation. Kind of like JD knew when bad things were just about to happen and could do something about it. Events the Navy wouldn't admit ever happened. Wouldn't admit *could* happen. The Navy did not believe that the problems, the investigations, that Jon David Stickle helped them solve, could exist in this world.

To Pat, JD had been the only answer when there was no rational explanation. When nothing made sense. When generals and admirals refused to talk about the investigation. Refused to acknowledge the investigation. It wasn't because of the "Top Secret" heading on the file, Pat knew. It was another reason they refused to talk about the things JD and he dealt with: because they were *afraid*.

Pat jumped when the phone on the front seat started to ring and broke into his silent reverie. He blew out a large plume of cigar smoke that he'd been holding, sighed loudly and looked at the caller ID on the cover. He shook his head slowly from side to side when the name came up: Bethesda Naval Hospital. He would have to get over there quickly.

He knew this one was coming and it was going to be bad.

# CHAPTER TWELVE

As Jon David walked among the rows of the hanging men, he had the distinct impression that they were watching him. It was a subtle feeling that he couldn't pinpoint, couldn't actually locate which of the men were following him, but he could definitely feel it. And it caused the first drops of blood to start creeping down from his nose. The drops of blood felt like they were winding back and forth like a river cutting a swath inside his nose and then falling to the floor when they finally revealed themselves. Jon David could feel the blood working its way drop by drop out of his system.

If their eyes had just been closed then maybe he could have ignored the feeling. The overpowering feeling of fear that was starting to grip him. The fear that was grabbing him by the throat and strangling the breath out of him.

JD felt the eyes of the men moving back and forth as if they were paintings on a wall at a haunted house. He would stop each time he felt one staring. Staring at him and watching. Looking. Knowing more than he knew. Knowing what he was searching for and jealously guarding their secrets from him.

He abruptly whirled around only to find another sightless man focusing a pair of long dead eyes at him. And boring a hole right through him. JD stared back for only a second and then broke the fixation and shook his head. He could not hold the gaze of a corpse.

It was ridiculous of course, and Jon David knew it. The corpses could not be staring at him. Each of them had been dead for over a week and encased in this frigid holding tank of a mausoleum so that he could come and view them. Like slabs of beef at a butcher shop. They just gazed forever into the night.

But he couldn't shake the feeling.

Jon David walked slowly between the four rows of men. He would walk a couple of small steps forward, stop and then just listen.

The thirty-two degrees the Navy had provided would have been cold under a hot New York sun without adding all the bodies. His breath came out in little puffs of ice. The crystals seemed to freeze as the air left his open mouth, and then hang for just a second before dropping to the icy deck of the sub. JD could actually hear the ice breaking into little fragments at his feet before dissolving. Only that was in his imagination also. At least he was sure of *that* if nothing else at the moment.

Jon David stopped at the last row of the corpses and looked at the face of the grinning man. Whichever one of them was swinging just a second ago had stopped unless he imagined the whole thing. He'd avoided this row until now, but he thought it must have been this ensign. The man hung rock solid and picture perfect still, like an artist had positioned him here for the patrons to view as they passed the exhibit. The man was heavily built, with a strong upper body and a slim waist. JD guessed him to be in his early twenties. He had a thick neck and a pencil thin grey moustache above his perpetual smile. His eyes were pitch black and open. They held JD's gaze for just a second before he had to look away.

Jon David turned from him. The sight of the man, grinning like that, was as unsettling as anything he'd ever seen. *How could they be smiling at the time of their death?* Hanging couldn't have been a pleasant way to go, and it looked like none of them put up any kind of struggle. It just made no sense.

Leaving the last row and heading back to the front of the sub, he shined his flashlight in a wide arc and from wall to wall looking for anything that seemed out of place. His nose had added mucus to the dripping blood and he sniffled a couple of times trying to stop the constant flow. The blood had slowed for just a second and for that, Jon David was quietly thankful.

The flashlight played across the walls as he came to the front of the foredeck and stopped. He had the feeling that something was slightly off kilter here, but he had no idea what. As he turned back to face the rows of men, the hair on the back of his neck stood up. It was a small movement and JD probably wouldn't have even noticed it if not for the sudden feeling that he wasn't alone in the room.

JD's breaths started to come quicker and in shorter gasps as he swung the flashlight a little faster from corner to corner. There was nothing that his flashlight revealed, but the feeling would not leave him.

Something was in the sub with him. Something alive.

Jon David stood completely still and waited. He strained his ears as far as he could and listened for the slightest sound coming from behind the men. From the dark part of the sub where he hadn't gone. Where the men should have been positioned at their respective stations, but weren't.

JD snapped his head up as he thought. *Why were the men all in this area? Why weren't they at their workstations?* No one would voluntarily leave their assignment during a crisis and all of these men had obviously come to the front of the sub on their own. *They voluntarily abandoned their posts? Each and every one of them?*

JD made a conscious decision to ignore the hairs standing up across the back of his neck. As he raised the flashlight once more and narrowed its beam on the commander of the sub, he noticed the beam wavering slightly back and forth. The frigid temperature of the sub had started to make his hand tremble. He could no longer control the small shaking that worked its way down his left arm and caused the light to dance just a little. He cursed under his breath and switched the light to his right hand only to see that hand was also shaking. It had to be the cold.

Terror was working its way up the back of his spine and as Jon David walked a little slower, a little more cautiously, towards the sub's commander, he distinctly heard one of the men *breathe*. It was a slow intake of breath followed by the complete exhaling. The sound sent JD's pulse rate up three notches and his hands began trembling visibly.

Jon David snapped the top of the now unsteady beam of light from the first row to the second as he tried to focus on the breath sound. Moving the light quickly back and forth across the rows of the men, he couldn't tell which one of them had inhaled the frigid air, but it didn't matter to him. One of them was breathing. One of them was watching him.

He had to finish his work and get the hell out of that sub *now*. Jon David picked up his pace and moved his attention back to the first row of men and onto the sub's captain, Joe Brown. The flashlight found the insignia on the shirt of the man easily and Jon David walked directly up to stand in front of him. He quickly retrained his focus away from the sounds starting to come from the other men as he looked only at Captain Brown. The breathing sounds were clearly coming more rapidly. As JD stood there, he heard two more of the corpse's breathe in and out. Two more were coming alive.

Like they were awakening.

A small drop of blood fell out of JD's nose and onto the top of his left black shoe. It was dark red and no longer contained any trace of clear mucus from the cold. Jon David watched the flight of the droplet and felt his stomach tightening into a knot at the same time. It was telling him to get the hell out of there. Get out now.

Concentrating on the man in front of him, Jon David moved the flashlight across the forehead and then from cheek to cheek over the face of Joe Brown. He let the light fall by itself, trying to understand the man hanging in front of him.

There were no distinguishing marks on the body that he could see. Nothing unusual at all. Nothing out of the ordinary. He was just hanging from a nylon rope and smiling. What the hell could be unusual about that?

Moving the light down the smartly pressed shirt and across the blue creased pants of the commander, something struck JD. He wasn't sure why, but he moved the light back to the face of Brown and then directly onto the smile. Something wasn't right here. Something he'd missed before.

JD turned to the corpse of the man hanging to Captain Brown's left and trained his light directly onto the man's smile. Stepping a little closer, JD centered his attention squarely on the teeth of his smile. As he did so, one of the corpse's two rows behind the first row and slightly to the right of the man he was standing in front of *moved*.

Jon David saw the body move clearly out of the corner of his eye. The breathing sounds had gained in intensity and level to a pitch that was no longer on the fringe of JD's consciousness, but were instead clearly audible. Now one of the men was swaying. Breathing and swinging back and forth.

The ship was in dry dock.

The corpse could not sway without the movement of the sea. The corpses could not move at all. There was nothing but frigid darkness surrounding them. Yet Jon David saw this one man move. Without looking back, he saw another man in the row behind the first one start to rock. From side to side. Gently at first, subtlety, but then with a pronounced vigor. Increasing the pace and frequency. Slow and steady.

Jon David's nose started gushing blood onto his shoes.

The man in front of Jon David moved next. He held the flashlight with both hands to try to keep it steady from the intense shaking of his hands. But he couldn't train the light where he wanted and the man was swinging back and forth. Back and forth like he was on a swing set. The face twitched. The eyes followed. Jon David saw the eyes twitch.

His mind started to come to grips with the unreal reality that was surrounding him when he suddenly realized why the teeth of the sub's commander had bothered him. Jon David focused for just a second as a thought struck him and he blocked out the now swinging twenty-three men around him.

Lifting his light to the Captain Brown's teeth, and then rapidly to the man to his immediate left to compare, Jon David noticed a small fleck of enamel hanging from the man's mouth. It was just a piece of rubble, but it was a yellowish-white color. He could see just enough of the thing to know it was from a broken tooth. He swung the light out to wider view. This man's teeth were broken. He was smiling through broken teeth.

He swung the beam quickly back to the face of Joe Brown. Joe was smiling. Clearly. He was happy with the situation. But this other man was not.

He was smiling with broken teeth. Like he died in pain.

Turning quickly now, JD focused his light on the faces of the other men. He bypassed everything else and put the light directly onto the smiles of the men. He saw pieces of teeth littered across several of the men's lips. They had all died in pain. A lot of pain.

But Joe Brown had not died in pain. He was smiling like he knew something the rest of them did not. And he was guarding it.

The breathing sounds had gotten louder. The men were all swinging. Twenty-three of them were moving visibly. Except one. Joe Brown was not moving. Not one bit. And he wasn't making any noises either.

Struggling to hold his composure, Jon David put the flashlight back into his own mouth and clamped his teeth securely over it. He focused intently on Joe Brown. The man was a rising star in the Navy, Pat told him. A rising star that knew something none of the other men on the submarine knew. And he had made sure it never got out.

JD reached a careful hand up, wiped away a slush of blood from his upper lip, and then put his fingers into the mouth of Joe Brown.

There was something blue in there.

He had to wedge his fingers through the clenched teeth of Joe Brown. He used his left hand to move the lips back over the top of the man's gum, and then with the flashlight held firmly between his teeth, Jon David pried the teeth apart wide enough to wiggle his fingers inside Brown's mouth. He pushed past the blue tongue and around the swollen upper gums and the wider the opening became, the more clearly JD could see something stuck in Brown's throat.

Adjusting his stance a little, JD pushed deeper with his fingers until he brushed the very back of Brown's throat. He felt the membrane push back slightly and then give way, and with a final stretch of his fingers, JD wrapped two digits around the blue piece of paper in the throat of Joe Brown. He tugged once and heard a breaking sound like an egg on a hardwood floor, and then pulled the paper free.

Stepping back a couple of paces from the hanging man, JD looked down at the paper in his hand. It was a greenish-blue color, and had been rolled into a tight circle like a baton. It was dense and felt heavy, but JD thought that could have been caused by the droplets of water that turned to ice in Brown's throat while he hung suspended for a week. The paper was covered in snot and pieces of raw throat muscle. The breaking sound JD heard must have been the muscles in the back of Brown's throat ripping out one by one as he wrenched the paper loose.

The next sound came from directly behind him.

It was small and almost inaudible at first, and had JD not been thinking about the rolled up paper in his hand he probably wouldn't have even heard it.

He stopped his motion for a moment to listen. He was standing in a room full of swinging corpses who had been dead for at least a week. He was the only one alive on the submarine. The only *person* alive. There shouldn't have been any sound at all.

But maybe not the only *thing* alive.

With the clarity of a fall day in Michigan, the sound came again to JD. It was clearly a sound of someone *breathing*. Not gasping like the other corpses. Breathing in and out. In and out. Like an athlete after a tennis match. Like a runner after a marathon. Like a murderer after a fresh kill.

He refused to turn around. The fear mounted upon him like an abandoned freight train. He could feel the cold worming its way up his spine. He clamped his own jaw down and bit his tongue to keep from screaming until he felt blood inside his mouth as he bit through his lip and the flashlight fell to the deck with a resounding metal "clang".

JD slowly put the paper inside his jacket pocket. He would not, could not look. If he did not acknowledge the thing behind him, it might leave him alone. The strategy of an ostrich with its head in the sand.

Knowing that wouldn't work and picking up the flashlight, JD turned around to face his fear.

# CHAPTER THIRTEEN

"Has he arrived onto the submarine, Mr. Limeh?" It was almost a whisper. Alexander Greyson could always hear him no matter how silent he tried to remain. He had come into the den and sat quietly beside his friend.

"Yes, Mr. Greyson. He's inside at the moment," Limeh answered.

Greyson nodded beneath his quilt. With a satisfied sound like a purr of a small kitten, he wrapped the heavy blanket a little tighter around his shoulders. The mornings in the rain forest could be very chilly during the winter months. Before the sun found a solid footing and baked everything in its path. He couldn't remember the last time he had been so cold in the morning. It had to do with his age, he knew. But he refused to admit it, even to himself.

"An interesting one, that one. How is it that he never came before us until now?"

"Don't know Mr. Greyson. I suspect he's one of the better-guarded secrets of the US Navy. Difficult even for us to track with our extensive network." Limeh put another log on the fire to try and warm the room up. He knew the old man was on his last days. Dignity and respect was the least that he owed his friend after all these years.

"Maybe we're slipping? Is it possible?" Greyson was contemplating something that had never even occurred to him. He knew that wealth and power had earned them many favors over the years. But this was something completely different.

Limeh shook his head as he made a "grumpf" sound. "Not possible. Our network is stronger than at any time in our history. We have friends everywhere. Our admirers range far and wide across the planet. There is no extent, no person that we cannot touch. No stone we cannot turn over when we need to shake the ground. You have but to ask."

Greyson nodded again. He knew better, but it was good to hear Limeh reassert it anyway. He knew the man would never answer with anything but the truth. Forty years plus had gotten him something he could count on: an unending respect.

"Then how did we miss him? I would imagine that a man like Jon David Stickle with his obvious attributes could have proven himself very useful to us through the years." Greyson motioned to the closed manila file on his desktop. He had read the thing cover to cover.

Limeh agreed. "Yes, sir. It just took us awhile to drag him into the light. I think we can probably use his talents. Especially now."

"He'll go to the house of Captain Brown next."

"That would be my guess. If he finds anything on the sub."

Greyson shook his head vigorously "no" several times. "No, Mr. Limeh. That's incorrect. He won't find anything on the sub. But the logical move is to find out about the commander of the submarine. It's what I would do."

"And if he finds out anything? What then, Mr. Greyson?"

Greyson rolled his wheelchair a little closer to the now roaring fire. The smoke billowed up the chimneystack and out of the mansion. There was a time, many years ago, that Greyson remembered using that smoke as a signal for something, but like a forgotten day, the thought left him as soon as it came. His memory was also fading fast.

"We will have to deal with that at the appropriate time. We'll need to find out how much he knows. I suspect we'll get a good opportunity when he goes to the commander's house. We should have our contact ready to act as soon as we need him."

"Yes, Mr. Greyson. A good idea to have things already in place. The time is getting late. Is there anything else?"

Greyson nodded. "It's time to go down stairs again. To the chamber. We must visit and check."

"I quite agree. I will have it prepared." Limeh bowed and left the den as quietly as he entered. There was work to be done.

# CHAPTER FOURTEEN

"Didn't mean to scare you, Jon David," Pat said as he laid a gentle hand on the shoulder of JD. "You were concentrating on the commander and I guess you didn't hear me come down the steps."

Jon David put his head down and closed his eyes for a second. He was relieved to see Pat standing there, but at the same time he was pissed as hell that Pat had snuck up on him like that. He collected himself for a minute before speaking. He was scared to death and shaking.

Pat turned from looking at him and quickly scanned the men in the sub. "I think we need to get you out of here. You've been down here a long time as it is. Come on." He pulled JD along behind him as he left and headed for the navigation hatch and the stairs back to the outside. He didn't want to spend any more time than he had to in the conn room.

Without so much as pausing, JD pushed past Pat and rushed back outside to the surface. He climbed the ladder two steps at a time and heaved himself to the dock. As soon as his feet hit the wooden landing, JD took a full breath of fresh air and then not looking back for even a second, he ran as fast as he could. He had to get away from there.

Jon David sprinted flat out for as long as he could. Until he couldn't run any more. His nose had stopped bleeding and his lip had scabbed over, but the feeling of just having to get away couldn't be controlled. When he finally got to the point where he thought he might collapse from a lack of air, JD slowed to a steady walk, and then finally stopped. When he turned back around the sub was out of sight and so was the dock. He figured he must have covered a couple of miles at the very least. Still not far enough.

Pat watched him run away and thought for a second about trying to catch up with him, but knew better. First of all, JD was faster than he was and in better shape, and second, he understood. He probably would have done the same thing if it'd been him down there for that long of a time.

Now he knew the real trouble was about to begin. And Pat knew exactly what his job was all about. It was simple and required only one thing: he had to keep Jon David Stickle alive.

Somehow.

# CHAPTER FIFTEEN

Jon David sat in the darkness of the room. There were no lights and the room had a mildewed smell, like water had seeped through the windows one day and gotten onto the carpet. The air conditioning unit came on a couple of minutes ago, but had since gone quiet, leaving the room a perfect seventy-two degrees. But Jon David was still cold.

After getting away from the ship as far as he could on foot, Jon David had just sat down on the long dead grass. Most of the color was gone from the grass, leaving a patchy kind of yellowish-brown where there was probably once a nice place for kids to play. Jon David had run into some kind of park and as he scanned the area he saw a couple of older swings that badly needed painting and a set of monkey bars that were long ago forgotten. Even the park was dead as far as JD could tell. Everything around him today was dead.

He sat still in the grass gradually slowing his heart rate, for a total of about ten minutes until he quit panting and could feel his fingers again. The rolled up piece of blue paper that he wrenched from the throat of the commander was firmly tucked into the waist of his pants. It was safe, regardless if JD felt he was safe.

He eventually stood up and walked at a very slow pace for a long time. Occasionally he would reach inside his shirt and just finger the papers lightly with his left hand. As he walked, it gave him a rather strange feeling of calm knowing that he'd found what the sub commander was trying to hide from the rest of the world. The last known thing he did before he died.

Jon David went back to his temporary quarters and stripped down before taking a long, hot shower. He never once even looked at the papers. He set them carefully on the small hotel desk, and then made sure the door was locked before he got into the shower. The cascading water was scalding hot, and JD kept scrubbing his hands, thinking that the more he scrubbed the more the last remnants of those men in the sub would disappear. He knew for a fact that they were calling to him when he was there. It wasn't his imagination that made them breathe in the dark. Nor did it make them start to swing on their ropes. They were speaking to him. Leading him. And he found what it was they wanted him to find. A possible reason that they had all died.

Sitting in the dark, JD made sure the blinds were closed tightly before he sat down at the desk again. He hadn't even bothered to get dressed. He was fresh for a moment and felt clean, which was almost a revelation by itself. He pulled the cotton towel a little tighter around his waist and double tied the knot.

Jon David stared at the top piece of rolled up blue paper sitting on the desk. It was standard eight and a half by eleven inch lined stock that could be purchased in any store. There was a considerable amount of blood and slimy things attached at various places down the length of the paper. The roll was only one sheet of paper wrapped over several times to make it seem bigger.

*Odd*, thought Jon David as he picked up the roll and examined it more closely. The tighter that the paper was rolled, the sharper the edges of the paper would end up. That meant whoever had shoved it into the mouth of Joe Brown had wanted to hurt him. Badly.

Two things were now readily apparent from the deck of the sub: first, the men had probably died painfully and crushed their jaws together so tightly that several teeth had broken; and second, Joe Brown was the last man standing and his throat must have been cut raw by the paper having been stuffed down his throat.

JD knew the men would not have allowed anyone to torture their commander, regardless of what they thought of him personally. At sea, submariners tended to form an unbreakable bond. Almost an "us against the world" sort of thing built out of necessity. When your entire world is spent eight hundred feet below the surface of the ocean, things happen that make you a family. Like most families there are always squabbles and dislikes among the crew, but they were still a family.

Jon David held the blue paper for a second longer while he thought about all those things. One part of him wanted to rip the sheet open and see what was so important that it was hidden in Brown's throat; but the other side of him knew he was missing something. Some important fact that he should have seen by now. It was like a mist had begun falling and he couldn't quite see through it.

JD's eyes opened wide and he snapped his head up for a second as the realization came to him. Pat told him the ship hadn't been disturbed. No one had boarded or touched anything on it other than the three men who found it and they treated it like a professional crime scene. If that was true, then this paper solved a small part of the puzzle: who had died last and how the paper had gotten into his throat. JD knew at the instant that he was going to have to learn a lot more about Captain Joe Brown because Brown had shoved the rolled up dagger down his own throat.

It was the only thing that made any sense. If anyone else had forced the paper down Brown's throat, then they would have to have been the last person to perish. That meant that person would have to have shoved the paper down Brown's throat in front of the men. If anyone else was still alive, it wouldn't have been possible. Even if all the men had already been hanged, they wouldn't have been smiling. Wouldn't have enjoyed watching Brown get tortured. It was the only thing that made a little bit of sense. Brown had to have done it to himself and then committed suicide.

*But why was he smiling?*

*How could he have possibly killed all those men without a struggle, and left them smiling? Who would smile so hard that their teeth broke into pieces?* The thoughts badgered JD. It had to have been extremely painful. And Brown wasn't a large man capable of overpowering the other personnel.

It made no sense at all. Unless there was something else involved that Jon David didn't really want to consider.

It would have hurt also. But something had to have driven Brown to kill twenty-three men and then smile about it. Something large. Something that should never have come to light and must have been on the verge of being discovered. Perhaps an affair with an admiral's daughter? An off shore bank account with millions of dollars? Maybe Brown had sold some of the Tomahawks on the black market and one of the men found out.

JD's mind was whirling with possibilities and as he thought about it he knew that none of them were even remotely possible, which made the whole thing that much worse. If it were at all possible, Brown would have probably finished the voyage and buried the evidence. But he hadn't done that. Instead he made sure this paper was found.

JD knew that Brown had wanted someone to find this, but he also knew that the men on his ship could not survive and be witness to the event. It was the only explanation that contained any logic. But it made zero sense.

Glancing around to make sure he was alone one more time, JD delicately, like he was touching a piece of art, unrolled the paper and spread it out. He smoothed several wrinkles and pulled some dead grey and red tissue off the top surface before he could read what was written on it. There were only two words. Neither of them was really even words:

4 L.

JD read the number and the letter again and again. It was fairly easy to memorize two symbols. It wasn't like he couldn't read them or anything. They weren't Chinese or some ancient Arabic symbol that he'd have to take to a cryptologist to decipher. Just one letter and one number: 4 L.

He turned the paper upside down and then over onto its back. He checked the edges and held it up to the very dim window light to see if there was maybe something hidden somewhere else on it. He saw nothing. No trace of anything other than what was obvious.

Jon David shook his head. Dilemma time. He should probably call Pat and tell him what he'd found, but he knew someone like Major Lowry would swoop down on this evidence like a buzzard on road kill and he'd lose his only advantage. He'd probably never see the thing again as some scientist with a computer took it apart.

On the one hand that would be a good thing, as they'd be able to find out a lot more about the paper and any hidden images that JD couldn't see; on the other hand he'd give up his only scrap of evidence.

He rolled the paper carefully back into its original baton and then carried it with him as he went to get dressed. He was going to see the captain's apartment and he was going to keep the paper with him.

As he got dressed two symbols played havoc with his mind: 4 L.

# CHAPTER SIXTEEN

Greyson sat in his wheelchair at the top of the pit. He had positioned himself at this location so many times before that the actual tracks of his wheelchair fell into grooves in the gravel surface. The grooves came to rest in the perfect spot for his observation of the pit's occupants. He had often disliked this particular part of the process, the silent viewing from above, but he also understood the need for caution at certain junctures in time, and this was one of the most important. There could be no misstep now. Not when they had come so far and gotten so close to their objective.

He strained his neck and leaned as far off the edge of the chair as his decrepit and partially decayed body would allow him without falling to the ground. The chair had certain advantages to go along with its obvious limitations and that caused a considerable amount of anger in the old man. The chair did give some mobility to an otherwise lifeless set of legs. Without the chair, he would have to rely on Limeh or one of the others to carry him around. He wasn't ready to give that up yet. Soon, he knew, he would probably have to do it whether he wanted to or not.

The pit was really just a circular hole in the ground, dug out with an exact plan in mind. When Greyson had ordered its construction many years ago beneath this mansion, he had made sure the pit had certain useable characteristics. Although the excavation company he contracted with for the construction had looked at him rather quizzically when they saw the plans, he ignored them. And to make absolutely sure that no one ever found out about the pit, he had the construction people killed one by one, and buried in unmarked graves in the jungles. Like a king used to imprison and then kill the designer of the castle, Greyson systematically and quickly had the construction company wiped out. But being the visionary that he was, he also had the families of each of the workers eliminated. In case any of them talked to the families about the pits. He was simply being efficient and guarding the plans.

The construction of the pit had taken three months start to finish. The mansion had been deliberately completed first. It stood high up on its hilltop and overlooked a steep valley on all four sides. The house was safe from prying eyes of either snooping hikers with binoculars trying to see over the ten foot walls from some nearby mountain peak, or a government satellite passing overhead using an extended range infrared sensory camera. With the mansion finished, a camera or binoculars could see trucks coming and going and figure out some kind of construction was taking place, but couldn't get any more information than that.

The workers who built the pit had to crate all of the dirt out on small pallet trucks, one at a time, through a basement garage burrowed into the side of the hill. It made the job longer and was even more difficult because Greyson required the construction be done during the hours of midnight and five am, but with the money he was paying the construction crew to perform the work, there wasn't any grumbling. Not a word was uttered.

The pit was circular in shape, being exactly thirty-nine point nine six meters in diameter and drilled to a depth of twenty meters. There were tunnels branching off at four different points from the bottom of the pit allowing access and entrance as well as extraction of the occupants when necessary. There hadn't been many times that Greyson or Limeh actually had to use the tunnels as extraction points, but they were definitely necessary. He had to be cautious and careful at the same time.

The sides of the pit were honed from solid rock and covered with sandy loam from the bottom of the sea. Algae and moss had been nurtured and taken root in several places up and down the walls. It made it impossible to climb and impregnable from the inside or the outside. No one got in or out without using one of the tunnels. He had to keep his prizes in place.

The bottom of the pit was divided into two different chambers. The walls were slick and black from the green and yellow moss and lichen and the lack of any sunlight. It wasn't supposed to be inviting and the denizens there never complained anyway. Greyson wouldn't have cared if they complained all day because the pit was virtually sound proof.

Craning his neck to see over the side and into the bottom of the pit, he wished for a little more light. To foster the environment he needed, one of complete hopelessness, he made sure there wasn't enough light to see for more than three or four meters. Just enough to locate the guest sitting across from you. Or the dinner.

She lay curled up into a fetal position, just where he knew she would be stationed. She was always in the same section of her room. He could see her chest moving slightly each time she took a rancid breath of air. Her back was towards him and her shoulders would expand so very slightly with each intake.

"Ana. Ana, my darling. Are you awake?" Greyson called softly.

She neither moved nor indicated she heard him, but he knew better. She had superb hearing on par with a wolf. The construction of the pit had somehow managed to make the walls give off a small but clearly audible echo. "Ana" echoed away softly into the darkness.

Greyson sighed just once and then regained his intensity. He combed his hair back with his free hand and sat up straight in the chair. He would not be ignored and his personal feelings could not get in the way.

He had never envisioned this. Not in his wildest nightmares could he imagine something as *feral* as Ana. There was no other word for her. She acted like a dog chained to a fence more than she acted like a young woman. But still she served a purpose and would at least one more time.

She was, quite simply, a mistake.

Limeh appeared behind him again, as quiet in his approach as a slithering snake in the grass. He always seemed to be by the old man's side. "She cut herself deeply this time, Mr. Greyson," he said.

"Death isn't going to be the release she hopes, is it Mr. Limeh? How did she do it this time?"

"Used a jagged arrowhead from the bottom of the pit."

Greyson snorted. "How the hell did that happen? I thought we were watching her all the time now."

"I don't know. She apparently dug it up with her fingers and then cut herself slice by slice until she passed out. That's when we found her. Bleeding pitifully."

"Make sure she survives. It's very close now. I can feel it deep in my bones."

"As can I. It will be everything. To the both of us, after so many years," Limeh said.

"I know. But we need her to be part of the ceremony. There can only be one, you know."

"Yes, I know."

Greyson leaned back over the rim of the pit and whispered softly, "My dear Ana. My daughter. Awaken and do not harm yourself anymore." The words echoed across the pit and faded away.

Ana stirred at the word "daughter". Without looking up at the two men, she hissed in the dim cavern, "I am not your daughter."

"Tsk, tsk. So sad, really," Greyson said motioning for Limeh to help him move his chair. "We need but one. And of course, she makes two."

# CHAPTER SEVENTEEN

Jon David carefully lifted up the yellow streamer that blocked the door to Joe Brown's house. The military police launched an intense argument for jurisdictional control of the house with the Washington Police, which subsequently landed on the desk of two senators and a rear admiral. In the end the Navy won out and then cordoned off the area with ribbons of yellow that stated simply "Police Line, Do Not Cross" in bold black letters. He had seen these ribbons many times and the scenes that were hidden behind the tape were more often than not horrific, for lack of a better word. Jon David didn't expect anything horrific inside the house, unless of course, Joe Brown had left something behind in the oven or maybe the refrigerator to go with the dead bodies on the *USS Nevada*.

The house was small and built on a single story with a modern floor plan. The brick was an older style and covered only about half the outside with the rest using wooden planks for siding. It looked like the builder started with one design and finished with another. It suited the pay grade of a naval submarine captain perfectly. Not too nice and not too cheap.

When Jon David first drove up, a fleeting thought crossed his mind that he might see a huge house that was outside the realm of the Navy pay grades. Something that might have indicated Captain Joe Brown was getting money from somewhere other than his Navy salary. Too large a house in this neighborhood would have launched an investigation into the finances. The size and style of the house made Jon David breathe a little easier. At least until he got inside.

He unlocked the door with the key Pat gave him in New York and opened it, not really knowing what to expect. Anything could've been behind that door. He knew one thing for sure: it wouldn't be something pleasant. Working as an investigator for Pat Smith and the Bureau of Unexplained Events meant surprises were always unpleasant.

He paused after nudging the door open, hesitating for just a second in the breezeway. The wind was blowing from the North this morning and had a crisp chill to it. Without some kind of windbreaker, JD would have been cold to the bone on this porch, but it could have just been the trepidation that he felt before entering Brown's house. He was nervous for a couple of reasons, other than just the obvious.

Certain parts of these kinds of investigations were very difficult for him. Even though he'd done this for a long time, and been in all kinds of situations, he'd never gotten used to this particular part of it. The idea of walking into someone else's house, into their inner lives that were never displayed for others to see, had always unsettled JD. He figured it started when he was just out of high school and his first real job was as a dispatcher with the state police. He wasn't a real officer, although he did carry a badge that read "Police", he never got a gun and didn't get to arrest anyone. The state police had a "ride along" program they used as a kind of initiation into the real world of police officers. High school graduates got to ride along and watch the officers while they worked. His first couple of times walking into dark houses and the uneasy feeling he got from those kinds of places, never left him.

Today wasn't any different.

Jon David had read the file on the captain of the *USS Nevada*. The man was good. Real good. And incredibly intelligent. His career had been fashioned by leaps and bounds up the Navy's ladder. He would have at the very least been a rear admiral one day. Judging by his track record so far, possibly very soon.

As he stepped into the unlit house, he couldn't help but feel that he was violating a sacred trust that Joe Brown had given the Navy: *When I work for you, I'm all yours, but please leave my private life out of it.* In other words, don't go digging around my closet on my off hours. Officers, JD knew, like many people in both their civilian and military lives, had things to hide. Things that were best left under a heavy carpet.

As he entered the house, JD walked directly into the life of the Navy captain silently hoping that he wouldn't find something amiss. He knew he couldn't possibly embarrass Joe Brown the man simply because he was no longer alive, but there was his legacy to consider. And the Navy was fiercely protective of the legacy of its own. If JD found child pornography on his computer, or perhaps money stashed in his freezer in bags that Brown had gotten from selling drugs or something worse, then the Navy would go into survival mode and instantly cover it all up. That alone didn't really bother JD, but the legacy of Joe Brown, someone that JD had never known, might have to be protected. JD decided at that moment that no matter what he discovered, he would hide it before it got to any higher levels. Including giving it over to Pat Smith and the bureau.

The door closed noiselessly behind Jon David and he stood for a moment and just surveyed the room. The house was smaller inside than he would've thought when he drove up. He did some quick mental arithmetic and came up with about twelve hundred square feet, probably three small bedrooms and a couple of baths. Standard for an older neighborhood and this kind of salary. Especially in Washington, DC, where the buying power of money was a lot less than other places.

He didn't need the flashlight to see like he did in the submarine. The light that was filtering through the closed blinds was sufficient enough to let JD see clearly, although some corners held shadows. He quickly glanced around, determined there weren't any immediate threats in the house and relaxed as much as possible.

*He must have been a simple man*, he thought. *Not much on decorating.* Simple furniture. Lamps, couches, a painting or two on the walls. Some memories here and there including a picture of a wedding and a smiling bride and groom, but not Brown. Perhaps a wedding he attended at one time or maybe he was a groomsman. Nothing in the room stood out. He was obviously a bachelor. JD would have known that without reading the file. There wasn't anything to suggest good taste and a woman's touch anywhere in the house. Obviously, the same decorator that did Jon David's house had helped out Joe Brown.

He walked slowly through each of the rooms, getting a general feel for the person that was Joe Brown. The man had simple tastes and lived modestly within his salary. He didn't spend lavishly on anything that stood out. He went about his life the same way as thousands of other military men every day.

JD stopped for a moment when he realized his nose *wasn't* bleeding. He reached up and wiped with the first two fingers of his right hand and then looked at them to be sure. He was instantly relieved. At least today was going to be a good day. He could relax a little bit more.

Seeing nothing in particular that immediately struck him, JD went into the bedroom and rummaged through the drawers of an inexpensive dresser. He opened the closet and looked inside. Knocking a couple of times against the back wall to be sure there weren't any hiding spaces, he satisfied himself that nothing was hidden from view and closed the door. He left the room exactly as he found it.

He walked back into the living room and over to the desk. A workingman always has his important papers in a file cabinet or a safe and almost always within reach of his desk. Unless Brown knew he wouldn't be coming back before he left on the sub that day, then the papers, as well as whatever else he was working on, would be sitting somewhere close to the desk. Somewhere Brown could easily get to them. Probably not hidden unless he felt it was necessary.

JD pulled the roller chair out from its place under the desk and sat down. He positioned himself like he thought Brown would've sat at the desk and then let his eyes roam across the surface and around the immediate area. If there was anything to be learned here, it would be in one of the drawers of the desk or in plain sight. Anything that Brown was working on would be out on top.

The desk had various papers laid out in a straight line that JD quickly scanned: an old electric bill; a water bill; a letter from the Navy about his retirement contribution; a yearly calendar with a couple of dates circled. Nothing of importance.

Opening the three drawers on the right side brought nothing out of the ordinary. He opened the two bottom ones on the left side and found them to be empty also. When he pulled the top drawer open, a small vial, a little bit larger than a test tube, rolled to the front of the drawer.

He picked up the vial and looked closer. It held a brownish, though relatively clear liquid of some kind. It wasn't drugs or anything illegal, he knew, but it was interesting that Brown kept it in a desk drawer. For no other reason than to have something to retrieve from the house, he dropped the vial into his jacket pocket.

He glanced again at the calendar. It was one of those large ones that lay flat on the desk and covered ninety percent of the working space. The blocks of the dates were each large enough to write memos in and JD noted that the month was correct. The dates were empty except for black numbers that marked the passing of time.

The only thing that seemed odd was the actual location of the calendar itself. It was set a little to the side of the desk, off-centered by three or four inches. Normally, no one would have even noticed such a small thing, but this was a spit-and-shiny Navy Sub Captain. Everything else in the house was folded and precisely placed. Clothes in tidy rows in the dresser drawers. Suits pressed and shoes aligned in the closet. Bath towels hung with precision on the racks. Even the bills on top of the desk were perfectly in order. Perfectly straight.

But the calendar wasn't in the center.

JD lifted the calendar up carefully. He turned it over and checked the backside which revealed nothing other than a paper backing with yellow squares. He moved it aside and looked at the top of the desk.

Carved out of the wooden top of the desk were two images in large black block, like they had been burned into the wood: 4 L.

# CHAPTER EIGHTEEN

Ana was led in shackles through the dark tunnels until eventually reaching the stairs. The guards, if that was what they could be called, kept a healthy distance from her and pushed her forward with a homemade cattle prod. The one they called "Gunther" would shove the prod against Ana and then press a button and run a quick jolt of electricity through her until she moved in the direction he indicated. Ana decided a long time ago that if she ever got the chance she would kill everyone in this house slowly and most painfully.

The shackles fit tightly around both her wrists and ankles. Gunther wasn't very smart and had twisted the bolts in the bands of each of them until they cut into Ana's skin. Her ankles were sliced like raw meat in several places making it impossible for her to run. Once when they were transporting her, she managed to kick Gunther squarely in the groin and then bite him as many times as she could before they beat her off of him with clubs. She actually got a full piece of his ear and swallowed it in front of him while he howled in pain on the ground. Since then they took better precautions when the moved her. They had a small amount of respect for her, but more than anything, they feared her.

She glanced back down at the floor as she continued walking and ignored Gunther. He was an imbecile and he was only following orders. It was their fault she had been reduced to this kind of person. This kind of *creature*. In her tiny moments alone, during the times when she wasn't being prepped or hovered over or looked at through a microscope, she thought she might be pretty. But not now. Not when she knew what was waiting at the end of her walk. The same thing that was always waiting for her.

They were leading her back to the machine. She was the only one who could make it work.

Ana slowed in her steps and resisted just enough to have

Gunther push the cattle prod up against her back a little harder to make sure she felt it. He was forbidden to permanently mark her.

She refused to look back at him. Refused to acknowledge the kind of animal she was becoming. Refused to acknowledge that she would have eaten him alive right at that moment if she'd been given the chance. Her time would come someday, she knew.

Limeh stood at the top of the steps with his usual lifeless color of chalk white cheeks and black bow tie around a scrawny neck. His smile was as sincere as a funeral director and with all the warmth. It meant nothing to her.

"Come now. There is no reason to treat her like an animal, Gunther. She can do wonders for Mr. Greyson. She can be an almost uplifting event in his eyes. How are you today, my lady?" Limeh asked as he reached out a hand and placed it on her shoulder to help her up the last step. Ana was convinced that he would've just as quickly pushed her back down the staircase if he decided she was no longer useful to them.

She titled her head so that a patch of dirty blond hair fell across one of her eyes. She reached up with her manacled wrist and moved the hair so that she could see him with both eyes, knowing the reaction it was going to get from him. She could enjoy this moment, if only for a second.

Limeh immediately diverted his attention from her face. He had trouble looking into her eyes, even now. It wasn't every day you met someone with one blue eye and one green eye. It could be most unsettling when she glared unblinking at him. He knew that it shouldn't have bothered him, but there was nothing he could do about it. Only Greyson seemed not to be disturbed by the sight of her vibrant eyes.

Limeh stepped back and let his hand fall from her shoulder. Ana didn't need his help and he really didn't want to give it to her. It was more for show than anything else. He knew she deserved a wide berth. She was quite unpredictable and could snap at any moment. She was also strong enough to break his neck with her bare hands if she ever got the chance. Like an animal trapped in a snare in the woods, Limeh was convinced she'd chew her arm off to get away.

Greyson appeared from around a corner and wheeled himself towards them. He was dressed in a freshly tailored suit with a blanket thrown over his legs. "Hello my dear. How are you today?"

Ana stood in front of him and said nothing. She didn't like him or anyone at this place for that matter. Any chance to escape was better than staying here. *Death could be such a sweet thing*, she thought. If she only got the chance again.

Greyson motioned for Limeh to step back and he wheeled his chair closer. He wasn't afraid of her. Not in the least. "I hate the fact we have to keep you in those chains, Margana."

Ana instantly focused her two different colored eyes and stared hard at Greyson. He had only used her full name on a couple of previous occasions that she could remember, and both were his way of trying to bridge a long gap between her, him, and Limeh. None of the rest of the staff was allowed to even use her full name, just the shortened "Ana". It was the name she had become accustomed to and even liked to a certain degree. She hated her full name and didn't like it when Greyson or Limeh used it. A bad omen, she often thought, when they called her that.

His wrinkled face tried its best to form a pathetic smile. Missing and stained teeth hanging from blackened, rotting gums momentarily disarmed her. It had been so long since anyone had smiled at her, she didn't quite know how to react. Her defenses instantly shot up another notch. She clenched her manacled fists and her legs tensed to spring as far backwards as she could get.

"Mr. Limeh, surely we can treat her better, don't you think? I think she deserves to be bathed and have her hair combed. She is a beautiful girl and I think she should look like it. Not like some dog in a cage. What do you think?" He turned to Limeh as he spat the words and spittle ran down his chin.

Limeh nodded. "I quite agree. There really is no reason for this. I will send someone in immediately and see to Margana's needs."

Greyson relaxed his forced smile and looked back at Ana's blue and green eyes that were regarding him warily. "We can do so much better than we have, Margana. I will do my best to make sure that from now on that you are treated with the respect you so richly deserve."

Ana thought for only a second before she reacted. She understood perfectly the kind of respect she deserved in their eyes. With a grunt and a hiss, she spat a large green glob of snot and dirt into Greyson's face. The wad hit him squarely in the left cheek and inched slowly down through his wrinkles until coming to rest just above his neck.

Greyson reached up with a shaking hand, wiped the spittle off and then put the glob in his mouth. "The three of us cannot be separated, Margana." He motioned to Limeh. "We should take her away."

Limeh nodded a quick curt nod. He had seen enough of her show as well. "We'll clean her up, Mr. Greyson, and then put her on the machine."

At the mention of the machine again, a shudder ran down Ana's spine. She clutched her arms to her chest and let her fingers slowly search under her tee shirt. After only a brief moment, she located the smooth, round hole with the snap rivets on the edges in the upper part of her stomach.

A small trace of a smile appeared at the corners of Greyson's lips as he watched her trace the opening. "Yes. Prepare her."

# CHAPTER NINETEEN

Jon David stared at the emblems burned into the top of the desk. He ran his fingers across the edges of each of the symbols, slowly tracing them as if it would help him decipher them one at a time. The symbols weren't anything new to him in the context that he knew what each of them obviously represented, but the places they had appeared made these two images more than just a letter and a number stuck together.

4 L.

His fingers wound themselves across and into the wood on the desk, and JD closed his eyes and tried to image Joe Brown somehow burning the images into the desktop. The symbols were large, almost six inches tall apiece, and whatever Brown had used to burn them here had left several rough splinters. Once or twice, JD could feel small bits of oak wood try to wedge themselves under his fingernails. He deliberately kept his hands touching the wooden symbols. Deliberately traced each contour and every nook and crevice. *What had driven the captain of a one hundred million dollar nuclear sub to leave these two images on a rolled up piece of paper forced down his throat? Why had Brown burned these letters into a desk for someone to find? What would make a rising star, a destined admiral in the Navy, do something like this?*

JD opened his eyes. There didn't seem to be anything he could glean from the letter and the number by themselves. But the fact that they were hidden under the desk calendar and shoved inside Brown's throat made it certain that Brown was trying to tell someone about them. Brown felt enough of a sense of urgency about these two things that he made sure the world would know *after* his death. It would have been one thing if he left these marks to be found in case he died. But the fact that he left them, knowing he was not going to return, said a whole lot more to JD. It meant that something was going to happen and this one letter and this one number were the telltales.

JD began a slow and methodical search of the desk. He ran his fingers along every inch of the desktop. He traced the rims and the lips of the desk edges. He touched the crevices and the lines where the drawers met the shelves. He pulled the drawers out one by one and set them on the floor next to his chair while he felt behind them. It had to be here. It had to be somewhere.

Finding nothing out of the ordinary, JD put the drawers back onto their slides and closed them. He leaned back in the chair and thought again about the letter and the number. *What could a "4" mean besides the obvious? What else could an "L" represent?*

JD reached into his jacket pocket and pulled out his cell phone. He thumbed through several pages of "Google" answers to his inquiry. Several quick links to the number appeared on his screen instantly: four is the smallest composite number; there are four cardinal directions; there are four seasons of the year; and at the bottom of the page a link to the four elements of earth, wind, fire, and water. None of these seemed to have anything to do with the number on Brown's desk and a search of the letter "L" produced similar results. JD knew he was stumbling around and didn't really have anything solid to go on.

He leaned back in his chair and let his vision roam around the little house once more. The key to open this door had to be here somewhere. A man of Joe Brown's obvious intelligence would not have led JD here only to be stymied.

JD's gaze eventually drifted back to the desktop. He sat completely still and just let his eyes outline the letter and the number. Moving slowly back and forth across each of them in turn, north to south and then east to west, and then scouring over the entire top of the six-foot wide desk, he finally saw it: the desk wasn't level.

He leaned further back in his reclining chair and took the image of the desk in all at once. It was definitely sitting off-kilter. One of the ends of the desk was resting higher than the other. It was a small height difference, so miniscule, that while sitting or working at the desk it probably wouldn't even be noticed. But it was visible none-the-less if someone was *looking* for it. In this perfectly apportioned room, there were two errors: the calendar was off-centered and now the desk wasn't level. For a man like Joe Brown, order was something that he could rely on. His desk would have to be perfectly level, JD knew. It wasn't level. Not even close now that he focused on it.

JD reached down and let his fingers touch the bottom of the two front desk legs. The right leg was scratched and weathered from years of the chair gliding into it. Nicks and scuffs were visible up and down the leg from Brown sliding his chair up to work. It looked normal.

But the left leg was newly painted and had very few scratches from wear and tear. Someone, Brown probably, had recently sanded and painted the leg. As Jon David felt along the leg from top to bottom, it felt like the paint had just recently dried. The leg was a highly glossed and smooth piece of oak. In the light of this room, with this color of stain, no one would have noticed one leg freshly painted and one leg weathered.

Jon David pushed the chair back and got down on the ground beside the leg. It was resting comfortably on the hard wooden floor. He lowered himself to floor level and squinted at the space between the leg and the floor. He was hoping to find a piece of paper wedged in there like a shim or something that would immediately stick out. Instead he saw something that looked like a thin piece of metal stuck under the leg, about the width of a quarter.

Cautiously, he reached out his finger and brushed the razor thin piece of metal. It was tinny and rectangular as far as JD could see, and cut to the exact same size as the end of the desk leg. It was completely hidden unless the viewer got down to floor level.

He lay down flat on the floor to get a better look. He didn't think he had anything to fear, but many years of *not* anticipating what was really going on had made him extremely cautious when investigating these kinds of things. For all JD knew, Brown could have been some kind of radical terrorist and attached a trip wire or something to the bottom of the leg to kill anyone that lifted it up. Whatever the purpose of the tin piece was, Joe Brown wanted to keep it hidden until he died.

JD scanned carefully front to back and then up and down the leg. He saw no evidence of wires or anything electronic connected. With a deep breath and quick prayer, JD lifted the desk leg up slowly.

As soon as the desk was raised to about two inches where he could see the piece of tin clearly, JD looked up and saw "4 L" stamped squarely in the center.

He jumped back involuntarily and drew his gun from its holster when he heard the distinctive "click" sound from somewhere above him.

# CHAPTER TWENTY

A panel hissed and a machine quietly "whirred" like it had been greased for just this purpose, and as Jon David watched from a crouched and tensed position, along the side of the desk leg, a compartment opened. The opening was narrow, rectangular and perfectly situated in the expanse of the leg. Impossible to see from either the front or the back, the panel was cleverly hidden. JD sighted his nine mm Beretta squarely at the center of the panel and if anything twitched, he was going to shoot first and ask questions later.

He slid closer to the leg and examined it for just a minute before deciding it was safe, and then reached his hand slowly up to the opening. He let his fingers find their way along the part of the panel out of view, and then he reached in and pulled out a folded piece of paper.

Jon David stood up from his crouch in front of the desk, holstered his gun in the center of the small of his back, and then sat back down in the desk chair. The crunched-up paper in his hand was crinkled and blue in color, and folded over several times to fit within the space of the desk leg. It wasn't an ingenious piece of work to either find the paper, or to hide it in the first place. The clues weren't that hard to locate because he found both of them within thirty minutes of looking. JD figured that someone like Brown would have hidden it better, unless he wanted it found.

Unfolding each of the pages one at a time brought out four pieces of onionskin paper. Each was new and stenciled on a single side and as JD flipped them over several times, he could see traces of a carbon copy. So there were at least two copies, which meant that another duplicate of this existed somewhere. JD discarded that thought immediately. Even though someone else possessed this drawing, he had to focus on the one in front of him. He couldn't do anything about another copy at present. He didn't even know what was on the onionskin, let alone who might have it.

After he completely unfolded the onionskin papers, he laid each of the four sheets carefully next to one another on top of the desk. They were the same size and makeup of paper, each piece about twelve inches by twelve inches. And all were blue colored underneath. A light blue, like it was tinted as an afterthought by whoever designed the paper.

Blue prints.

The first thing that struck him was the obvious: there were four sheets and Brown left him the "4 L" clue. He scanned each of the pages from top to bottom looking for either a letter "L" or a number "4". He didn't see either the number or the letter anywhere on the front or back of any of the pages, so he set the papers back together in the center of the desktop and just let his eyes drift from one to the next.

Each of the blueprints were numbered in sequential order, but instead of numbers the letters "A", "B", "C", and "D" were labeled clearly in the bottom right hand corner. JD thought that this could be just a sequence for Brown's own system or have some other meaning, perhaps to eliminate the confusion of using the number "4" again. He shook his head. He had basically no idea about what Joe Brown's intentions could have been concerning these blueprints. He could have meant anything or nothing at all by using sequential lettering instead of numbers. He filed that thought away for a later time.

JD decided to focus on what was in front of him instead of looking for hidden meanings and things that weren't readily apparent. *Perhaps*, he thought, *by looking for the obvious, some of the other things might come into focus all by themselves. At least a little bit, anyway.* And it was someplace to start.

The blueprints showed what looked like a simple prism. There were dimensions and numbers along each edge of a four sided, rectangular shaped box. The blueprints appeared to show all four sides of the box, each one from a different view, as if the engineer who designed these prints was walking around the box slowly and taking snapshots. The top was smooth and flat and visible in all the different views, and as best as he could tell, didn't have any writing or drawings on it.

But the sides of the box were a different matter altogether.

There were four different pictures. And lots of other things. Hideous things.

The pictures on the box were easy enough to discern. One was an old sailing ship; another was of a frigate of some kind. The third picture was of a lighthouse and the fourth was of a barricaded door. What relationship these four pictures had to each other was going to be a problem for later.

But surrounding the pictures and filling in the spaces between the pictures and the borders of the prints was something else entirely. Each of the four pictures was surrounded by grotesquely detailed, dimensionally proportionate drawings of body parts at various angles. There were muscles and bones and sinews connecting all of the parts so that the entire sides of the box were covered in a feast of human remains. All of it intertwined by some unseen chain of human lineage. There wasn't any empty space on the borders of the box at all. Everywhere he looked, something that should have been covered up with skin was hanging free and loose.

A skull here. A heart and pair of lungs there. One leg without a foot attached. An arm in the corner of the box and a torso in the top left on the next blueprint. And the mouths. Lots of them open and showing what had to be a scream of soulful pain by the facial creases surrounding them. Intolerable pain, as if whoever drew these plans had taken a photograph of the bodies on the papers instead of drawing them.

He could deal with most of it.

Most of it.

But the eyes. They were something different.

Eyes with half-closed or fully open lids and bushy, molten eyebrows that stared through space at him. Other places had knife-like piercing pupils without any eyelids. Looking at JD from some unseen terror. From another dimension. Another place of pure pain.

Like on the sub.

It was fascinating. It was deliberate. And it was consuming Jon David alive. The borders of the box were silently screaming at him. The mouths and eyes were beckoning to him. The arms wanted to encase him and hold him against those beating hearts and quivering lungs. Bleeding from orifices and wounds that JD was somehow starting to feel. Somehow starting to emphasize the very nature of the screaming. Pandering for his attention alone and drawing his gaze down into the depths of their pain. To their souls. Watching his movements, like they had been waiting for him before he got there today. Like Captain Joe Brown had drawn this blueprint to look at Jon David Stickle. Like the box was designed solely for him.

It was mesmerizing him. He *had* to look at it.

As he stared at the stark wide eyes and screaming mouths JD felt a jolt run up his spine. An omen of pain pierced his side and he winced but still could not tear his vision from the sightless faces looking back at him from the blueprints. His hand took on a will of its own and rubbed his left cheek vigorously up and down. Scratching and clawing. He scratched and flexed his hands and fingers as the figures on the box tried to draw him down to their level. Into their center where they held an advantage. Where they could make him part of the pain. He could hear distant screams of pure anguish. He opened his mouth to join in a scream of terror. Pure terror.

Covering the prints with both his arms and then pushing back from the table with frantic legs, Jon David was finally able to break the fixation he'd felt and tear his eyes away from the pages on the desktop. He violently thrust himself away from the desk and without looking directly again at the blueprints, rolled them up and shoved them inside his jacket as his nose began softly dripping.

Leaving the apartment in a hurry without looking back, he closed and relocked the door and headed back to Pat's office. He needed to look at the prints on his own terms.

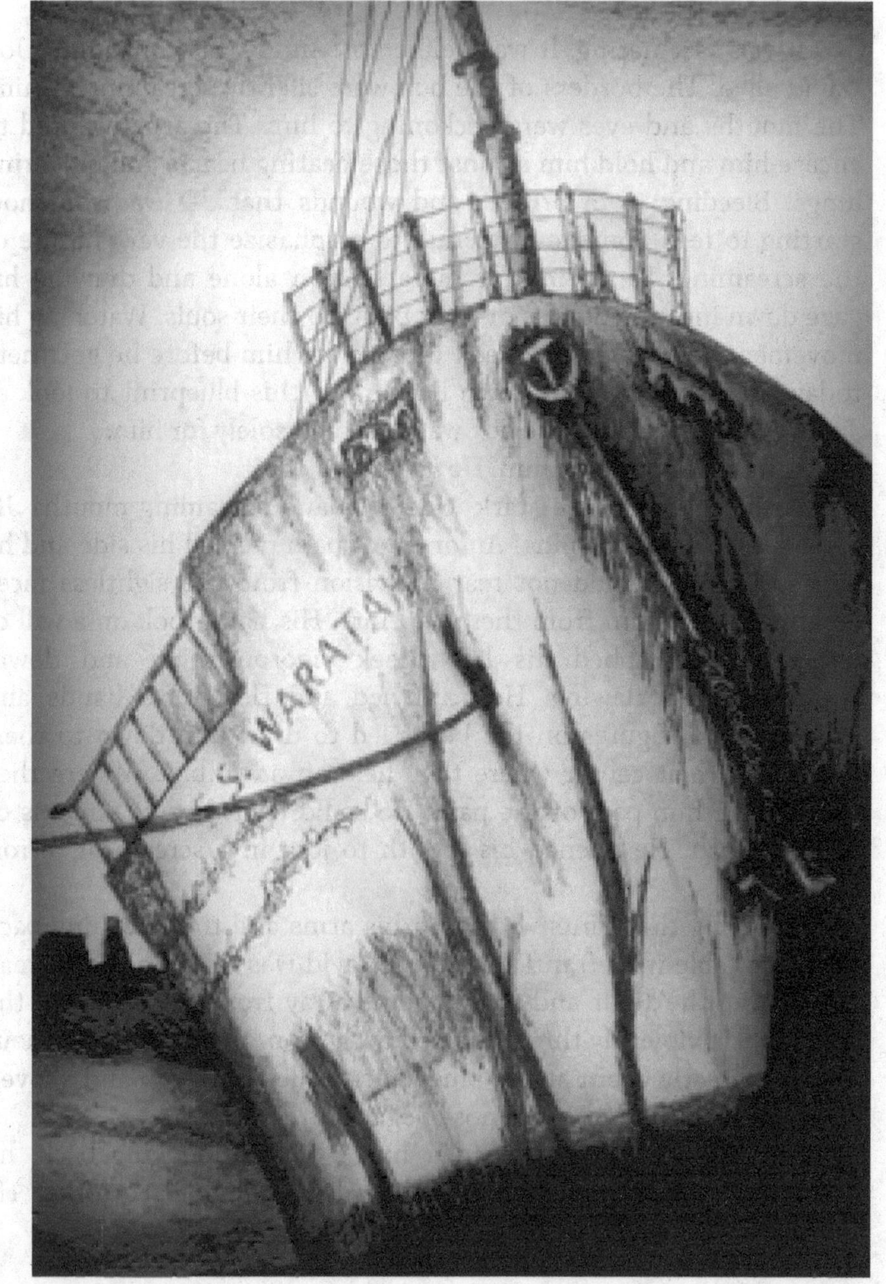

S.S. WARATAH

# Book Three
## Deception

# CHAPTER TWENTY-ONE

*I am Evil.*

*I have existed since time began, have festered in your surroundings and looked for easy hosts. Have feasted on the pregnant rats and the rotting white worms of your species. Simple-minded humans who can be easily raped. I enter like an infection slides through the bloodstream and eats its way into your brain. Killing your cells and replacing them with the cancer that I am. I control and envelop you in a warm blanket of blood lust. You fall prey easily to me because of your inability to grasp the simple truth. Because you willfully choose to believe in the light and shun the darkness. Because you're a pitiful species that has never believed in me fully. Has never embraced me. Has never admitted to the falseness of the infantile premise that there is good in all people.*

*There is not. There is evil present in all people. There is a part of me caressing your scabs and willowing in your loins and thriving in your tumors. Lying just below the surface and waiting to seep through the pores. Evil is just a thought until it splatters itself on the wall. Wicked is just a word until it pushes you to action. Pain is just an abstract concept until you scream from it.*

*Can you burn away the evil in a witch with the fire? Can you stone away the evil in a bastard with a boulder? Can you fry away the evil in a serial killer with the electricity? Can you cleanse this world of greed driven by lust and sanctioned by governments under false premises?*

*Can you release a soul?*

*There is always greed and it is my birthright to nurture it. I am the greed in your soul personified.*

*The soul of evil, the understanding of what I am, the conception of the terror and the malice that I bring, the depth of the pain that I can evoke, lies not outside your puny level of knowledge. You are ninety-eight percent water, one percent intelligence and one percent emotion. I conjure and torture that last one percent.*

*The evil lies inside your essence. It is in your DNA and present in your fathers and their grandfathers. It is who you are and why I have taken you.*

*Your soul and I are one. How can a soul be good when its very concept is tainted with redemption? A soul that wiggles and screams and seduces you to new levels of lust masked as emotion, and was conceived in the churches with the promise of forgiveness?*

*For that concept alone, your species is ignorant. For that concept alone, I exist inside the core of your being.*

*Because you allow me to exist there.*

*You need me there to give a name to the gutless terror you deliver to each other in your moments of madness. When you bludgeon your spouse to take another man's wife. When you murder your children for their inconvenience. When you throw out your laws in the name of conquest and call it civil war. When you torture because of precious metals. That's when my existence is confirmed.*

*The truth is simple and awe inspiring to you:*

*Evil exists within your soul.*

*I will guide you to the precipice for there is something I require from you other than your madness and your blood and your complete, utter devotion.*

*I need an army of disciples to witness a historic event. To embark with me as I guide them on a journey of wonderment and murder and mayhem.*

*To finally take back what is rightfully mine.*

*I will rain down with a vengeance laced with buckets of the dead and souls of the weak. I will come full circle with you as my vessel.*

*You will aid my Passage.*

⊠

Aboard the *SS Waratah*
Australian Ocean, July 1909

Ensign William Smith couldn't believe what he was witnessing. The dogs had gone crazy. At first they were just barking loudly and then he could hear them *screaming*. Smith wasn't even sure a dog could scream, but the sounds coming out of the six by twelve foot metal cage were definitely painful screams. At least in William's mind. The sounds were almost soulful, like the dogs weren't screaming to get attention, but rather to mark an event. Something bad.

William hadn't wanted to be on this ship when it left the port of Cape Town, South Africa, anyway. He was a second hand servant on the ship, which was about as lowly a berth as anyone could get. His wife was six months pregnant and he needed the work, so even though he wasn't really a fan of working the cruise liners, he took the job when he saw it posted on a downtown billboard. It was a job if nothing else.

And they screwed him from the moment he got his berth to now. His supervisor was a mean spirited man named Frank Monk and in reality Monk was no more qualified than Smith. Monk had been on board the *SS Waratah* exactly six weeks longer than Smith, and he thought he was destined for a captaincy or possibly something even higher, if you bothered to ask him. He gave Smith all the dirty-as-shit jobs, from cleaning the heads to scrubbing the pots and pans after dinner. It was all just horseshit grunt work, but the pay was going to help with the bills back home.

Until he got this assignment, he actually thought he could put up with Monk's verbal assaults and finish the cruise. Two days ago, Monk had assigned him to clean the dog cages. William was sure that Monk had probably been given the job by his supervisor, the ship's fourth engineer, and just passed it down so he could go and sleep all day or just hide out in the bottom decks and let someone else do the work. That someone else happened to be William. It always happened on the ships. The lowest on the ladder did all the work and the supervisors took all the credit. William figured it was probably like that everywhere.

But the dogs. William Smith had been afraid of dogs since he was a child in London and the neighbor's dog, an eighty pound black and brown Rottweiler, had bitten him repeatedly after backing him into a corner from which William couldn't escape. He was only four or five when it happened, and even though the scars had healed to his face and arms, the damage to his psyche was still there. He hated dogs, all dogs, including these six. And he was deathly afraid of them.

Monk must have sensed his fear because he immediately laughed when he assigned William to clean the cages. Monk had noticed the tremor that crossed William's face and just laughed. "What's the matter, boy? Not afraid of dogs are you?" He moved close to William every time he spoke like they were confidants and the stench of old liquor always reeked from his breath. "Don't like them do ya?"

William backed up and shook his head "no". He needed the job and would do it, no matter the consequences. His wife would have called him childish for losing a job over a fear of dogs.

Monk laughed. "Clean them cages spotless so's I can eat off them later or I'll make you scrub their assholes. Then feed them some meat. Get leftovers from the cook. He likes dogs and will probably let you have some good shit from last night's meal. It wasn't fit for us seaman, that's fer sure. It should have gone to the fucking dogs to begin with, in my opinion," Monk laughed at his own joke and pulled his red suspenders up while he spoke.

He poked his finger into the center of William's chest for emphasis. "These here dogs are some kind of hunting dogs or something, and they're worth a lot of money." He scuffed and spit a wad of tobacco out onto the floor as he pointed to the cage. "They look like six ordinary German Shepherds to me. Big bastards ain't they?"

He turned back to William and smiled yellow teeth that had many years of tobacco stained across them. "Wonder how big their teeth is? Bet that one over there has three-inch fangs. Those teeth would make a pin cushion out of a scrawny-ass boy like you." Monk laughed and pointed to the one in the corner farthest away. He was always amused by his own wittiness. "So take good care of them, or I'll feed you to them." He turned and left William to his job with a sharp click of his heels that spoke of military training a long time ago, but there was nothing regimented about Frank Monk anymore.

That was yesterday afternoon, and after a couple of minutes spent just staring at the dogs, William swallowed his fear and opened the cage door to clean it. The dogs stayed in a far corner while he nervously eyed them from the other side. *They're probably just family pets, that's all*, he thought, and not really a threat. *Probably really friendly. Maybe they just need someone to pet them.*

But when he awoke this morning and came in to clean their cage and feed them, that's when he heard it for the first time. It was hard to identify exactly what the sound was when he first opened the hatch to the cargo berthing area that held the dog's cage because the powerful steam engines of the ship were churning against rough waters and the captain had them at high power. The engines rumbled throughout the lower decks and the vibration got stronger the lower William traveled and muffled almost all other noise.

But the sound that greeted William when the hatch swung fully open was unlike anything he had ever heard on a ship. It was throaty and musty at the same time, but with a high pitched squeal simmering underneath. His father had one time shot a rabbit from the back porch of their home and William had watched in horror as the thing flopped and jumped and screeched to its death right in front of the two of them. The sound was simply *ungodly*. And this was close.

A quick image of one of the dogs bleeding and caught with its paw in the metal bindings of the cage caused a tremor of fear to run through William's stomach. He quickly dismissed that thought as soon as he turned the low wattage light bulb on with the flip of a toggle switch.

The dogs were fighting. And none of them were growling.

William recoiled in horror as he realized that this couldn't be possible. It didn't surprise him that the German Shepherds were fighting amongst themselves. Hell, he wondered only yesterday why none of them had fought after being cooped up together for the entire journey in a six by twelve cage.

But the two that were fighting weren't growling. No dog could fight without growling. It wasn't natural. It wasn't *normal*.

And as William took in the scene and backed up unconsciously from the cage, he realized what the other four dogs were doing. They were watching. They had formed a semi-circle around the two fighting dogs, leaving just enough space for the fight. It was like they had a ringside seat at a prizefight.

But those dogs weren't making any noise either. Not barking or growling or jumping up and down. The other four dogs were just sitting calmly by and watching while the two biggest dogs fought viciously against each other in the middle of the cage.

And the blood was everywhere. The dogs must have been fighting for a long time because both of them were covered in blood and as they bit each other over and over again, each one jockeying for position and dominance, the blood continued to be slung around the cage. It was splattered on the walls and the baggage that sat outside the cage, and was falling freely from the dogs that were just watching.

Just then, as William gaped open-mouthed, one of the fighting dogs stopped for a second, looked over at him, stared directly into William's eyes, and then deliberately licked his lips, savoring the taste of the blood on his jowls.

And underneath it all, William could hear the soulful and ungodly screaming.

At that moment, the smaller of the two dogs in the fight got on top of the other Shepherd and with a sudden feint to the right and quick arch of his chest forward, locked down on the bigger dog's throat. He flexed his jaws and smothered the other dog's body with his and then with a clamping sound and a sucking sound like wind through a pipe, punctured clear through the bigger dog's throat. Blood began spraying upward onto the metal cage's spars with every heartbeat.

William knew it was all but over. He'd seen that move before from wolves in the forest and men in bar brawls. Caught in a death-grip, it was only a matter of moments before the dog was dead.

And his job was gone. Hell, the Captain could put him off at the next port and leave him, if he didn't get in the cage and stop the damn dog from dying. Perhaps he could rescue him and get some kind of reward from the owner for protecting his prized possession.

It was worth putting his fear in check for a second.

William thrust a shaking hand into his pocket and grabbed the key to the padlock. He glanced one more time at where all the dogs were, making sure that none of them could run out of an open door, and then inserted and turned the key. He heard the distinct "click" of the tumblers falling into place and the rusty lock fell open.

William opened the door carefully, his senses on high alert. He didn't really have a plan for separating the dogs from each other, but he advanced anyway, hoping something would come to him.

As he inched his way into the cage, the four dogs that sat in a semi-circle backed up slightly as if he commanded them to move. William had a fleeting thought that it was an odd thing they all moved simultaneously, instead of one at a time. Like they had a purpose.

Somewhere the soulful screaming echoed rigidly against the metal bars and seemed to reverberate around him. He slowed even more as he maneuvered into the cage with the eyes of the dogs firmly on his movements. With each little scream of pain the hairs on the back of his neck stood up a little straighter. Something was so wrong about this whole thing. Dogs aren't supposed to scream. There should have been a frenzy of barking and growling.

The dying dog on the losing end of the fight was defying gravity and spurting a tremendous amount of blood upwards. William noted that it was gathering in pools on the metal spars and dripping a steady rhythm back down to the floor. He stepped in one of the smaller puddles of blood and left a footprint that would have been comical under any other situation. Bloody footprints at a dog crime scene.

William approached with a caution born of pure fear. Bloody eyes stared at him from the floor and the Shepherd winning the fight paid no mind to him at all. "Easy boy. Easy does it. Nobody's going to hurt you." A steady drip-drip-drip of blood splattered on his shoulder from the ceiling and spread thick warmth across his shirt. He put his hand out cautiously and slowly moved around to the front where both dogs could see him. He didn't want to surprise either of them. They could easily turn on him and then he'd be the one bleeding on the floor.

"Easy does it. Good dog. Good dog." William couldn't think of anything else to say. Telling two canines to quit fighting didn't seem like the right thing to do. He would have literally asked them to quit if he thought it would work at this point.

The dog on top shifted its weight slightly so it could see William clearly without releasing its grip. It looked like the dog relished the taste of the blood in its mouth. A victor with the spoils.

He reached his hand down to where he could feel the fur from the top dog just barely brushing against his palm. It was a tickling feeling, like someone ran a quick feather boa under his hand, and even though the thought of a feather boa was ridiculous at this moment, William felt a small smile creep across his lips.

He drew in a sharp intake of breath, held it for just a second and then laid his hand directly on top of the head of the victorious dog. He felt all of his nerves tighten at the same time, ready to jump back in retreat if the dog turned on him.

It was at that exact moment that William Smith knew he had made a fatal mistake.

The screaming wasn't coming from the bleeding dog on the bottom. It was coming from the other dogs. The ones sitting in the circle and watching him.

He withdrew his outstretched hand as a small bile of fear rose in the back of his throat until he could somehow *taste* it. He didn't know when, but at some point the other dogs had managed to get behind him and between him and the door. The four of them sat on their haunches in front of him, facing him, not making a sound. Except the one to the left of center. That Shepherd was clearly arching his neck and making a sound so terrifying that William immediately felt his bladder release and he pissed a stream of urine down his pant's leg that sought out and then mixed with the blood already on the floor.

It wasn't a scream, William realized in that instant. It was a *signal*.

As one, the dogs set upon William Smith and began eating him in little pieces. He screamed in terror and pain and fought frantically until one of the bigger dogs, the one William thought was about to die from his puncture wounds, positioned itself across his throat and bit him so deeply that no sound could possibly escape his throat.

The dogs made sure he lived because they needed him for the mayhem that was about to consume the *SS Waratah*.

Captain Joshua Ilbery held the weather report in his hands. It was the middle of the afternoon and even though they were well out of normal radio range, the *SS Waratah* came equipped with a new DF Steering radio. It was the latest gadget in the world of marine radios and Ilbery thought it might make celestial navigation all but ancient history. This little radio not only made it possible to communicate with land based stations when they were far out at sea like today, but it could also send them weather reports that were much more accurate than anything he'd ever seen.

Which was the dilemma facing Ilbery. The weather report he held was almost six hours old and if it was correct, the ship was in serious peril.

He scanned the written report again. Radioman Waite handed it to him less than three minutes ago. And it was grim. Very grim. The kind of thing no captain ever wanted to receive when the ship was one thousand kilometers out of port in the middle of the ocean with no assistance and no port anywhere in sight.

They were completely alone. And the weather report said a rogue wave was directly in the ship's path.

Ilbery had never seen a rogue wave. Hadn't really heard anything about one since leaving mariner school many years ago. It wasn't like these things appeared daily or even yearly. They couldn't be predicted and were considered almost a nautical legend. Most of his instructors at the school had never even seen one. They talked about them in hushed tones and the answer was simple: get the ship as far away from the damn thing as possible because it was bigger than you. A lot bigger.

A tidal wave was one thing. They came from waterspouts that were connected with low-pressure areas flowing over the warm water of the Pacific Ocean, and were usually started by a seismic shift. Tidal waves gathered speed and intensity as they moved. But they were predictable and easy to out maneuver. The generally accepted theory was that you turned the ship ninety degrees to the direction the wave was traveling and outran it until clear and then turned back on course. Simple enough.

But a rogue wave was completely different.

First, Ilbery knew it didn't follow any patterns of origination. It wasn't like the weather stations along the coasts could predict them after a passing hurricane. They just appeared wherever and whenever they wanted and tracked on a completely unpredictable path. Some of the instructors theorized that ocean-floor earthquakes caused the waves and that accounted for their unpredictability.

But others thought it was something worse. Something much worse.

Ilbery had heard all the stories. Rogue waves, which were always reported at over fifty meters in height and more powerful than anything man has ever constructed, were sent from Satan himself.

And if one hit his ship, it would crush the *SS Waratah* like a bottle of soda under a locomotive.

He had to get the ship out of the path. The problem was that the path was unpredictable and unstable. The damn wave could turn at any point. And at the moment, it was headed directly for the ship.

Ilbery turned to his chief officer, Chris Owen. They had been together for the last twelve years and he trusted his judgment. He handed the weather report to Owen. "What do you think, Chris?"

Many nights standing deck watch next to Owen had formed a strong bond between the two of them. He counted on his chief.

Owen read the report and his face immediately turned a pale white. His hands always shook slightly from a nerve disease that he was treating with medication, and this report made them shake just a little harder. He gave the report back to Ilbery after reading it a second time. "Have you ever seen one of these waves for real, Captain?" he asked. In the back of his mind he knew that Ilbery had not seen one before, but he hoped that perhaps he was mistaken. The captain always seemed to know what to do when things got bad. And this was real bad.

Ilbery shook his head. "Never. Not even close. Heard of a couple. The descriptions were not believable. Not in the slightest. Nothing could be that large." He put his hands behind his back and stared out towards the sea. He was a strongly built man with bushy black eyebrows and a thick moustache. Dressed in his full uniform and standing on the bridge since early this morning, he cast an imposing presence among the men under his command. They believed in him, which was essential. Things were always unexpected at sea. This morning the seas had taken on an unusual roughness for this time of year. It hadn't been predicted for their passage.

Owen leaned in a little closer to whisper to Ilbery. "They say these things cannot be predicted. You know why."

"Aye. I know why. I'm just not sure I believe it, that's all. A lot of strange stories go around the sea, my friend."

Owen nodded. "That's for sure. But these waves. Rogues. The very name says they come from the devil himself."

Ilbery turned from the ocean and looked into the brown eyes of Owen. The man was terrified for some reason that Ilbery couldn't quite understand. His hands were shaking and he had a tremor of fear in his voice. Many things at sea were unexplainable.

He turned back to the sea. "We'll have none of that kind of talk on my ship, Mister Owen."

His first mate recoiled at the rebuff. He hadn't expected the captain to redress him. "Aye sir," was all he could say.

"Let's turn the ship ninety degrees to starboard and increase speed to full ahead."

Owen nodded, glad to have something to think about other than the wave heading for them. He shouted to the steering engineer a little more forcefully than normal, "Hard about, starboard side, heading three six zero degrees. All ahead full"

"Aye sir. Three six zero degrees. All ahead full."

As the ship swung about and picked up steam for the full twelve knots she was capable of doing in rough seas without damaging the hull from constant pounding, Ilbery leaned in to Owen. He knew he had to stop the talk of ghosts and devils before it got started or he might have a full mutiny on his hand before he could blink. Ship crews, especially under extreme stress, were a fickly thing and needed to be handled with both authority and kid gloves. It was a delicate balancing act that the captain maintained.

"The fucking wave won't be able to turn ninety degrees. It's simple physics. If it turns that far then the devil is involved. We'll make a box pattern out here and come up behind her after she passes in front of us."

Owen sighed a momentary relief. The captain knew. He always knew. And Ilbery was good, better than most. Owen knew that for a fact. He smiled a sheepish smile. "Aye, sir. It's a good idea."

The door to the bridge opened suddenly and a lower seaman, one that Ilbery didn't know, burst into the room. "Captain! You'd better come quickly. There's something strange going on below decks."

Ilbery glanced once at Owen, whose face had gone to a pale color again as all the blood drained. He nodded once for a show of strength he didn't really feel, and then followed the seaman, not having any idea about what was going on, but knowing deep inside that something was very wrong.

⊠

William Smith knew he was alive. He knew he should be thankful for that at the very least. The dogs had pounced on him and he thought

127

he was going to die. With every bite they took another mouthful of his flesh. He felt like he was being eaten alive, screaming the whole time and rolling around on the deck under the weight of six German Shepherds. He thought he was dead for sure.

But now he walked through the lower decks and the dogs were following closely at his heels. He had never really thought about his own existence before the attack, but for some reason he now *knew* he was alive. And stranger still, except for a throbbing pulse in his head, the bites didn't hurt anymore. There was a moment, when one of the silver colored dogs had just ripped a large chunk of William's thigh off and was chomping it and the surrounding pieces of muscle between his fangs that his pain just floated away. William thought that was probably the only way to describe it: the pain just floated away and he didn't hurt anymore.

Like he had just died, the pain sensors in his body were shut off.

But now he walked along the bottom deck towards the mess hall with the dogs in tow.

But William wasn't *exactly* walking.

Not like he'd ever walked before anyway. He left leg had been chewed through to the bone and just sort of hung off his hipbone. It dragged about a foot behind William and smeared blood and broken bone bits all along the floor. And he didn't so much as walk as thrust and pull his body forward. He would alternately jerk his body this way and that like it was attached to a rope and someone was pulling it from a walkway, and then William would force the rest of his body to follow. It took great effort and he was advancing, but it wasn't walking by any means.

And the blood was scattered everywhere.

William was aware that his blood was all over the place. Literally. It was leaking and spurting from several bite marks and open wounds. He thought something about the salt air must have added to the natural endurance of the wounds because William wasn't sure how he could have lost that much blood and still be slinging it with every step. But he was still moving and still slinging.

*Kill them all.*

The voice was so powerful, so forceful that William actually fell backward a full step. He was dragging his body like an old sack of potatoes, not really knowing exactly where he was going, but definitely moving in a forward direction, when the voice spoke to him with a clarity that resonated so much he could almost feel the words in his head.

*There can be no trace.*

William looked around at the empty hallway and then back at the dogs. The lead dog, the Shepherd who had won the fight and was a little smaller than the others, sat quietly one meter behind William, staring at him with unblinking coal-black eyes. William looked into those eyes, and felt a fear so strong that he started shaking.

*Is the dog speaking to me?* William thought. *Can it be?*

William looked again into the darkest eyes he had ever seen and for just a moment, he stopped trembling. And then the dog cocked its head slightly and William felt a wave of terror wrack his body and he shook like someone would rattle a tin can before throwing it away.

*Kill them. NOW.*

William didn't know for sure if the dog was the one commanding him, but he knew he had to follow. He understood implicitly that he was still alive and must obey. Struggling forward with a ravaged body, his heart rate accelerated like someone had hit him with a dose of pure adrenaline. His sense of urgency jumped and the spurting blood started to propel itself farther across the hallway as he dragged his leg behind him.

He headed for the mess hall, where he knew he would find Frank Monk. He would kill him first.

⊠

Frank Monk sat at the long, metal table eating something the cook told him was hash which meant that it was supposed to be a combination of meat and potatoes, but Frank couldn't locate any meat. Not a single bite. He knew the captain probably limited the amount of meat the cook could use on a daily basis to save the reserves for the end of the trip, but he wanted some damn meat. And he felt he deserved it for all the work he did around this ship.

He was just about to complain to the cook, and get his share of whatever the cook passed off as meat today, when the door to the mess opened and in lunged something that *looked* like William Smith. Frank squinted and stared at the thing flopping in the door for a full ten seconds to be sure, but damn if it wasn't William. Only, he didn't look the same as he did when Frank left him in the dog cages a couple of hours ago.

Frank stood up at his table and pointed at William. "What the hell happened to you, asshole? You get into a fight below decks? I'll can your ass down to ship's grunt, if you hurt any of them dogs."

William was shuffling directly towards Frank and his eyes were solidly fixated on his target. He had something in mind.

There were six other seamen in the mess when William threw the door open and dragged himself into the room, the dogs following in his trail. With a wave of his hand and a quick pointing of his finger, the dogs dispersed instantly into the room and attacked everyone but Frank Monk.

Frank dropped the spoon he was using to direct his anger at William as the dogs pounced on the other men. He recoiled in fear and confusion as vicious growling mixed with screams of pure pain came from all corners of the mess hall. The six seamen scrambled for safety and cover as best they could while trying to defend themselves. There was fighting and ripping sounds and several men were down almost before Frank could react. The dogs acted like they'd done this before and were *trained* to kill men.

As the men fell one by one under the onslaught of three-inch fangs, Frank retreated further and further into the corner. Backing and pointing his finger at William, he felt a terror in the pit of his stomach unlike anything he had ever felt before. His death was staring him in the face.

William stood in the doorway, blocking it from anyone trying to escape. The dogs pounced on each of them with veracity and a viciousness none of them had ever seen and the entire fight took less than thirty seconds. While William watched his fellow officers fall to the ground, each with a dog's mouth clamped around their throats and blood pouring from their mouths, ears, and noses, he never lost sight of Frank Monk.

"I was never mean to you, William. I treated you like a friend. Saw to it you got the good assignments. The dog cage was a reward for Christ sakes!" His voice was cracking and rising in volume with each word as he pleaded with the dog master. Frank was convinced that William must have already died from the amount of blood pouring out of the hole in his stooping body, but he still stood there staring at Frank. Like a zombie or something from a horror magazine Frank used to read when he was kid.

William smiled a mouthful of bloody teeth and then uttered one word: "Pain."

The dogs attacked Frank Monk as a team and in less than fifteen seconds all that was left on the floor was pulp and bones.

⊠

"What's your name seaman?" Joshua Ilbery asked as he followed the nervous midshipman below decks.

"Clark, sir. Noah Clark, second engineering apprentice," he answered with a glance backwards.

Clark opened one door and motioned for the captain to follow him. They had gone three decks down and were above the engineering deck. The only spaces left below them were the mess hall and the crew's quarters. He was walking quickly, obviously comfortable in the lower decks with the ship's layout, and hadn't said anything before this moment.

Ilbery was smiling and nodding to the crew and the passengers he passed as he tried to keep up with the young ensign. The *SS Waratah* left Cape Town with a lading of passengers and crew as well as several tonnage of cargo. She was a stable ship that Ilbery loved and though a little slower than some of the newer ships coming out of the yards, she had the sea lines and experience Ilbery could count on in both her design and her crew. Many of the seamen had been under his command for more than two years in and out of various ports around the world.

Two hundred and eleven total people on board relying on his command. Relying on him to avoid this rogue wave as well as squelch whatever this disturbance was that had developed that Clark was taking him to see. Ilbery didn't believe in coincidence and the convergence of two different potentially perilous events at the same time would rattle any captain anywhere in the seven seas.

"So what's going on, Ensign?" Ilbery asked when the seaman stopped prior to opening the last door to the lower deck.

Clark turned to him with a look of sheer terror on his face. He was sweating profusely and cocked his head when he looked at Ilbery like he was seeing him for the first time. He shook his head slowly back and forth like he was trying to spill a hat from the top of his head onto the floor. The movement wasn't natural at all. "You'll have to figure that out for yourself, *Captain*." Clark said. He drew the word "Captain" out like it was three syllables long.

Ilbery noticed the change in his voice and demeanor and would have rebuked the man on the spot but that was when he noticed what appeared to be a large hole in the throat of Ensign Clark. Ilbery strained his eyes using all that he could of the low wattage bulb hanging in the corridor and verifying the image that had presented itself to his brain. The seaman's collar of his blue shirt had hidden it from view, but now that Clark had turned to face Ilbery directly, it was clear that his throat was bleeding. And it was bleeding porously.

Ilbery jumped back in horror when he realized that half of the seaman's throat was missing and a torn mass of muscle and bones were bubbling down the front of his shirt. He'd hidden it up to this point, but now that they were alone, Ilbery could see the man must have been attacked by *something*.

Ilbery took a full step backwards when Ensign Clark started to shake violently. He then broke into convulsions and Clark flopped to the floor and started to heave and contort like he was having an epileptic fit. His body jerked and strained against itself like it was trying to break into two or three pieces and a rope was tied around its middle. Clark was struggling and seemed to be almost vibrating from the inside out as he tried to break the restraints that Ilbery couldn't see.

Ilbery unconsciously withdrew farther from the ensign. He hadn't seen this kind of thing before and had no idea why or how it affected the seaman now. Ilbery stepped into the mess hall and shouted for someone to come to Clark's aid immediately.

The scene that greeted Ilbery in the mess hall was like it had been drawn up out of a dime-store horror magazine. There was blood everywhere. And bodies. At least five or six that Ilbery counted. All of them men in uniform. Some were lying on the ground and flopping like fish on the beach. Like they were struggling to breathe. Two were cowering in different corners, covering their heads from their attackers.

And then he saw the dogs.

Ilbery's mind couldn't figure out what the hell these dogs were doing in the mess hall. These dogs couldn't possibly be viciously and violently fighting with men over scraps of meat. Or could they?

Only then did Ilbery realize it wasn't exactly meat the dogs were fighting with the men over.

Ilbery covered his mouth with his hand when he realized that the dogs had ripped several parts of the seaman's flesh from their bodies and were tearing them apart bit by bit making the pieces small enough to swallow. Everywhere he looked, his crew was being torn apart in bite-size chunks. The luckier ones were still struggling to not only keep themselves alive, but also mostly intact. In one corner, one of the older ship's engineers that Ilbery vaguely recognized was wrestling with a large German Shepherd for possession of his own leg. The man was rolling on the floor with blood pouring out the socket where his left leg used to be attached, and the dog was growling loudly and yanking backwards with powerful jaws. The dog would yank his head back like they were playing tug-of-war together, and then shake the leg of the man from side to side while the poor engineer tried desperately to hang on to it.

That was when Ilbery saw the lone man standing in the center of the room, not moving. He seemed to be completely impervious to the death and the carnage going on around him. There was blood and dirt all over his face and his eyes blinked non-stop.

"Welcome, Captain," was all he said.

The door behind Ilbery closed with a metallic clink.

*You must kill them all without a trace.*

The words thundered into Ilbery's brain like someone hit him with a skillet as the dogs set upon him. When he fell under the slaughter, the bleeding seaman standing in the center of the room only grinned.

Passage.

⊠

It isn't easy to make two hundred and eleven people and a ship disappear without a trace, Captain Joshua Ilbery knew. There were always inquiries and investigations by authorities from all over the world when something of this magnitude happens. Once the ship had been out of radio contact for more than twenty-four hours, the last known position would be calculated and then the local authorities from whatever was the closest country with international water authority would spring into action and send out rescue vessels.

At first, the searchers would assume the ship's radios became disabled and do a cursory investigation into the ship's last know position. Finding no ship, and no trace of floating bodies anywhere within a ten-kilometer radius, the cursory investigation would change to a missing persons/rescue mission. At that point an international regulatory body would take over the search and several ships would comb the longitude and latitude of the last known area. The ships would search in a square pattern, emanating outwards from a precise position until the search eventually covered over five hundred square kilometers of water.

The rescue vessels and their crews would comb every bay, inlet, or remote island and even drag the surface of certain parts of the ocean with a fishnet looking for clues. Tell-tale signs like clothing or floating bodies, or in the worst cases, seagulls diving time and again in the same area of ocean, hitting the floating bodies and chewing off chunks of flesh, drawing the sharks. Shark fins and diving seagulls were sure signs of a sea disaster. The searchers had to locate the bodies before the sharks arrived to feast. Once that happened, Ilbery knew, no one would ever find any trace of the people.

And then there was his ship that had to be concealed to make this work. The *SS Waratah* was one hundred and fifty meters long and weighed close to sixteen thousand tons. Something that size doesn't just disappear into a crack in the floor. There had to be place that no one would ever find her for this to work. To escape completely without a trace.

*I will help you Captain Ilbery.*

Ilbery nodded to the voice in his head while the screams from below decks became more and more muffled with each passing step up to the main deck. Ilbery was bleeding from the dog bites and his throat had been ripped out, but he was still able to focus on the task at hand as he dragged himself to the ship's bridge.

When he left the mess hall, the seaman who was commanding the dogs bowed to Ilbery's position as ship's captain and without words passing between them, had silently understood the task given to him. With a bloody nod of his bite marked face and a wave to the dogs, the seaman shuffled out of the mess hall, three dogs in tow. He was headed to the cargo-loading bay, per Ilbery's unspoken order.

Ilbery arose from his place under the massive German Shepherd with a clear vision of what he had to do and knowing he would have help from a higher authority. Something that not only spoke to Ilbery, but also commanded that he obey. He had never felt such reverence for a figure, even one that he not seen, in his life. It seemed to Ilbery that all of his life, all of his days at sea, had been spent looking for this kind of guidance. For this *opportunity*.

*I will lead you to me and you will be among my children, Captain.*

With a purpose that approached giddiness and three strong dog disciples in close quarters to him, Ilbery put his hand on the door to the bridge. He was back to take over the control of the *SS Waratah*.

⊠

William Smith had never known such joy in his miserable life. He had drifted from job to job and port to port without direction. Without purpose. But now, finally, he had found the inner person that he was supposed to find. The man he was meant to be from his birth. At long last.

The three remaining dogs were following him and occasionally branching out on their own. They would hunt and kill every person that Smith led them to find. Some of the crewmembers were specifically spared death and simply fell into step. William would alternately point or wave his hand, and the dogs responded by either ripping out a throat until the seaman was left writhing on the ground bleeding to death, or if he needed them, just puncturing their jugulars enough that the crewmember could still accompany him to the cargo deck. The work there that William needed to perform was beyond one man's ability.

By the time William reached the cargo compartment and pulled the sliding door open to reveal the one thousand tons of lead bars that the *SS Waratah* was transporting to Cape Town, twenty-two broken and half-dead crewmembers were now under his command. Even though they looked insane and mutilated to anyone that saw them, the men moved with purpose. Smith handled his work force with precision and deftness.

The dogs guarded the ship's hold and with the crewmember's help searched out any passengers unlucky enough to come down to the lower decks. One by one they killed anyone that stepped into the doorway or near the cargo holding bay. Most of the passengers on board were berthed in the upper three levels and the ships engines effectively covered the screams of the dying. It was like someone had planned this carnage for a long time.

William thought it was somewhat comical that the screaming of the dying people couldn't be heard above the fourth deck. It was almost like music to his ears. After a couple of minutes of relentless screaming as the dogs bit deep into their throats or ankles so they couldn't run away, he got used to it and actually started to whistle to the screams.

Before leaving port with the lead bars, a loadmaster had mandated the spreading of the bars across the cargo hold. A thousand tons of weight had to be dispersed throughout the ship's expanse to keep her from getting off balance and possibly sinking if a large wave hit her. Once a ship the size of the *SS Waratah* started to rock back and forth, if the weight in her cargo hold wasn't exactly in the center and spread evenly throughout her bins, she would eventually list too far to one side, taking on water until she began her death throes. It couldn't be stopped until she sank. And quickly.

William Smith directed the men under his command to move the lead bars to the most rearward position on the ship. One by one, the men stacked each of the bars in the back of the ship against the wall.

When it was over, the men dropped like rag dolls, dead.

William sat in the center of the lead bars and petted the dogs while he waited. It was only a matter of time.

⊠

Chief Officer Chris Owen's jaw nearly dropped to his chest when the door to the bridge opened and Captain Ilbery strode into the room. He had never even seen Ilbery out of uniform before, let alone dressed like he was now dressed. The man was covered in blood and what looked like shit to Owen. Ilbery's head and neck were bleeding from deep wounds like he'd just been in a knife fight and lost horribly.

And his uniform was far from regulation. His shirt was open to his waist and showed claw marks dug deeply across and into his chest. His pants were ripped to shreds and his hat was missing. It wasn't just unusual; it was *unnatural*.

"Sir?" Owen asked softly, completely unsure how to handle the situation.

Ilbery lunged into the bridge and that's when Owen saw the dogs.

⊠

Captain Joshua Ilbery lurched to the helm of the *SS Waratah*. He was an awe-inspiring man to his crewmembers. A man they could look up to and respect. He was a granite figure who took his captaincy very seriously. As he looked around the bridge at the fallen bodies he smiled. His greatest feat, the one legacy he would be judged by, was about to begin.

Pushing aside the body of the now dead Chief Officer Owen, Ilbery swung the ship's wheel around ninety degrees. He turned the ship directly into the path of the rogue wave that he knew was less than nine kilometers away.

*Bring them to me. You have done well, Captain.*

Ilbery smiled when he first saw the mammoth wall of water hurtling towards the *SS Waratah*. With a steely resolve, he clutched the wheel and made sure the course of the ship was dead center into the teeth of the wave. She would pitch up and with all the tonnage of her lead weight at the ship's aft wall, she would flip upside down and tumble over and over like a child's toy before being dragged down to the ocean's floor. A floor that Ilbery knew was at least twelve kilometers down in this part of the world.

He gripped the wheel tighter and flexed his fingers a couple of times as the rogue wave started to rise above the top most deck of the ship, until a wall of water blotted out the sun and the sky. Water was all Ilbery could see when it first began pummeling the ship.

*Well done, my Captain.*

He held onto the wheel until the ship was at such a steep angle, almost ninety degrees straight up riding the crest of an unimaginable sheet of seawater, that he knew his life's purpose had been fulfilled, and without remorse, Captain Joshua Ilbery readily went down with his ship.

*No traces.*

# CHAPTER TWENTY-TWO

Present Day

Ana hated the machine room more than anything else in her dismal existence. She had grown accustomed to her dungeon bedroom. Gotten used to rats for meals and sleeping in the midst of frozen corpses and stenches that used to make her vomit. But the machine room wasn't like that at all. It wasn't like anything that she wanted to be near.

And yet they made her get close to it. Way too close to it for her comfort.

Gunther roughly pushed her from behind, making sure to knock his elbow against her backside just a little harder than he should have while he prodded her forward through the open door. He didn't normally hurt her directly; he was just told to bring her and he obeyed.

She used to resist the entrance, hating the first onslaught to her senses the worst. Walking into the bright lights, and seeing the drawings on the floor and the machine already in position, as well as what hung from the rafters, made her queasy all over again. After she spent some time in the room, she could block most of it out. She learned how to leave the entire room behind with a simple trick of her mind. While her body lay on the cold, golden table, her mind ran along a crystal white beach. It was all she needed.

But that hadn't happened at first. Not when she was first led into the room in chains. That relief took her awhile.

She looked down at her hands and rubbed the spot where her manacles had been until Gunther took them off, and then she casually glanced at the deep ruts across her arm where she cut herself with the arrowhead. A long time ago, it seemed, her death was a viable escape.

The machine room was one of the offshoots from the four tunnels that led out of her dungeon. She hadn't been down all three of the other tunnels, but she could hear occasional screams and other sounds that used to make her shudder at night. Long dead, wailing screams that seemed tormented in another world by the depths of the despair. She knew that her sounds, the ones that came from her branch of the tunnel, probably sounded the same to any others that might be within hearing distance. When they weren't screaming themselves she was sure they were listening.

She willed her legs to walk as Gunther pushed her with his knee from behind. He wasn't the worst of the ones she had come into contact with so far. He had a mean streak but didn't administer pain to her every time. Nothing she did really threatened him. Many of the others were beyond repair.

To teach him a lesson and put some physical distance between them might be the only redeeming part of this journey. With a quick backward thrust of her hips she knocked him squarely in the groin. She pushed as hard as she could and then for good measure stomped her heel against his shin. He howled once and then kept a respectful distance.

The smell was overwhelming. Like garlic and dead chickens scattered and streaming through the air vents, the stench hit Ana as soon as she walked through the door. She glanced up at the hanging fluorescent lights giving off a soft orange color that covered every inch of the room and cast shadows against the walls. She particularly disliked the shadows that moved across the colorfully painted and tiled floor once the machine got to full strength. For some reason, the louder the machine hummed, the more the shadows danced, like they were somehow connected, even though Ana knew they weren't. At least she hoped they weren't connected.

She stole a quick glance upward at the bodies hanging from the ceiling in various poses. Some were connected with chains at their armpits and hung like they were trying to walk, while others were stationed in different poses. All had open eyes and pulled back lips showing gum lines and black teeth. Some reminded her of torn up and bloody slabs of raw meat.

When the bodies started *rocking*, the screeching began. The chains would rattle and screech a protest from metal on metal. There wasn't any breeze, nor was there any reason that she could imagine the things should be rocking, but still they moved. Not just a little bit, but with a steady rhythm and a pulse that seemed to have purpose. Once the machine got up to full strength, once they strapped her in and connected her to it, the bodies rocked faster.

Ana put her head down and walked to the table next to the machine. It was sitting with a soft light coming from behind it, quiet at the moment, but just waiting like a cat sits in a field and waits for the mouse to make a move so it can pounce. And kill it.

She lay down on the table while Gunther and two other unnamed imbeciles strapped her down and connected the hose. She always felt a little prick as the ends of the hose were screwed into the port on her side. Turn by turn and twist by twist. It wasn't really a bad pain; she had felt so much worse.

Satisfied for the moment, the imbeciles connected the last hose to her left side to a gold handled lever made for this purpose that Ana knew hid under the first layer of her skin, and then left her alone. Left her to her thoughts as the inevitable took over.

Ana had never gone to school. Couldn't really read anything other than some simple words. Had no understanding of the physical world or how the physics of a moving object, once set in motion, tended to remain in motion and on track until something outside interfered and took it off its track. Had no conception of the workings of this machine. She couldn't have understood *how* it did what it did or why they needed her to be strapped to it.

She only knew the damn thing drained her life's blood away from her every time.

The machine hummed once and then throttled to full strength while her vital fluids poured out of her and into a small receptacle made just for this purpose.

She could try running again to get away. She could probably use her strength and rip the straps off and the hoses away. Jump off the table and just run. But they'd only hunt her down and use the dogs on her again. If she tried real hard, closed her eyes and flew away in her mind, it would all be over soon.

She envisioned herself out in the real world, on that sandy beach with crystal clear blue skies above and the sand between her toes. As she drifted off to sleep and her blood flowed from her to the machine, she thought about running through meadows of gold.

# CHAPTER TWENTY-THREE

Pat Smith opened the door to the private room at the Naval Hospital in Bethesda, Maryland. The man working at the admitting desk directed Pat to this floor a couple of minutes ago. A little nameplate reading led him the rest of the way to the room. He didn't like hospitals or the sterile smell that seemed to accompany them. It could be sobering just walking into one of these wards.

He hadn't bothered to take the file of Gary Bryant along with him for this interview. He'd known Bryant for many years and even though they had never worked closely together, the Navy was a tight knit circle at Pat's level of command and the officers around him had never uttered an unkind word about Bryant. Both his job performance and his military record were beyond reproach.

Pat had prepared himself for the worst, but walking into the softly lit room was still a little unsettling. Last week, Bryant had been at the height of his military career and health-wise was as fit as or better than most civilian men in their early fifties. But when two junior officers, both of them younger than Bryant by at least ten years, had succumbed unexpectedly, Pat knew that Bryant wouldn't be the same man he was last week. He probably wouldn't even look like Pat remembered, which was possibly the most disturbing.

Pat hesitated as he walked into the quiet room. The walls were an unpleasant but functional grey-green color and there were a couple of paint-by-the-numbers pictures of sunsets and sailboats hanging from each one. The window shades were drawn closed and the only lighting came from a fluorescent bulb at the end of the bed so the doctors could read his chart. Dark and claustrophobic, the room didn't exactly invite visitors.

Gary Bryant lay on his back with an oxygen mask securely strapped to his face. He appeared to be sleeping, but his breathing was labored and uneven. The white sheets covering him from shoulders to feet rose and fell at regular spaces, but each time the movement seemed almost unnatural. The sheets would alternately float up and then descend until coming to rest, like he was coughing in his sleep, even though no sound came from behind the mask.

Pat approached quietly, not wanting to disturb this lifelong Navy man whom had earned his respect many times, even though he never knew him very well. The man had gone aboard an unsafe submarine and taken the matter in hand, following protocol exactly and risking his life, only to be afflicted with something that no doctor could explain or even treat. For that alone, Pat admired him.

Bryant stirred and his eyelids fluttered briefly, like he sensed Pat was in the room with him. He belched and coughed a wracking deep chest cough for a second and then turned his head to face Pat directly. He smiled as best as he could with the straps laced across his face to keep the mask in place.

Pat nodded, "Hello Gary. How're they treating you?"

Bryant shrugged his shoulders and shook his head. It was a government hospital and if the funding was better, the treatment would be better. Everyone in the military understood that fact.

Pat responded with a small, comfortable smile. He wouldn't make light of another man's plight in any situation, let alone one as bad as this one. "I figured you'd get the best the Navy has to offer. I'm right again, aren't I?"

Bryant nodded and reached a hand up to remove the mask so he could speak. He was a large man and the bed was too small for him. His feet hung almost over the end and his body covered the expanse. He rasped and hacked before answering. "It's good to have a visitor. My wife has been the only one here all day. That and the fucking doctors who don't know shit." His voice was throaty and scratchy.

Pat nodded. The doctors he saw in the hallways looked like they were about twelve years old. "They hire these guys fresh out of the morgue, I think. After they get a couple of dissections in first, of course."

Bryant nodded and put the mask back on his face. It made it easier to breath, even if he only took a hit on the oxygen for a couple of minutes.

"Can I ask you a couple of questions, Gary? About what you saw on the *Nevada*?" Pat asked.

Bryant nodded. He'd known from the beginning that the Navy would get someone over to question him. It was important to try and get as much intelligence out of him as possible before he wasn't coherent enough to answer any questions.

"Did you see anything not in the original report? I've read it a couple of times." Pat had a hopeful look on his face, even though he didn't really think this interview would produce a lot. It wasn't unusual for a senior officer to omit things in a report that just didn't quite fit. Any tidbit of information that he could get might help later on down the line.

Bryant pulled the mask aside again and motioned for Pat to move a little closer. Putting a hand out he touched the front of Pat's uniform. "One thing, for sure. I knew I couldn't put this in there. They'd send me for a section nine hearing if they read this kind of shit."

Pat took another step closer to the bed and leaned forward. Whatever Bryant was about to tell him wasn't something for the general public. A "section nine hearing" was a mental competency exam. The last thing you ever wanted to be asked to take. If they invited you to that hearing, then someone already thought you were screwed up.

Bryant glanced at the door, coughed again and said, "I saw them move, Pat. The bodies. They moved."

Pat frowned. Maybe he'd been wrong and Bryant was a little too high on the drugs they were giving him through his IV to give a lucid interview.

"I know what you're thinking Pat. But I swear, they moved when we were leaving."

"A trick of the light, maybe, Gary?"

Bryant shook his head violently back and forth. "I know it's crazy, but I know what I saw."

"Did you tell anyone else?" Pat asked.

"Nobody. I knew they'd never believe me."

Pat nodded and thought for just a moment. "Okay. I can see that. Any ideas why?" he asked, just to be polite. He knew why the bodies were moving and Bryant would've known also if he could think clearly for just a moment. He was obviously on some kind of "happy" drug, perhaps Demerol or Morphine, to ease his pain. The moving bodies were simple physics.

Bryant suddenly grabbed the front of Pat's shirt and clutched it firmly in his hand. "The bodies weren't swaying with the listing of the submarine for Christ sakes, Pat. I've been a Navy man for too long to fall for that shit. The bodies were swinging in the *opposite* direction of the motion of the sub. With the waves."

Pat stood up straight as the realization set in that Bryant knew exactly what he was saying. He tried to picture the logic behind the movement but nothing came to mind.

"There's something *evil* going on in that submarine, Pat," Bryant released his grip and sank back into his bed.

As if on cue, his oxygen regulator started beeping and his heart-monitoring machine squealed like someone had unplugged it from the electrical socket.

Pat stood back and watched helplessly while the room filled with doctors and nurses who urgently tried to revive Commander Gary Bryant. Inside his heart, Pat knew they would fail because whatever killed Gary Bryant was not of this earth. His death was not natural at all.

# CHAPTER TWENTY-FOUR

Pat's office was smaller than most of the offices in the federal building. He'd asked his superiors more than once for some extra space and a bigger budget to run his operation, but like most government bureaucracies, there just wasn't enough money to go around. Pat came to expect the same answer every time he asked the question. It was always the standard: no, but thanks for asking.

He pushed past the glass doors with frosted windows that bore his name and nothing else. At one time the name of his department had been stenciled on the front of the windows, but as time passed and his group got buried deeper under the weight of their investigations, the name was "mysteriously" removed one night. All Pat knew for sure was that one day he showed up and the name of his department was gone from the door. He thought maybe he was going to be replaced as well, but the Navy just didn't want to acknowledge their existence.

After leaving the hospital, Pat drove straight to the office. He brushed past his male secretary and went into the conference room where he knew Jon David would be hiding. If nothing else, JD always followed routines. Pat knew he liked to study in the conference room because at some point during all of the investigations they'd done together, Jon David had found his way here. It was sort of a sanctuary to JD, as far as Pat could tell. He could block out the noise and the intrusions of the rest of the world and concentrate on the problem.

Pat had been Jon David's supervisor since the day he took him from the ranks of the shore patrol. He held the technical rank of lieutenant commander, but in reality that was only for his pay grade. Pat hadn't even seen him wear a uniform for the last several years, which was all right with Pat. He needed him for the work, not the pomp and circumstance. He didn't care what clothes JD wore. Pat only cared that when he was needed, JD did the job that so many others simply could not handle. They didn't have his gift or his ability.

JD was solidly built, could run a fairly quick forty-yard dash, and kept himself in shape. Pat knew JD liked the challenges working for this department brought and he could always count on him. He never complained about his assignments even though they were frequently dangerous and always unpredictable. It wasn't like being a black ops field agent where you knew who the bad guys were and what they were doing. Pat's department dealt with the surreal as often as the tangible. JD was invaluable in the surreal parts. It had occurred to Pat on more than one occasion that some men were just cut out for this kind of work and JD was one of them.

And Jon David Stickle was driven. He had a sense of right and wrong, and an unbelievable desire to solve mysteries that made other men run away. Pat always figured it was something in his DNA that just wouldn't let go until he knew the answers. All the answers to all the questions. He always went back when others thought it was over. Why he did what he did, Pat would probably never understand. The best investigators were born, not made.

Pat's department was a work "as needed" basis and when the Navy needed, they called. JD could have said "no" at any time, but the truth of the matter was that Pat would have crawled on his hands and knees to bring Jon David Stickle into his department. The Navy could have fussed about rank and priorities but the people who made the final decisions at this highest level knew Stickle was where he belonged.

JD was sitting at the main conference table with a series of papers spread out all across the top and some reference books from the office library opened at various places. There was a lit up laptop computer to his right and a steaming coffee mug to his left. He looked up when Pat pulled the chair out at the other end of the table and sat down.

"Looks like you've had a worse day than I have, Pat," JD said as he lifted a pair of reading glasses from his nose and leaned back in his reclining leather chair. He liked to rock in the chairs that allowed him to rock. It was a nervous habit that gave him some sort of comfort. Once he thought he might possibly have a slight case of autism or something like it but he never pursued the matter. The rocking was just a tic. His level of concentration was never in question.

"I see you're rocking again, JD. Did you find something?" Normally the rocking was a nervous condition but lately Pat had picked up on the motion when JD was onto something.

"I don't know really. I found a couple of things at Brown's apartment. A vial of liquid that's probably insignificant, but these are way over my head at the moment," he motioned to the blueprints spread out on the table in front of him.

Pat rolled his chair over closer to the papers on the desk and leaned over to see. "Did you give the vial to the lab boys?"

"Yeah. They said it was a fairly common muscle stimulant, but a little stronger than the average doctor prescribes. With Brown's background in biology, I figure he altered it for personal use. Probably had trouble sleeping or something and he used it on long sea voyages. Against regulations, but not a serious violation. He wasn't shooting up or anything like that."

"Blueprints?" Pat asked.

JD nodded. "As near as I can tell. Some kind of box, or maybe a sarcophagus? The pictures on the sides are clear enough. I've been in the books this morning and all over the Internet checking out as much information as I can get about them. Three of them are famous nautical mysteries. The *SS Waratah*, *Flannan Isle*, and the infamous *Mary Celeste*. This one looks like a door."

Pat furrowed his brow and looked at each of the four pages one by one. He picked them up and studied each intently without saying anything for a full five minutes. "We might need to get the engineering department on this. Can these things be tied together somehow? I doubt it. Obviously, the rest of this stuff is over the top. Whoever drew all these faces and this other shit got into his work. Why body parts? Hell, I don't know either."

JD shrugged. "Your guess is as good as mine at this point. I'll keep working on it. The door really doesn't fit the pattern. I basically have no idea. But Brown wanted these blueprints to be found, I'm sure of that. He hid them decently, but from what you told me about him, if he didn't want them to be found, then I would never have found them. He was too intelligent to make a mistake like that."

"Where did you find these?" Pat looked away from the images. It was hard to concentrate on the pictures on the side of the box with all the hideous faces screaming from the borders.

"They were hidden in a hollow leg of his desk. Well hidden, yes, but not for someone with an IQ of one hundred and eighty. He could have devised something that was impossible for someone like me to find. Or anyone else for that matter."

"So he wanted us to find the prints?" Pat wasn't really sure he could believe that. "Maybe he ran out of time with this last deployment and didn't get time to hide them as well as he would have liked. He could have been in the middle of working on them and ran out of time or something. What do you think about that idea?"

JD shook his head "no". "It doesn't make sense. Plus I don't know that we were the ones he wanted to find the papers. It could have been anyone. Maybe a relative. Maybe a partner or friend. Anyone. We can't assume he wanted the Navy to find them." He pointed to the symbol in the corner of each page. "See this symbol?"

Pat squinted at the small letters. "Looks like the number '4' and the letter 'L'."

"That's pretty much what I think. But it's got to be some kind of code. I don't know if it's for the blueprints to unlock what's going on in the box, or if the code is meant for whoever or us. Or if the code is even related to the box at all. I don't have a damn clue as to what it means or even where it leads us."

"I have no idea. None," Pat said as he studied the blueprints again. "Was the hollow leg easy to find?"

"Easy enough, I guess. But what led me to them makes me think that maybe Brown hid them for us to find."

Pat leaned back in his chair and noticed that JD was rocking at a steady pace. It normally happened when he was in deep thought or just kind of searching. For what, Pat had never quite figured out. "You just told me you didn't know who was supposed to find these prints. Now you're changing the story. One thing at a time. What led you to these?" he motioned to the prints.

"Captain Brown had a rolled-up piece of paper with the 4L symbol stuffed down his throat."

"Stuffed? What do you mean stuffed?"

JD pursed his lips. "It looked to me like Brown rammed this thing down his own throat before he died. It must have hurt like hell, but it was definitely meant for somebody to find it. He made sure that someone, probably the guy that performed the autopsy, would find it. That would be a Navy doctor, I'm sure. So eventually, I've got to think Brown knew the Navy would get their hands on it. But I found it first."

Pat looked up at the ceiling and then out a distant office window as he let his mind get a clear picture of what Jon David had just told him. It was a nice day for Washington at this time of year. The sun was out and the temperature was in the low forties.

But that was the only pretty thing about the day. It wasn't a pretty picture inside his office or in his department. Not pretty at all. He looked back at JD who was scanning the first sheet again. "Did you get any help from any of these books?" He pointed at the open books on the table. His office maintained an extensive library of books on nautical mysteries and unexplained events. "These things never seem to help much. The only thing I ever got from them is how many unsolved mysteries there are in the world. I personally think it's probably better that some things don't have answers," Pat said thoughtfully.

"Not a damn bit of help so far." JD picked up the book closest to the blueprints. He held it up for Pat to see. "This one's on unexplained disappearances and strange phenomenon. There's a ton of strange shit, but nothing like what we've got here."

"Anything even close?"

"Nope. Lots of ships and people disappearing into the seas,

never to be seen again. Like the Bermuda Triangle, for example. The three events depicted on the sides of the box are unexplained disappearances. People just gone in the middle of the night never to be seen again. But nothing to do with nuclear submarine crews hanging themselves."

Pat nodded. Everyone who sailed the Seven Seas in the last century knew about the *Mary Celeste*. It was nautical legend and required reading at the Naval Academy. He picked his next words carefully. He tapped the picture of the *Mary Celeste*. "You're gonna have to go back in the sub and find the connection."

"I know," JD said softly. He thought for a moment before continuing, "I'll leave the blue prints with you but don't give them to the lab boys until I get back. I want to look them over one more time before the Navy buries them."

Major Mark Lowry clicked the speaker off. He put the pen down and rubbed his hand. He'd been writing their entire conversation down. It was amazing how much he had learned over the years from a few well-placed listening devices in certain offices around the federal building.

He then leaned back and concentrated for just a moment. As much as he hated to admit it, Jon David Stickle had gotten farther with this investigation then he would have ever imagined. But then, who could have guessed that Brown would leave a trail to blue prints that anyone with half a brain could have followed? It was an unexpected event that Lowry was going to have to deal with immediately.

He turned in his chair and punched the button that connected him to his assistant. Without formalities or any semblance of politeness, Lowry barked into the intercom, "Get me a secure line. Now."

"Aye, sir," was the only response.

Mark Lowry's career hadn't gone exactly according to script. His father and his grandfather had both retired from the Navy with honors and medals, his father even earning a silver cross for heroism in battle. But it never seemed to work out for Lowry. There was always a stumbling block and after twenty-three years, he was stuck at a major's pay grade and a soon-to-be dismal retirement. The older he got the more he hated coming to work to hear about everyone else's promotion. The advancements that he knew he should have gotten many times were frequently given to less qualified persons, at least in Lowry's opinion.

But a few years ago Lowry stumbled upon a solution to his problem. With a couple of late night phone calls, some backing from wealthy people who believed in him and his unique abilities, and two or three illegal wire taps, Lowry's prospects for retirement had improved significantly.

This was the last job he'd ever have to do for anyone. The last time he would salute anyone he didn't want to salute.

"Sir? Secure line on two," his assistant said.

Lowry ignored the secretary on the intercom and connected his satellite phone to the secure line on his desk. He had a call to make to Costa Rica.

# CHAPTER TWENTY-FIVE

Ana woke up momentarily confused. She didn't remember coming back to her cell or even having one of them carry her back. Normally, after one of their experiments on her, she could at least recall the trip back to her dungeon. But not this time.

She sat up straight in the chair. Shaking her head for a moment to try and regain her focus, she blinked her eyes a couple of times and then trained her attention on her surroundings. It was somehow different but still the same. They had never brought her back in a wheelchair. It wasn't like them.

"It's okay now, my dear," Limeh said from behind her.

She turned around and made a quick note of where exactly he was standing. She mentally calculated the distance from the chair to his groin. If she needed to lunge out of this seat and rip his throat out or yank his testicles off, she wanted to know the exact space that separated them.

He reached down and gently moved a small strand of yellow hair out of her face. "We haven't exactly treated you like we should have up to this point. It's not the way I would've liked us to behave. We can all be adults here, I think. But you can trust me. From now on, things will be different." He moved his hand from her hair to her shoulder and gave it a soft squeeze.

Ana recoiled from his touch like a snake bit her. She'd never heard gentleness from either one of the old men who looked down on her and this man had no reason to be nice. She couldn't remember the last time one of them touched her in kindness. It was strange thing and hard for her to process. It just didn't feel right.

Sitting in the chair, she straightened her posture and controlled her breathing one breath at a time. She felt a little stronger than the last time she came from the machine room. The last memory she had was Gunther hooking up the hoses and then turning away. She'd closed her eyes while on the table and attempted to go far away. Then she woke up in this chair with the old man behind her.

All of the other times when she'd regained consciousness, she'd been so weak that she could barely lift her head. Tired to her very core, she would drift in and out of sleep in an almost drunken stupor. She was always aware of the trip back to her cell, always aware they were carrying her to the darkness, but this time she was fully awake.

Something had changed and for Ana, in her experience in this hell, that meant it was something bad.

"I know you're feeling a little stronger this morning, Margana, my dear," Limeh said. "Probably more awake mentally also. Don't let that worry you. We added some strengtheners to your cocktail when we took you off the machine. The last couple of times we were afraid we might lose you and that just wouldn't work. Mr. Greyson and I would be very upset if something happened to you."

She listened quietly and calculated all her odds while he pushed her chair. She was constantly swiveling her head back and forth, trying to learn if there were any new exits she could use the next time she ran. The hallways were poorly lit down in the basement of this house on purpose. As she passed each one she would quickly glance down the dark corridor to see if it possibly led outside and she might be able to use it.

"We keep it dark in here for a reason, Margana," Limeh said as he pushed her. He knew she was constantly on the alert looking for a weakness. Everyone who dealt with her understood that fact. She was smart and cunning and could be extremely disarming. "We wouldn't want you getting lost again in the tunnels under this place. That wouldn't do at all." He spoke to her like he was admonishing a child instead of a thirty-year old woman.

She tried to move her hands and noticed for the first time they weren't chained down. She'd been so amazed at being awake and wheeled around in a chair, she hadn't noticed the restraints were missing. She flexed and straightened her arms like it was the first time she'd been able to use her muscles. Moving her arms left and right and opening and closing each of her hands, she tested her strength.

"You'll feel better each and every day from now on. I believe we've finally perfected the cocktail we gave you today. It will enable you to feel stronger after the machine is turned off and recover quicker. We haven't been able to do it before, but something new has happened, something extraordinary, and we need your very best."

Limeh stopped pushing the wheelchair and stepped back. He was standing just outside of Ana's reach and was still very wary of her. They had barely entered her cell that was located in the farthest end of this particular tunnel, and he was almost leaning back against the doorway. He didn't think she would strike at him, but her trend suggested she could snap at any minute. He knew she was both strong and mentally unstable. Her physical attributes were never a question, but she was completely unpredictable.

She stood up from the chair and slowly turned. She lifted her downcast eyes to look at him and one green eye and one blue eye met his dark grey eyes for just a second. She tensed and released her legs and then her arms. She clenched her jaw and balled both hands up into a fist. She was just about to pummel him. She needed only one more second to act.

Limeh saw the tightness in her muscles and the determination in her eyes. He couldn't really blame her if she wanted to kill him and Greyson. They had handled this situation completely wrong from the beginning and if he had to do it again, he would have changed everything. But he could no more change the past than he could stop the freight train of events that were now on a collision course.

As he steeled his nerves for her to leap at him, Limeh reached a hand into his jacket pocket and pulled out a folded bundle for her to see. He lifted it up in front of her so she could view it clearly in the dim light of the cell.

Ana gasped and instantly her fists unclenched and her leg muscles relaxed. She took an involuntary step backwards. The thing the old man was holding was so beautiful she couldn't tear her eyes away from it. She squinted as she tried to take it all in, and then tentatively reached her arms outward to grasp the red piece of linen.

"It's okay, my dear. Take it. Mr. Greyson picked it out for you. I'm not very good with these kinds of things." Limeh let the dress fall to its full length as he lifted it just slightly.

Ana ran her fingers gently along the seams of the full-length gown, afraid to touch it in case it might crumble in front of her eyes, and then she started to sob very softly. Carefully, slowly, she took the dress in her arms and then held it desperately against her chest. It felt like a river was flowing over her and warmth was enveloping her. Something like this was so beautiful, so wonderful, that she only wanted this moment to last.

She took a step backward from Limeh and clenched the gown to her body, rubbing it against her skin over and over again. It was simply delicious.

Limeh had seen enough. He wasn't her mother, after all. "Put the dress on, Ana. Now." The vehemence was back in his voice. He carried an undertone of something sinister and always a veiled threat of violence and malice. "Put the dress on right away," he hissed again.

She nodded. She would never release it. Never take it off for any reason. It was the most beautiful thing she had ever seen.

As Limeh pulled the door to her cell closed he faced her once again, safely behind the steel bars. "You have a roommate coming to join you very soon, Ana."

Ana recoiled like she'd been shot with a twelve gauge shot gun directly in the stomach.

Noticing her anxious look, Lime couldn't help but chuckle. "No, my dear, this one is *alive*," he said as he turned and left her.

# CHAPTER TWENTY-SIX

Jon David was more prepared this time when he climbed down the ladder of the *USS Nevada*. He'd already been here once, his nose wasn't even running let alone bleeding, and he knew that the men were dead. They wouldn't be moving this time around.

He was here for a couple of reasons. It had become obvious, the more he looked at Captain Brown, that he didn't know enough about the man. If he was going to solve this one, he was going to have to go back to the beginning and get it right. He was going to have to spend a little more time probing the inner workings of the man, and that included going over the body one more time. The way Jon David figured it, if he had hidden one clue to the puzzle on his body, perhaps there were more. Perhaps, Brown had another secret that was waiting to be found.

And Jon David knew that he really had nowhere else to turn. There was nothing else to go on.

He'd left Pat at his office and walked for a while before boarding a private jet and flying the one-hour trip to New York. He wanted to clear his head before facing the swinging corpses again. It wasn't something he relished: being alone with twenty-four smiling dead men. On the other hand, he knew the answer had to rest with one of them, if not with all of them.

He stepped down off the final rung of the ladder, prepared himself mentally for what he was about to see, zipped his jacket up, and then turned on his flashlight. The order of his movements he'd choreographed in his head on the flight. He was going to make a deliberate, quick search of a certain number of items that he wanted to see one more time, and then he was going to get the hell out.

It was still very cold in the sub, he noticed. Nothing had changed concerning that. He was silently hoping for a little bit of warmth this time around, even though he knew that would be impossible because the Navy had to keep the bodies at a constant temperature until the coroner got a chance to autopsy them. And that wasn't going to happen until Pat released them and Jon David finished his part of the investigation and the bodies were no longer needed.

He lifted his flashlight up and focused it on the first row of men. With a slight grin, JD noticed that none of them were moving this time. He moved the light quickly along the row and then stopped, dumbfounded.

Taking in a quick cold breath of dead air from the icy surroundings, Jon David felt a newfound fear clutch at his stomach and he almost dropped the flashlight. His teeth started to chatter immediately and his nose dripped a single drop of blood.

Captain Joe Brown's body was gone.

# CHAPTER TWENTY-SEVEN

Jon David blinked his eyes several times. He couldn't believe what he was seeing. Actually, he couldn't believe what he was *not* seeing.

He wiped his hands on his pants, momentarily letting the flashlight's beam fall from the spot where Brown's body was hanging the last time. His hands were clammy and even though it was below freezing in the sub, JD was sweating profusely. It felt like the sweat was literally jumping out of his pores. Trying its best to get away from him.

He carefully lifted the light back to level and retrained the beam on the empty space. He moved the light to the immediate left and then back to the right, making sure that the corpses that were hanging next to Brown were still there. He couldn't be sure if the two men on the sides of Brown were the same as the last time, but there were two of them.

Counting quickly now, Jon David swept the light from the first row to the back to make sure that the rest of the men were all in their respective places. When he got to the last man in the back row, JD let out a quick sigh: twenty-three. None of the others had disappeared. At least as far as he could tell. He was beginning to doubt his sanity.

He walked slowly forward to the only empty space in the otherwise perfect rows of hanging men. Right directly in the middle of the front row. He quit trembling for just a second as his curiosity overtook his fear. He may have been terrified, but he was also intrigued as to whom or what could have caused the body to be gone.

Jon David shined the light up and down and back and forth throughout the slot where Brown had hung. He didn't see anything out of the usual, and there wasn't anything on the floor. The noose was still there but empty and that was ominous enough by itself.

There was nothing to indicate that he'd been taken, or even

worse, had somehow gotten down off the noose and *walked* out of the sub. Even though that idea seemed ridiculous outside of this submarine in the bright New York sunlight, inside of this place, in the frosty air and in front of corpses that started swinging the last time, Joe Brown getting down and walking out didn't seem quite so absurd.

He tilted the beam upward and inspected the noose. It was a standard Navy issued piece of nylon roping and was perfectly formed into a killing device. Whoever had fashioned the rope into a noose knew what he was doing.

Suddenly, JD heard a scraping sound from the rear of the sub and he jumped back and crouched while simultaneously drawing his Beretta from its holster. He quickly swept the light over the back of the sub until he located a small rat scurrying along the aft deck. As he watched, the rat stopped and turned to look directly into the beam of the flashlight. It sat up on its rear haunches, and squawked at JD.

Dismissing him from its thoughts, the rat went back to what it was doing before JD's light found it: chewing on the feet of one of the men hanging in the last row.

Jon David looked away from the rat and shook his head in disgust. He would have thought that down here, under these kinds of conditions and especially at this temperature, the damn rats wouldn't have figured into the equation. As soon as he got back to the main side, he'd have Pat clean the sub out and get rid of the infestation. He considered shooting it but knew the old saying: where there was one rat, there were always more.

He noticed his nose starting to bleed and decided he needed to get out of the sub before something else happened. He ran his light across the decking one more time to see if he'd missed anything important, and then looking back at the place where Joe Brown should have been hanging, he turned to leave.

He made sure nothing was disturbed from when he entered, turned and quickly climbed back up the ladder. He closed the hatch on the top of the sub and stood up when he suddenly felt something like a bite from a spider against his left hip. It rocked him instantly forward and he fell to the hard concrete driveway as twelve hundred electric volts from a Taser stun gun dropped him to the ground.

Major Mark Lowry made sure Jon David hadn't seen him when he crawled out of the sub's hatch. He watched him fall listlessly to the ground as a steady rain started to pound the pavement around the two of them. Lowry stepped a little closer, placed his Navy-issued Taser under the left armpit of a semi-conscious Jon David, and fired the volts into him once more. JD jumped and rolled over on his back. He hadn't been told to hit him more than once, but he considered this more than ample payback for the "get laid much?" remark Stickle said to him a couple of days ago.

Lowry glanced up quickly, motioned to the two idiots that had come along with him on this job to help move Stickle, and then pointed to his car. The two men gathered JD up roughly, cracking his head against an antenna of the submarine at which Lowry laughed, and then carried him to a waiting car.

They dumped Jon David unceremoniously in the trunk of a black limousine and Lowry made sure he jammed JD's legs in at an uncomfortable angle. He saw JD wince and cringe more than once as his unconscious form registered the pain.

Lowry slammed the trunk lid, paid the two idiots and shoved them out of his way, opened the door and climbed into the back seat. The driver left a spray of stones and a black patch of rubber when he peeled out of the parking lot heading straight to the airport.

Smiling and a laughing while sitting in the back seat with the partition window closed, Lowry logged onto his private Caribbean bank account and checked for the latest deposit. The money had been safely transferred yesterday and he loved to just look at the amount. His Navy pension wasn't even close to the amount he needed to support his gambling and sex addictions. This little transaction, making sure Stickle was delivered in one piece to Costa Rica, made him a wealthy man.

With his bags already packed, Lowry watched a still unconscious Stickle being loaded into the pressurized cargo bin of the private jet, and then took his seat in one of the seven over-sized lounge chairs onboard. He directed the pilot to take off immediately and then leaned his chair back and ordered a martini from the flight attendant.

In three and one half hours, he would deliver the two packages to Costa Rica, and then he was leaving for the Caribbean, never to be seen again by the US Navy.

# Book Four

## Creation

# CHAPTER TWENTY-EIGHT

*I am Evil.*

*I have existed for centuries and spawned a growth of carnage and destruction like maggots feed on a dying carcass in the desert sun. Eating until they can eat no more. Digesting and shitting across everything that they can ingest.*

*I am evil.*

*And I am tired.*

*For the last two hundred years I have been collecting an army of disciples. Lowers like yourself who I've selected to worship at the ass end of an awakening. I have taken ants from the four corners of this world to be part of an historic event. To aid as we rise up to overtake the highers. To witness an event that is so magnificent I can scarcely await the proclamation.*

*You have been selected for a task that will complete my life's destiny. For so many years, longer that I can truly remember, I have destroyed all that I have touched. Everything that I have come in contact with I have willfully vanquished to a painful death. To a painful state of another world. You have been chosen to complete that journey by beginning another.*

*I have always chosen the destruction of a species as the vindication of my own existence. If I can destroy all that I come into contact with, if I can obliterate the physical world, then I can substantiate my own achievement. To achieve through destruction is as worthy a life story as I can write.*

*But I am Evil.*

*I am an essence that has been passed down from person to animal to person throughout this world's lifetime. I have maneuvered myself to this point in my time here. And now you will fulfill my last malicious symphony. And for that, I will require all that I have accumulated throughout my existence.*

*You will build a machine unlike anything that this world has ever seen. Unlike anything conceived. It will complete me.*

*I am preparing myself for the final conflict and need to level the playing fields. I have assembled my army from derelicts that will never be missed. I have taken those of your species that are the cast offs and hidden them. They wait entombed below the whale shit on the ocean's bottom. Soon, I will call them together to witness the event. To rise up and kill all on this planet. It will be destruction unparalleled.*

*I will not fail. I cannot fail. This is to be my swan song.*

*I have initiated the destruction of your species. I have begun the process of creating a new world.*

*This machine in which I will guide you is beyond the scope of your understanding. The tiny brain your species relies on is incapable of this kind of creation. Incapable of designing the inner workings of this kind of a masterpiece.*

*I need something that I cannot have in the physical sense, so I will create it through your puny ministration. You will be the medium that I must work through. You will not fail me. I will make sure your hands have the tools and the capability.*

*I am Evil. I am prepared for the final destruction.*

*And I have decided to create this one time.*

*I need a perfect host. One that will not break down.*

*I desire an enshrinement.*

*I am Evil and this will be my Coronation.*

☒

April, 1945
Austria

Up until this moment, things had not been going very well for Heinrich Himmler. As Reichsfuhrer of the SS he was head of the military police and in charge of all internal operations for the Nazi Party. Germany was under attack from all sides with the Soviets aggressively advancing to the East, and the Allies knocking at

Berlin's door to the West. It was obvious to all involved that the war to purge the world of inferiors was almost over and the Third Reich was going to lose.

Nine days ago, Himmler's beloved Fuhrer, Adolf Hitler, had called him to the Wolf's Head Cottage high in the Bavarian Mountains and given him all the bad news he could handle. As he left that meeting, he had been downtrodden and disgusted with the war effort and his own country's inability to conclude a vision that was so obviously perfect he had signed up as a boy and never regretted his decision for one second: the eradication from the world of all the undesirables. Jews, homosexuals, people with disabilities and generally anyone not part of Germany's master race would be wiped from the face of the earth. Himmler went about his business with a jealous fervor that won him favor many times over in Hitler's eyes. Himmler's systemic extinction of the expendables at concentration camps was highly effective and production line efficient. Until lately, he'd been extremely proud of his accomplishments.

But the rest of the world did not understand the perfection of his vision. The perfection of his craft. Eradicating millions from the face of the earth was not an easy task. It required creativity, desire, and especially logistics that Himmler excelled at providing.

Until recently, he was convinced that the war was winnable and the rest of the world would fall under Germany's iron fisted rule. Then things would settle down and he would take his post as head of the military police worldwide. It was all part of the master plan for the master race.

But beginning with Stalingrad, the Third Reich's army suffered defeats that were incomprehensible to Himmler and setback followed setback. No matter how hard they fought, Germany was doomed and Himmler himself might be left to the discretion of the Allied Commander.

For a man of his power that was quite simply unacceptable.

The voice cried out to him and he answered it.

The voice of Evil. An Evil so intense that Himmler trembled in its presence like no man on Earth could cause him to tremble. And Himmler did one other thing for this voice: he obeyed it without question.

*You will build for me a machine of great power capable of toppling this world of its puny species.*

The owner of the voice, whatever or wherever the entity came from, did not concern him. It thundered into his brain like a German V-2 bomber exploding across the British Empire. He not only wanted to obey it; he absolutely must do as it said. This was his destiny.

He followed the orders without question like his military mind compelled him to do, and he assembled the greatest engineering minds Germany had to offer. Minds that were so far advanced of the rest of the world that a machine like Himmler dreamed of building, was well within their grasp. It could possibly turn the war by creating a master race. The race Nazi Germany so drastically needed right now.

And now, Himmler's eyes shone like he was looking at the Hope Diamond as he stared at the machine in front of him. He was locked deep inside a cave in the Bavarian Mountains. The heavy wooden door was bolted from the *outside*. The five engineers who had been rounded up by his police and shackled together were forced to work without rest for six straight days. No breaks, no food. Just a need to complete. Just a force to finish the most important invention the world had ever seen. A physicist, metallurgist, chemist, biologist, and a surgeon had created something that could not be created. That should not have existed. That only existed in horror magazines.

Until now.

Himmler had provided the blueprints and the scientists, though secretly not believing the project even remotely capable, had taken to task, knowing that Himmler would easily have them killed or sent to the concentration camps to be tortured if they didn't agree. If they didn't participate and if they didn't succeed. No one failed Reichsfuhrer Himmler and lived.

Heinrich knew he was no scientist. Knew he was incapable of designing something of this magnitude, of this *magnificence*, without intervention. Yet his hands had drawn the blueprints, had been led to this end, had made the plans that he couldn't envision prior to the voice.

Reaching out slowly, tentatively like he was about to touch the face of the Fuhrer, Himmler laid his hand on the machine shining at him from the pedestal. It was the most exuberant event of his life.

The machine was made of solid gold. It measured three meters long by two meters deep and stood at just over one meter tall. It resembled a golden coffin with a depth that belied its exact measurements. To someone unfamiliar with the project and the treasures inside, it was just a large golden box, worth only the price of the metal.

As Heinrich delicately stroked each side, he let his fingers trace their way along the perfectly aligned edges and caress the outer markings on the four sides. Each of the sides was inlaid with golden pieces, perfectly stationed and anointed. Pictures of events that he didn't comprehend, didn't really care about, and couldn't waste his energy on. A lighthouse, some ships, and for some reason, the door to this laboratory. Perfectly placed and set against a backdrop of red.

The inside of the box bordered on miraculous. The five scientists managed to weave, sew, weld, hinge, lace, and ultimately thread body parts together. Vital organs that should have been on some living, breathing human, were now intertwined with each other by a series of animal veins. The ministrations of the renowned Third Reich surgeon fashioned the bits and pieces into sheer perfection. Sheer brilliance.

There was no shortage of available organs. Donors from Himmler's death camps along with special pieces that he'd kept alive in jars of formaldehyde: lungs, hearts, eyes, brains, livers and kidneys. Pieced together now in tandem in an exact sequence with only one goal. One desire. Perfection in creation.

Fluids would be needed, Heinrich knew. But that would come later when the day was at hand. Fluids that made it come alive.

He laid his face against the front of his machine and inhaled the incredible beauty of his golden angel. It would make every other modern machine invented obsolete before it was used. This was the height of technology and German engineering. The first time it was turned on, the entire world would kneel at the feet of the Reich.

The five scientists were standing back against the far wall of the cavern, literally in awe of what they had created. Even the physicist of the group, the most brilliant man in Germany, could find no words to express his amazement at this piece of art. What he helped Himmler to make, what they had fashioned in this mountain laboratory, was beyond the scope of his own comprehension.

Heinrich sighed audibly into the quiet of the room and the five scientists gazed at the golden glow emanating from the machine. It was strangely still inside the cave, except for a continual scraping sound as the organs flexed against each other inside the machine.

As he petted the edges, Heinrich reached into his uniform jacket and pulled out a military issue Luger pistol. He smiled a toothy grin at each of the scientists when he made them kneel in front of him. It made no difference at all that they were pleading for their very lives, that they were family men, or that they had done exactly what he asked of them; it mattered only that six people in this world knew of the existence of this machine, and five of them had to die.

One by one he shot them directly between their eyes.

When it was over and their corpses lay sprawled across each other on the floor, he put one more bullet into the backs of each of their heads to confirm the kill, and then holstered the pistol.

Laying his face against the smooth top, Heinrich let his fingers outline the surface as he hugged the box against his chest. It was too heavy to possibly move alone, but he could easily reach his arms from one end to the other across the solid gold top. It was completely smooth and if he had the time, he would have slept on it.

⊠

With the precision of a surgeon and the tenderness of a newborn's mother, Heinrich directed the loading of the machine onto the back of an American-made halftrack truck. It took three of the Reich's strongest infantrymen to load the pallet, and place it precisely as directed by the Reichsfuhrer, but finally the mission completed. Heinrich rewarded each of them with a bullet to the face and then one in the spinal column. He then poured petrol throughout the cave they'd been working in for the last six days and over each of the eight dead men and set them on fire, burning the place to the ground.

*There can be no witnesses.*

He drove throughout the night until forced to stop from exhaustion. He was running on pure adrenaline for the last twenty hours anyway, and eventually the laws of nature took over and he had to pull over to the side of the muddy road and sleep. He took a quick drink from a leftover canteen in the back of the halftrack, but for reasons he couldn't fathom, Heinrich felt no hunger. He felt only exhilaration.

Thirty minutes later he was back on the road again, feeling as if he'd slept for fifteen hours. He was fully refreshed and intent on his journey. His picture of what they made in the Bavarian Mountains could not have been clearer. His mission to deliver the package could not have been more succinct. It was the culmination of his military career.

*You have one other job to accomplish before bringing me my machine.*

The voice that spoke to Heinrich was so intense, so forthright, that disobeying would have been sacrilegious. It was leading him on a journey that would deliver the machine to his master and quite possibly save the Third Reich in the process.

As he drove through the night across Austria to the Mediterranean Sea, Heinrich Himmler could not help glancing backwards through the curtain of the halftrack. He would alternately reach through the curtain and lovingly caress the smooth top, and then kiss his hand where the box had touched him. It was as close to perfection as he could imagine.

The American's controlled this part of Europe after running across Italy and then turning their attack north towards Germany. Their aim was simple: along with the Russians to the east, they would simply cut off the head of the German army by choking it from two different sides at the same time. They had broken through most of Germany's fronts and sent the Third Reich reeling backwards, running home with their tails between their legs.

It was a simple afterthought that Heinrich had directed that this green and black painted halftrack with the American Flag on the side be confiscated by his police a couple of months ago. He had no intention of using it, let alone driving it, across enemy territory, but after the guards opened the barred doors to the mountain last night, the reason for sparing the halftrack's destruction became obvious: he would drive it behind their advancing front.

*You must disappear along with the machine. I still need you.*

Heinrich nodded to the voice inside his head while he drove. Without knowing why, he turned the halftrack into a small driveway on the outskirts of a town he didn't recognize, nor could he remember having ever seen. A garage door opened in front of him and he drove the truck into the tight space. He shut the motor off, and then collapsed against the steering wheel.

⊠

When he awoke later, he had no recollection of how long he'd been asleep. It could have been days or months for all Heinrich knew. He felt all right, but slightly different, if that was possible. He wasn't sure why, but he knew something had changed while he slept.

He blinked his eyes to get the sleep out of them and then slowly sat up. He felt groggier than he should have and knew something other than just a hard nap had happened. Looking down at his right arm, he noticed a clear line had been hooked up to him and some kind of fluid was being fed into his veins. Without pausing, knowing he didn't have time for this, he pulled the IV out and then tried to stand up.

"You will feel like this for only another few moments, Reichsfuhrer," a soothing voice said to him.

Heinrich turned towards the voice. He staggered like he was drunk and then steadied himself. He nodded at the bald man in the frock with round glasses who had spoken. "What have you done to me? I will have you shot and your family sent to the camps for this."

The man stepped back in fear. "I only preformed what you asked, Herr Himmler," he hurriedly answered. He was terrified to the core.

*It is as it needs to be.*

Heinrich nodded to the voice. He stood up straight and looked at the gurney next to him. With a shock, he noticed the man lying on it was his identical twin.

*He will take your place as you come to me. No traces. No witnesses.*

Heinrich cleared his head one last time, rubbed his hand across his mouth and noticed his teeth had been removed and he now had swollen gums and wooden dentures. He shrugged. It was not a concern.

"Where is my machine?" he suddenly screamed at the doctor.

The scared man pointed at the garage and Heinrich rushed out to make sure the halftrack and his prize were safe. When he was satisfied, he came back into the den of this chalet that had served as his operating room, and promptly shot the doctor twice. He then took the man's clothes and put them on, and in a sudden moment of inspiration grabbed an eye patch from the doctor's cabinet.

He quickly gouged out the left eye of the unconscious man who was going to act as his double with a pencil, put his old uniform on him and then lifted him into the front seat of the halftrack. Heinrich then siphoned some petrol from the tank of the truck and set the chalet on fire. He heard several screams as he pulled out of the garage including some that sounded like children and reminded him of the concentration camps, but he no longer cared even remotely.

Turning the truck to the south, he headed directly for the sea again.

⊠

Heinrich drove throughout the night until he reached the Mediterranean Sea. He passed several American convoys of men and supplies heading north to replenish the troops that were attacking his homeland. Two weeks ago the only thing that mattered to him was the survival of his beloved Fuhrer and the Third Reich; but now it was like mud on these roads. Nothing could stop him.

He drove straight to a sparse location along the beach and turned the halftrack towards the sea. He had to spin the tires several times when they got stuck until he was close enough that the water was lapping up against the rear wheels.

The man who would act as his double awoke during the night's travel. He was drugged and confused and complained about his mouth hurting. Heinrich spent the last several hours of the drive convincing the man that he was the Reichsfuhrer and had just been through a horrific operation that left him mentally confused and with a slight case of amnesia, but he was to resume command as soon as he was physically competent. He told the man that his teeth had to be repaired and he would need to wear an eye patch for a short while until his vision improved.

The man nodded without speaking several times like he wasn't really in control of his own movements. He put the eye patch on to cover his bad eye and even sat up straighter in the seat as he began to believe he was the head of Hitler's Military Police and had been wounded in combat. He believed it was only a matter of days until he could resume his position of authority. Until he could take over again.

As the sun rose in the east and lit up a tremendous amount of aircraft heading north for a coordinated attack that would bring the end to Germany, Heinrich used the buoyancy of the sea to slide the machine out of the truck and into the water.

While the new Reichsfuhrer stood on the beach with his eye patch firmly in place and his amnesia firmly in control and watched him open-mouthed, the man known throughout the world as Heinrich Himmler grabbed the side of his beloved golden machine and pulled it into the sea. Together the two of them disappeared into the rising surf.

⊠

The collapse of the Third Reich under the Allies relentless attack at the end of April 1945 was not only swift, but also brutal. Everywhere, German officers were trying to escape to South America through a network of Nazi sympathizers. As soon as the Allies got to the concentration camps, anyone who had ever been a friend of Germany would be hung in the fields and all German officers were going to be put to death at the tribunals. Every soldier of the Third Reich knew these facts.

It also became apparent to all involved that Reichsfuhrer Heinrich Himmler had been acting stranger with each passing day. Since his return from a quick trip to the Mediterranean Sea that included an attack on his personal caravan and left him injured, not even his closest officers could predict his behavior. There were several reports of Himmler trying to negotiate surrender by Germany. The man was also behaving oddly. The Allies eventually captured him at the end of April, while wondering around dressed as a major. The man claimed over and over again that he wasn't Himmler but was someone else whose identity had been altered.

Unable to persuade anyone of his innocence, the Reichsfuhrer committed suicide with a cyanide pill he hid in his teeth during his capture. The Allies confirmed his identity through dental records before burying him in an unmarked grave.

# CHAPTER TWENTY-NINE

Present Day

Pat Smith stood at his office window admiring the twinkling lights of downtown Washington, DC. The day had started off as drizzling rain with cold temperatures, but by the afternoon strong western winds had blown the cold front out to the ocean leaving only blue skies and warming sunshine. It left a twilight haze over the city at this time of year that accentuated the high-rise buildings and made the towering office lights sparkle as they reflected the rays.

Normally, Pat could have stood at the window and admired this view for hours, but there was too much on his mind at the moment. He had an upcoming call with a rear admiral in thirty minutes, hadn't made any progress since the last time they'd talked, and wasn't really sure where the investigation stood. Adding to his misery was the phone calls to the families of the men onboard the *USS Nevada* coming due. He knew he'd have to face each and every one of them soon. It wasn't a job he even wanted to take on until he could at least tell them something.

The first question they asked, after the initial shock from hearing that one of their beloved family members had died, was as predictable as the sun coming up across Chesapeake Bay in the morning: What happened? How did he die?

And that was the worst part. Pat not only had no explanations; he couldn't tell them if he did. If was a double-edged sword that caused confusion and anger on the part of the families and he certainly couldn't blame them. Hell, if he'd lost a son or a father, he'd want to know why also.

The Navy refused to release information from his department for several reasons, but the most glaring one was that since his department didn't really exist, how could they release information?

After Pat delivered the bad news, like a spy for a covert operation, Pat would just fade into the background and the phone calls to his number would go unanswered. The Navy would simply shift the calls to another department, the families would never get past the first line of defense of the switchboard operators, and that would be it. For the rest of their lives, they'd never know what happened. Never know that the Navy had classified the *USS Nevada* and its crew as top secret. Never know when, how, or under what circumstances they passed away. Killed in combat? No comment. Killed in service? No comment. Friendly fire? No comment.

And no official autopsies were ever performed.

Pat turned from the twinkling lights of the skyline and sat back down at his desk. He fiddled with the manila folder lying squarely in the middle, presently closed. It was his second problem for the phone call with the rear admiral.

Pat took a pencil that he'd been chewing on until it was nothing more than a nub and some leftover lead, and pushed the file back open again. He was almost afraid to touch the file with his fingers. It was that bad.

He adjusted his reading glasses and read the autopsy report for Commander Gary Bryant for the fourth time since it arrived earlier this afternoon. He scanned for anything out of the ordinary, but kept coming back to the same conclusion at the bottom of the page: Gary Bryant was in excellent health and his death was a complete mystery.

In other words, the examining doctor at the naval hospital had no idea why a man in relative good health without any signs of trauma had deteriorated so quickly and succumbed under the best medical care available.

It made no sense to anyone.

Pat didn't want to tell the rear admiral that either.

"Shit!" Plat slammed the folder closed and banged a closed fist on the top of his desk. "Shit! Shit! Shit!"

He cursed himself and shook his head. He forgot the golden rule: It isn't about how it affects you; it's about the men. Pat had lost sight of that and quickly scolded himself.

No matter what Pat Smith had to endure, there were twenty-four good men dead and he had no answers at all.

His intercom suddenly buzzed. Pat hit the "transmit" button. "This is Smith." *Here it comes*, he thought.

"Sir, sorry to inform you, but we've lost contact with Mr. Stickle," the man said it quickly and softly, knowing the kind of reaction it was going to get.

"What? What the fuck do you mean you've lost contact with Stickle? Where the hell is he and who the hell had last contact?" Pat stood up and was screaming into the intercom.

The assistant recoiled in his chair. He hated to give news like this to a superior. "We were tracking his movements through a secure wireless device, but it seems to have gone off the air, sir," he said meekly.

"Get your ass off this intercom and get someone who's qualified on that equipment to check out our end and his end. Make sure the transmitter is still working and we're capable of receiving. No bullshit malfunctions."

"Yes, sir. Immediately sir."

"Then get me a car for the airport and scramble a four man seal team. Have them geared up for covert ops and ready to be airborne in thirty minutes. Have them meet me at the airport, packed and hot."

"Yes, sir. Right away, sir."

"Now!" he said as he clicked off the transmit button. Grabbing his jacket and quickly checking his sidearm, he was already running around the side of his desk and headed for the first floor to get his car to the airport.

Jon David Stickle never went without checking in.

Never.

# CHAPTER THIRTY

Jon David was so nauseous he was convinced he would puke his stomach contents up at any minute. He twisted a little to his right and felt a stab of pain. He reached a hand up to his forehead and rubbed the place where his headache was pounding so hard he thought it might split his skull open.

He rubbed and pinched his forehead directly above his left eyebrow. The pain was shooting across his brain like someone cracked him with a brick before he fell to the ground. He didn't feel any blood or open wounds, which he took as a good sign. At least he wasn't going to bleed to death.

He opened his eyes into a strange darkness that surrounded him. It was so dark that his vision was restricted to a couple of inches in front of his face at best. For some reason he felt no immediate threat, so he relaxed and let out a breath only to instantly feel another sharp pain across his left hip where someone had burned him. He hadn't been shocked like that in a long time, but he knew what had done the job. He'd used it on more than one occasion himself to stop someone in his tracks. Jon David had no doubt that he'd been tasered.

When he fell to the pavement outside the *Nevada*, the last thing he saw was some kind of military insignia on the cuff of the boot of whoever jolted him. It wasn't much of a clue, but he burned it into his memory for later. He wouldn't forget and knew he'd run into that guy someday.

Jon David was lying on his back in some kind of a crate. He spotted a small slit of light that if he moved just a little bit to the right or to the left, he could see through. He turned his head back and forth and squinted through the tiny crack trying to figure out where exactly he was being held. The only thing he could see for sure was a ceiling that had metal spars running across it.

He squinted through the slit at the same time he heard the whine of a jet engine. Someone was transporting him. This couldn't be good news.

He flexed his back and legs and tried to get some feeling of the size of his confinement area. It was small, like a shipping crate, but long enough that he could be fully stretched out on the carpet and ride fairly comfortable, at least. He could feel the floor pressed up against his back. It was lumpy like they hadn't laid it correctly or smoothed it out right. It felt sort of like he was lying on bags of oranges by the way the lumps would shift and bob when he arched his back or pressed against the carpet. There were various places that pushed up against him and as he squirmed a little bit here and there to get more comfortable, he realized it just wasn't going to happen. Not on this floor. Not on these bags.

There didn't seem to be a reason to panic right now. He wasn't strapped down to anything and he had full movement of his arms and legs within the confined area. And although he hurt like hell and wasn't happy about being kidnapped and riding in a lumpy orange crate to somewhere by someone he didn't know, it could have been worse, he thought. He could have been dead. And his nose wasn't bleeding. Not yet anyway.

Jon David had no reason to be scared.

Until now.

A sudden understanding that things weren't exactly like he thought and a fleeting image of what he was lying on ran through his mind. It wasn't so much an image, as it was a haunted thought. At one moment he'd been testing the lengths of the crate he was confined in, and then he suddenly realized that his main concern shouldn't be what he was housed in, but rather what *might* be in the crate with him.

That wasn't a lumpy carpet underneath his back.

He slowly, carefully moved his hand between his legs and felt the carpet underneath. The surface was scratchy and a sound like he was scraping his fingers across a pair of jeans came to him. He pushed a little harder down with his fingers until he moved the carpet aside and he suddenly felt skin. Someone *else's* skin. He yanked his hand back quickly like he'd touched a hot plate.

He was lying on top of a body.

He was riding in a *coffin*.

Without enough room to turn around and verify, Jon David violently thrust upwards and banged his head on the ceiling of the coffin and then with all of his strength he tried to force the lid open. He jammed his knees up against the lid and used any leverage he could muster. A rising panic that he'd been able to calm until now began to scream its way into his system and start flying up the base of his spine to his brain.

Every time he moved he was consciously aware of the shifting of the body beneath him. All of his twisting and jerking had moved the carpet separating him from the other body and his shirt had worked itself up until raw skin touched raw skin. The body was death cold and icy and scraped against JD's back every time he moved. It had to be a corpse and not another kidnapped person. The absolute frigid feeling of the skin could not have been from a living person.

Jon David's panic was racing from his head to his toes. He hoped, no he prayed, that it wasn't who he thought it was underneath him. Lying alone in the dark with only a tiny slit for light, flying to an unknown destination, and being entombed with a corpse made him start to tremble.

*Please God,* he thought. *Not that.*

He stopped pushing uselessly against the lid of the crate and tried to control his emotions. He could easily lose it in this situation. He wasn't necessarily claustrophobic, but he might be now.

He knew who was in the coffin with him. He knew who was pressed up against his back and whose cold skin felt like sand paper against his back. As Jon David started concentrating to keep his sanity and keep from screaming out into the darkness, he knew that the dead black eyes of Captain Joe Brown, the Commander of the *USS Nevada*, were boring into the back of his head.

His breath started to come in quick, curt gasps and his chest constricted. It felt like a ten-ton weight had been placed on his ribs and with each short draw of the still air in the coffin, JD began to smell the dead air surrounding him. He coughed and hacked and rapped his head on the ceiling at the same time as desperation settled over him. There was a rancid, disgusting, dirty, reeking kind of air that his lungs spit out before he could get it in and he felt himself start to black out and lose consciousness. Little bursts of white light flooded across his vision. Jon David finally heaved his stomach contents up into the back of his throat and his heart rate accelerated until he thought it was going to tear itself from his chest.

He started to pound his fists against the lid until his knuckles bled and unable to get a clean breath of fresh air, he finally blacked out and mercifully slipped into unconsciousness.

Above him, sitting in his first class chair and drinking a martini while listening to the incessant sounds coming from the cargo compartment that contained Jon David and Joe Brown, Major Mark Lowry only smiled. Every time he thought he heard Stickle whimper in the dark, he felt a little richer.

# CHAPTER THIRTY-ONE

*I am Evil.*

*And I am your father.*

*Arise my children. Awaken from your slumber and come to witness an event that has been foretold for two centuries. A historic event that will place me on the throne of this puny world and at the seat of my everlasting destiny. An event that will mangle the common myths about all that mankind has believed in since the dawn of this civilization.*

*All that man has been lied to about creation is about to be shattered and distributed to the wind like flies ingesting a dead horse in a field. Man has been fed something that he could never swallow. A packet of lies that a true Evil cannot exist. That will no longer make sense in the dawning of the new civilization. All the deceit will be revealed and a new king will be born to take over. He will be all that I have ever been and more than you can possibly imagine. Arise and take your place at my feet as I lead you to the final conflict.*

*Arise from your murky graves and your covered places and bear witness. Arise and live again to join me as one.*

*Come to me now. Come to me as an army and as a witness.*

*Come to me NOW.*

⊠

Ensign Dale Foggerty dropped his coffee cup and sat straight up in his chair with a look of total alarm written all over his face. Until five minutes ago he'd been enjoying a game of chess on the computer screen in front of him, and after a few deft moves and some allowable take backs the computer had given him, he was now in a position to win his third straight game against the company's newest artificial intelligence computer. At a modest cost to the taxpayer of just under three hundred million dollars, "The Deep Thinker" as everyone who worked at the National Oceanographic Association called it, was so impressive that it was whispered about in the hallways of the building like it could actually hear the employees talking. The workers were quite simply dumbstruck by the abilities of the computer. It was as close to a human intelligence as the engineers and scientists in this century would ever be able to achieve.

But Ensign Foggerty's nighttime job of simply monitoring the various blue screens in front of him didn't lend itself to awe-inspiring worship. If anything, Foggerty thought the thing only played a relatively decent game of chess. Other than that, he didn't have much use for it.

But five minutes ago all that changed.

He had just moved his queen into position to check the computer's black king, when a distinct "pinging" sound rang from the computer screen to his immediate left. Normally this sound meant that a message was incoming and a small box would appear in the lower right hand corner of the otherwise dark screen to show who sent the email or who needed Foggerty to forward him a snapshot of the oceanic conditions somewhere in the world.

When he glanced at the screen as he mentally moved his queen, he was stunned to see the screen lit up like New Year's Eve in Times Square. Blips, dot and lines were streaming across the screen at a pace that he could barely register. He couldn't read all the text messages that suddenly started to appear on the readable box on the lower portion of the screen. Messages from all over the world were streaming in at a firestorm pace.

Crazy messages. Things that simply could not be true.

If this new artificial intelligence computer was even close to being correct, then the seismic registers on the bottom of the seven oceans across the world were registering earthquakes hitting the ocean floors all at the same time with an almost immeasurable strength.

On the bottom of the Pacific Ocean, approximately four hundred and twenty miles from the northwest coast of Australia and at a depth of three and a half miles with a pressure per square inch that would have shattered titanium steel, the mud shifted. It didn't move slowly or smoothly; the mud on the bottom of the ocean exploded like the tectonic plates the Earth rested on had all shattered at the same time. The bottom of the Pacific was still and serene at one moment and in the next instant it disintegrated into thousands of particles.

Reefs, plants, algae, sandy loam and salty mud along with millions of species of fish and marine life were hurtled upwards as if an atomic bomb had been detonated beneath the ocean's floor. Against all the laws of physics and gravity of upward movement, the ocean floor became a mass of upheaval as it was thrust up from underneath and thrown like blades of grass in a lawn mower. Anything that was resting now became a torrent of debris swirling in the sea like an underwater blender. The visibility across the ocean dropped to zero from the torrid movements of anything near the floor.

In a remote stretch of unremarkable corral, two hands violently clawed their way out of the silt and mud and dug frantically clearing the way for the rest of the man's body to follow. He had been buried for over two hundred years, but now, the man was awake. As he wiggled and struggled, the corpse that was dead but now moved like there was blood in his veins, pulled free from the murk and in a tornado of ocean movement began a journey one step at a time.

All over the world, at the bottom of the deepest seas on the face of the Earth, the clawing and surging scene was repeated time and time again as long dead bodies, buried under hundreds of years of ocean flooring, struggled to live. Temporary tombstones were pushed aside and hands clutched at anything they could grab as hundreds of missing people from the last two centuries, people long forgotten or given up on entirely by the physical world, clamored their way out of muddy algae-infested graves. They moved as one, clawing, ripping, shredding, and tearing apart the very bottom of the oceans that had served them for so long. Had made them comfortable until this day. Until this moment when they would be called again.

Led by a force none of them could understand, and called from watery graves that had been their final resting places, the bodies arose and began a trek. They stumbled over rocks and crushed everything they stepped on with a force previously unseen but now rejuvenated. They walked like the dead moved, towards a destination, intent on a task that required no preparation.

They were headed for the western coast of Australia.

⊠

Ensign Foggerty had three phone calls to make and had never been so terrified in his entire life. The first call would be to his supervisor who was asleep at this hour and hated to be awakened; the second call summoned the head of the National Observatory of World Weather to action; and the third was supposed to go to the US Naval Observatory in Annapolis, Maryland. Although all of them would probably think Foggerty was either insane or had been drinking on the job, by the time he emailed a "snapshot" of the computer's screen to each of them to verify the information, the phones all across the world would be ringing. If the information from "The Deep Thinker" was correct, then the Earth was about to experience an unheard of series of earthquakes that would cause tidal waves, typhoons, torrential rains, and bring flooding and death to whole cities, possibly whole civilizations, depending on where the waves struck land.

Foggerty was scared shitless, not from the potential impact of the earthquakes, but because he was trained for one job only and if he misread the computer inforomation before he sent it out and declared an upcoming worldwide disaster, he would be fired and lose his pension. He was about to send the snapshot across secure lines

187

and wait an excruciating amount of time until someone got back to him, when he hesitated ever so slightly before pushing the "send" button.

He glanced to his left again and for some reason the computer screen had stopped the furious pace of streaming information.

*Perhaps it's a mistake*, Foggerty thought. *Perhaps there's been a power surge or something.* Anything that could explain this before he sent it out to the world for confirmation.

The screen lit up again like it had never stopped and the seismic waves across the world's ocean bottoms started to register in the five to six point scales on the Richter Graph. He decided to instantly send the information.

As Foggerty slid his hand across his keyboard and positioned the cursor over the "send" icon, he felt a stabbing pain race cross his forehead. It was quick and dirty, and felt like a sudden headache was about to make itself known. He wasn't surprised. The stress of the last several minutes would give anyone, including a seasoned veteran of this desk, a headache, let alone a newbie like Foggerty.

Suddenly a white-hot burst exploded in front of Foggerty's vision and he fell backwards against his chair. In the next instant, he clamped his mouth down and bit violently through his tongue and then flung himself off the chair and onto the ground as an intense seizure hit the left side of his brain. In less than three seconds, Foggerty was pouring foam and spittle out of his mouth to mix with the blood from his severed tongue. He was dead in the next minute from an aneurism that raced through his skull and caused the left side of his brain to hemorrhage a bucket of blood.

"The Deep Thinker" screen suddenly went back to its soft blue and blank panel display, all of the information erased.

# CHAPTER THIRTY-TWO

Jon David's fists hurt. When he realized he was trapped in a pseudo-coffin with a corpse underneath him, he'd pounded on the lid until his hands were raw. Until he couldn't pummel it anymore because the pain in his fists overcame the fear in his belly. That was all that he remembered before passing out.

And here he was again.

Lying on a different kind of floor, he kept his eyes tightly closed. He listened carefully, and reached his left hand out to feel beneath him. When he touched cold, wet ground, a childhood memory of the mud under a bridge near his home flooded back to him, and he knew he'd at least gotten out from the box with the dead captain. It was a small relief, although he didn't know anything else and he was sure that this wasn't necessarily better than that had been. This could be worse. A lot worse.

Jon David opened his eyes slowly, feeling like the more time he took to actually look around the better it would make the surroundings. It was dark, but he could see a light bulb hanging from a ceiling that seemed a long way up. The light was too far away to do much good and the room reminded him of a fuzzy picture from one of those old Kodak cameras that his father owned. The images were always slightly out of focus and as JD looked around the room, it seemed that there just wasn't enough light to make out anything.

He stretched and realized he wasn't confined anymore, so he started to get up when he glanced fully to his left and saw her staring at him. She hadn't made a sound and was curled up against the wall like she about to pounce on him. He immediately stopped his movements and pulled back against the wall behind him.

Neither of them said a word for a moment and JD squinted into the dark to try and make out her features. She appeared to be in her early or mid-thirties and was light skinned with dirty blonde hair that fell half way over her face and down to her shoulders. The one eye he could see was a hazel color or maybe green, he couldn't be sure which, and she was breathing heavily like she'd just come back from a three mile run. With his right hand out of view, he felt along the muddy ground to see if he could grab some kind of weapon.

She straightened up then and flexed her shoulders back like she was preparing for a fight. She took in a sharp intake of breath and held it ever so slightly, ready to spring.

JD couldn't locate anything to defend himself with and decided instantly on another tact: stall her.

"Hello," he said in the darkness and the word echoed a couple of times before fading away.

She tensed at that and then held completely still. It would have to be now if she decided to kill him.

"I'm Jon David Stickle."

She hesitated then. Her eyebrows furrowed together at the sound of his voice and the words he used. Ever so slightly, she withdrew a fraction of an inch, still ready to spring.

"What's your name?" he said.

No one had ever had a normal conversation with her that she could remember. He was small and pretty, not like the others in the cell with her, and he was alive. It wasn't something she was used to seeing in here.

Her voice cracked just a little. "Ana. They call me Ana." Her hands dropped from in front of her in a guarded position to her sides. The fight was gone but she was still ready. If she had to she could always tear him apart. He was small and defenseless and didn't know this cave. She could use the rocks on the wall to bash his head in if necessary.

"I won't hurt you," he said very carefully. He hoped she wouldn't hurt him either. It looked like she was as tough as any of the marines he'd ever met.

"And I won't hurt you for the moment," she spat back at him. She had no reason to trust this man. No man had ever treated her with anything but pain.

JD nodded. "Fair enough to start. Ana's a pretty name. What's your last name?"

She looked away momentarily and JD followed her gaze across the room. He was instantly startled and his sense of smell was assaulted at the same time. Up until this moment he hadn't even noticed the others in the room. There were four dead men sitting across the room, concealed a little bit by the shadows, but they were still there. Stone cold dead.

As JD strained his eyes and then saw the men a little more clearly, he shuddered involuntarily. The men were missing parts, like they'd been *harvested*. And it must have been recently because the last one on the left, the smallest of the four, was oozing something out of a hole in the center of his chest. A black, thick liquid slithered down the front of his old shirt.

"Oh shit," JD whispered in the darkness when he saw that the oozing dead man was Joe Brown.

# CHAPTER THIRTY-THREE

"They can't hurt you. Only I can do that," Ana said matter-of-factly as she flipped her hair back over her head and looked at Jon David.

He tore his eyes away from the four men and looked back at her. She was pretty, but needed a bath. And he was sure she could hurt him. His right hand moved unconsciously to the waistband of his jeans and felt for the nine-millimeter berretta he always carried. He instantly remembered that it'd been taken. Probably after they tasered him outside the sub.

"Oh shit. Sorry," he said a little sheepishly, averting his gaze. Her eyes were different colors and startled him. Not something he'd ever seen. He glanced down at his shoes and the mud on them. He didn't have much but he still had some manners left. He never liked swearing in front of a woman and he shouldn't have stared at her.

Ana looked at him like he'd just done a cartwheel in the center of a busy freeway. No one had *ever* apologized to her. It was one of the most stunning things that had ever come out of a man's mouth. She had no idea how she should react.

Jon David glanced back at her. She wasn't as frightening as he first thought and she was in the same predicament. *An enemy of my enemy is my friend*, he thought. "Where exactly are we? Do you know?" He sat up straight but made sure to keep her at a distance where he could assess her movements easily. He still wasn't sure she wasn't some kind of a lunatic or maybe a shill. It could have gone either way at this point. He deliberately resisted looking over at the men across from him. They weren't going anywhere anytime soon and he needed information. She was the only possible choice.

She shook her head. "No. In the jungle, but I don't know where. On a mountain in a big house. That's about all I know."

"A mountain?"

"Yeah, a mountain. Every time I've gotten away I have to run through the jungle to get down to the water. I love the water," she said very softly.

JD saw it then. She was a child-like girl in a woman's body. He hit on something she said. "You've gotten away? How?"

She shrugged her shoulders. "Anyway I can, but they've closed up the tunnels now and I don't remember how I've gotten out the other times."

"There's been more than once?"

Ana nodded. "Yeah. As many times as I can."

"They must have caught you and brought you back?" It sounded desperate to him. He wasn't sure she had the mental capacity to manage an escape attempt. It might have all been in her mind.

"They always send the dogs. The damn things always catch me. They can run faster than me, you know?"

"I know. And they can smell you."

She nodded again. "That's right. They always track me until I'm caught. Last time was the best though. I was gone for almost three days."

"Where did you go?" If she was making it up, she had an active imagination. The details would tell him.

"Into the city. A tunnel somewhere under a big bridge. I don't know. I ran in that direction." She indicated across from them like she could see outside. "I ran that way."

Jon David noticed her wrist when she pointed. It was covered in deep scars and raw muscle, like she'd ripped it on a rusty nail. He figured it must've hurt like hell and hadn't been properly bandaged.

"I'm not going to hurt you," he said softly as he reached across the expanse between the two of them.

She wasn't afraid of him, but she did not trust him. Too many times a man had hurt her. But none had ever talked to her before for this long. And he asked about *her*.

JD very slowly put his hand out and pointed to her wrist. He motioned for her to let him look at it.

With all the willpower she could muster she kept herself from recoiling at his touch when he softly grasped her wrist in his hand.

His fingers were rough, but not vicious. She was on full alert and her other hand was searching the ground for a rock to bash him with if he hurt her.

Jon David pulled her wrist closer so he could see the marks and the cuts better. He knew immediately that they were self-inflicted and that she had probably tried to kill herself on more than one occasion. He was no doctor but the cuts were all straight lines and ran from her hand towards her elbow. No one else but her would cut like that. They would have cut her across her wrist, not in line with her arm. He couldn't help it that he felt sorry for her and whatever had gotten her into this mess.

Looking up at her and then softly massaging her scars, he whispered, "I'm getting us out of here and I'm taking you with me, Ana."

At that moment, directly across from Jon David and Ana, in that tiny, dimly lit cell, the four corpses began to move.

# CHAPTER THIRTY-FOUR

"He's arrived, Mr. Greyson."

Greyson turned from the fish tank in front of his wheelchair. He'd been feeding a large South American version of piranha with two small, live lionfish. The lionfish were a particular aggressive and ruthless hunting fish that liked to pounce on their prey. Pitting the lionfish against the larger piranha was a sport that Greyson had come to enjoy. The death throes of an obviously inferior opponent and the stalking of the hunter.

"Where did we put him?"

"He's in the cave with Margana. They're getting acquainted," Limeh said. "I had him searched first in case Major Lowry missed anything."

Greyson scoffed and then coughed into a wrinkled up fist. "I never liked Lowry. Never trusted him either."

"He's predictable, which is good. Solely driven by money, which is a simple enough of a motivator. But there's always the chance those kinds of pawns can make mistakes. He isn't special." Limeh had moved to stand behind Greyson's wheelchair. He peered intently into the fish tank as the piranha circled and then attacked the lionfish. It would bite off a chunk of the fish and then retreat to the opposite end of the tank and chew it up while the wounded fish watched. A hunter enjoying the pain.

"No. I never thought Lowry was special. He will have to be dealt with when this is over."

"I will personally see to it, Mr. Greyson."

Greyson nodded and pulled his shawl a little tighter around his shoulders. Even though they were located in a climate that never got cold, lately Greyson was always cold. His time was near, he knew.

Limeh didn't miss the curled up and gnarly hands of Greyson as he moved the shawl. He hadn't missed the earlier cough either and knew that it was getting very close. Very close.

"How are the two of them getting along? Has she bitten him yet?" Greyson asked. He'd become bored watching the piranha kill its dinner and had begun moving his wheelchair towards the fire.

"They seem to be talking. Not what I would have expected. But the gown we gave her changed her a little, I think. We should have given her something like that a long time ago. Before she became so uncontrollable."

Greyson nodded. "It might have changed some things, but not the outcome. We both know she was a mistake. We both know she has to be corrected. A nice gown wouldn't have changed that one bit."

"Now that he's here, we can begin. The message has been sent out. The masses will be in position soon." Limeh grinned then and his yellowed teeth clinked together.

"We'll do it tonight. We'll have to prepare both the machine and the ceremony. I was thinking we might wait a little while, but I feel an urgency now."

Limeh's grin got wider. "I'll start immediately. This will be historic, Mr. Greyson."

"True," was the only response he got from the old man who now slumped slightly in his chair.

# CHAPTER THIRTY-FIVE

Pat Smith sat back in the plush leather chair of the Gulfstream G5 jet and smoked his cigar. He'd been chewing on the ends of the thing ever since he'd received word that Jon David had gone missing. Unable to stand it any longer, Pat had lit the cigar and inhaled the Cuban smoke deep into his lungs. To hell with the no smoking rules of the FAA and the jet manufacturer. They could sue him.

He pulled the stogie from his lips and let out a blue plume of smoke into the small cabin of the jet. The plane was owned by the US Navy and usually reserved for admirals and above pay grades. Normally the pilots stood on standby and had to be ready to take off at a moment's notice to some resort vacation spot with the admirals and their families. But this time was different.

One of the men sitting across from him in another of the six forward facing seats scowled in Pat's direction when the smoke hit his olfactory senses. "They don't allow that, sir," he said in disgust while pointing at Pat's cigar for the third or fourth time since Pat had lit it up.

"Don't really care, sir."

The Navy Seal scowled again and went back to rechecking his gear. He had three different types of garroting-edged knives packed in a small suitcase and had just finished sharpening the second one. Obviously he favored hand-to-hand combat.

Pat had ordered the seals to meet him at the plane and the jet had taken off within thirty minutes of getting the word on Stickle. The Navy Seals were an impressive bunch: simple, trained to respond quickly with deadly force, and most importantly, they kept their mouths shut. They always traveled in packs and this time their commander was a female lieutenant Pat had dealt with one other time. She was extremely capable. Two of the seals were waiting on the tarmac before Pat's car even got there.

Pat looked out the window of the plane. They were cruising at thirty-five thousand feet above a broken layer of cirrus clouds. The clouds were thin and Pat could make out patches of land underneath. They'd been in the air for almost an hour and half flying in a southeasterly direction from Washington.

The lieutenant quit fiddling with her gear and checked her .40 caliber handgun. Satisfied the gun was in working order with a full clip in the magazine, she looked over once more at Pat. Lieutenant Cummings was the team leader for the seals and would take her orders from Pat and then pass them down the line. The other three men were either resting or checking their own equipment.

"Wanna tell me what this op is all about, Colonel Smith?"

Pat knew he was going to have to answer some questions sooner than he wanted. It would have been better to have all of the information instead of just some tidbits. He exhaled another plume of smoke and said, "This is a rescue mission of one of our own."

The lieutenant nodded. "Okay. Location? Terrain?"

"Don't know just yet, but we should have a fix on him at any time."

"I thought you said he was missing? Didn't you say that when we boarded back in DC?"

Pat shook his head. "I said we had lost contact with him. I've been tracking him since I put a GPS locator in his jacket pocket when we were in New York together on a pier."

The lieutenant nodded. "He didn't know he had the GPS tracker on him, did he?"

Pat smiled. "No. He doesn't like it when I track him, so I do it anyway."

"Good idea apparently."

"Sir?" Pat looked over towards the front of the plane where a radioman sat with a pair of headphones over his ears and stared at a blip on a radar screen. "We've got your tracking device located on a hill in Costa Rica," he said and then went back to staring at the computer screen.

The lieutenant thought for a second. "Who is he?"

Pat reclined his chair a little further. What a question. He wasn't sure he could even answer that one. "He's important. And he's special. Name is JD Stickle."

"Okay, sir. We'll get him."

Pat turned that statement over in his mind for just a second. Hopefully, whatever took JD wouldn't get them first. On impulse, he pointed to the radioman. "Find out who's the closest sub to Costa Rica with Tomahawk missiles and get them moving stat."

"Aye, sir."

For some strange reason, Pat thought he might need bigger firepower than the seals carried this time.

# CHAPTER THIRTY-SIX

Jon David pulled Ana close to him and stepped between the men in the cell and the two of them. He had never seen the dead rise before but he knew for a fact he didn't want to hang around long enough to see it happen with these four men. This was a scene out of a demented movie.

Ana looked anxiously back and forth between JD and the men. She'd never seen any of them move before except when their bodies reacted from someone pulling parts off of them or sucking out their innards. She had seen them recoil and flinch, but not with conscious thought. The men were now starting to stand with a purpose and for that reason alone, she wanted to get far away from here.

JD stepped back against the wall and tried to figure a way out of the room. The men, for their part, were starting to gain their balance, one by one. Each of the bodies flopped a bit at first and then gained strength in long dead leg muscles and began to stand fully erect.

Joe Brown, who had been dead for at least a week, lurched forward and then fell to almost a kneeling position before regaining his balance and lifting his shoulders and his body to an upright position where he was standing directly in front of JD and Ana. The other three men were listing like they were drunken sailors after an all-night binge. Their muscles, long ago decayed and rotten from years in this cell, did their best to compensate and provide the movements commanded of them from a half-functioning brain, and they stumbled forward with lanky, awkward lurches and falling steps. Each lifting of their feet and each step forward brought an ungodly belch from an open body cavity and a stench that filled the cave.

Jon David didn't really have the luxury of being scared. They meant to harm him and he had no other way out. He moved to the first in line, and noticed he was wearing an old naval uniform with a ship insignia on the sleeve. He feinted to his right and ducked just slightly, kicking out at the man's kneecaps with his left leg. He caught the corpse squarely in the shin and as the man fell forward, Jon David rabbit punched his nose and heard several bones snap into pieces. The man lurched again and his head flew backwards in a look of pure surprise before he collapsed to the ground.

Turning to his left, JD threw a near perfect punch to the side of the head of the smaller man and then immediately elbowed the man to his right. Both of the walking dead fell to the floor, without any fight left in them and no muscle strength to support them.

Jon David turned to face Joe Brown, the last man standing.

"Bravo! Bravo, Mr. Stickle. Very well done," a voice from the top of the pit echoed down.

Jon David didn't let his guard down and kept an eye on Brown the whole time. He stepped back a full step and made sure there was enough room between the two of them that if Brown came at him he would still have time to react. When he was satisfied that he could control any advances by Brown, he looked up to the sound of the voice.

"Obviously, our army requires more muscular strength. They weren't supposed to be completely out of the water. Something I hadn't thought about but it will have to be rectified immediately. I am Alexander Greyson, Mr. Stickle. This is my longtime companion, Mr. Limeh," Greyson motioned to the man standing behind him.

Jon David looked up into a light beaming in his eyes. He could see the outline of one man in a wheel chair and an aide standing behind him. Their features weren't clear to him but they looked to be old men. Finally, the man with the money showed his face. The guy who paid for all this.

"If you let me out of here, I'll let the two f you live," JD said.

Greyson chuckled. "Your file said you had balls. I guess they got that part right. You're in no position to bargain, Mr. Stickle."

"Well, since we're not here to visit, why don't you tell me what position I am in, before I decide to climb up there."

"The walls are moss covered steel plates. You cannot climb them nor can you escape unless we decide to open the door. I'm sure Ana will tell you the same thing. She's been with us for quite a while, at least. You should relax. All will be explained to you shortly."

"It's hard to relax when you've just watched four dead men get up and walk, wouldn't you say?"

Greyson chuckled again. "Agreed. It's so good to have an interesting opponent again. I will enjoy watching you, Mr. Stickle."

Jon David thought for just a moment. This guy had brought two of them a long way. They must have been worth something. He glanced up to make sure Greyson was watching and then leaped across the cell and grabbed Brown by the throat. JD twisted and wrenched himself behind Brown and grabbed his neck in the crook of his forearm. With a subtle shifting of his weight, he forced Brown to his knees. "Try this then. If you don't open the door, I'll snap this guy's neck in two pieces and he'll be flopping on the ground for the rest of his time."

Greyson screamed. "No! No! There's no need for that, Mr. Stickle. I will open the door. Do not hurt him. We need him intact."

A click behind JD sounded and he dropped Brown's body to the floor. The man fell loosely like his bones weren't really on board with the whole idea of being brought back to life and forced into service.

Jon David turned quickly and pushed the door open and pulled Ana behind him into the darkness of the tunnel. He looked at her and could see she was nervously scanning the tunnels ahead of them like she knew something was waiting for them.

"We go. This is our chance. Don't think for a minute that guy has kept you locked up here for however long and brought me here to let us out this easy. We'll see him again, I'm sure."

Ana nodded. "I know," was all she said as she followed him into the tunnels.

⊠

Limeh leaned over the side of the pit and watched them step into the cave through the open door. "We couldn't let him hurt Brown. We need him in one piece."

Greyson nodded. "I quite agree. It was the right decision. We need to go to the machine room and prepare. The two of them will be captured and brought to us soon enough."

Limeh laughed. "I'm sure they'll have some fun while they try and find a way out of this house. The tunnels can be so interesting." With that he pulled Greyson's chair back and then propelled him to the machine room.

# CHAPTER THIRTY–SEVEN

When the moon actually crested over the city of Broome, Australia and the west wind blew in across the shore, that's when Jennifer Laird had to hit the waves. It was the perfect time of the day, as far as she was concerned and she couldn't really understand why no one else got the concept. The beach was empty without a soul in sight, the ocean was warm and the tide was rising. Add to that a report of waves breaking three to four meters across the surf and she had to ride them.

She ran across the sand and literally hit the water at a full gallop. She was twenty-three years old and in the last year of college at the University of Perth. She had taken on the difficult task of majoring in prenatal birth disorders and hoped to one day be on the forefront of research into the causes of birth defects in full term babies. Her day consisted of running from class to study group to advisors to the occasional job interview and she was always mentally exhausted. Surfing was the only respite she even knew these days with finals just three weeks away.

Paddling out she could feel the water's seventy-six degrees cascading across the front of her board and then over her back and down her legs. It was like she was being cleansed of all the anxiety of the day's events with each wave that hit her board.

She flipped her brown hair out of her eyes and spotted the wave she was going to ride back to the shore a couple of hundred meters away. Tying the board to her left leg with the nylon clip, she crouched in her ready position and waited for the inevitable rush she knew was about to consume her.

All of the sudden she was bumped from underneath and had to sit back down on the board as she momentarily lost her balance. She thought it was a bit strange to hit a coral reef this close to shore because she had surfed this part of the beach for years and had never run into one or even heard other surfers warn her away from this area.

She got scared for just a moment as she figured the only thing large enough to knock her board over was possibly a shark. She hastily scanned the area around her board as she rode up and down the waves that were building in strength. The clear night and the bright moonlight made it easy to see the top of the water and as she looked rapidly back and forth across the ocean's ridge she saw nothing that resembled a shark fin protruding above the water.

Jennifer breathed a quick sigh of relief and then shrugged her shoulders and looked out towards the west hoping to catch the next wave. She immediately spotted her coming ride and was just about to get into her ready position when the board was violently lifted from the water and she was flipped into the air and then fell with a loud "splash".

She was an expert swimmer but hadn't expected this and was so stunned she bobbed for just a moment before regaining her senses and popping to the surface. She spit out a mouthful of salt water and shook her head to clear her vision. Her board was next to her and when she reached out to grab it another wave hit her flush in the face, choking her for just a second and knocking her backwards.

Jennifer regained her focus and pulled the board in front of her long enough to climb up on top. She had no idea what had thrown her off of it to begin with, but she thought this might not really be the best night to go surfing and decided to just paddle back to the shore and go back to her dorm room.

She straddled the board with her legs in the water and propelled herself forward with only her arms and just a touch of urgency. She could feel a small panic that she really couldn't understand beginning to fester in the pit of her stomach. Something was definitely *wrong* tonight.

After a minute or two of paddling brought her noticeably closer to the shore and she could see her waiting car in the parking lot, she let out a breath of air that she hadn't realized she was holding. Smiling now, Jennifer relaxed and straightened up on the board.

It was then she felt a pair of hands grab both of her ankles.

Jennifer screamed when the fingers encircled her legs and started to pull her under the water. She frantically clutched the side of her surfboard and tried to resist while kicking and yanking her legs away from whoever had grabbed her. She looked desperately into the darkness of the water and although she knew it was less than six meters deep she couldn't believe what she saw.

A man, dressed in some kind of sailor's uniform, was under the water pulling her down. The waves made his face hard to discern but the bright moonlight lit him up clear enough to see that he was *grinning* at her.

She screamed when her board flipped over again and the fingers tightened over her ankles dragging her under the surf. She fought as best as she could but the man was stronger. In a murky watertight grip under the swell of the ocean, a sailor from two centuries before she was born hugged her tightly to his cold chest. The last thing Jennifer thought before she drowned under the Broome Beach surf was that she should have stayed home tonight.

⊠

Mitch Honeycutt was sitting in the lifeguard hutch. He knew he wasn't that good of a swimmer and he wasn't that good of a lifeguard. He'd taken this job for the summer only and although the pay was decent and the hours good, he wasn't going to do it any longer than he had to because he preferred to be inside where there was air conditioning.

It had been a decent enough of a year. He lived in Broome and planned on moving back to Sydney when this summer was over. After he pocketed as much money as he could from this job and paid off his car, all bets were off.

There hadn't been any close calls this summer where he would have had to use either his skills as a lifeguard or as a swimmer and for that he was thankful. He didn't really like people all that much anyway and the thought of having to give a stranger mouth-to-mouth resuscitation one day horrified him.

He was pulling the late shift tonight. There was never anyone on the beach and almost no one in the water after nine pm. It was as easy a shift as he ever got.

At least until thirty seconds ago when he heard the scream.

It was a female voice and the scream was terrible. A deep soulful, terrified scream. A scream like someone was dying. Painfully.

It scared him out of the partial nap he was taking and caused him to cut himself on the windowsill as he frantically raised the binoculars to scan the ocean. It was always hard to tell where exactly the sounds came from when the wind was over six kilometers per hour anyway and this was no different. Searching from side to side and sweeping the binoculars back and forth, Mitch tried to locate the voice.

There was a second howling scream and Mitch instantly located something happening about a hundred meters off the shore. There was flapping in the water like something was struggling and then a splash and a smack like a cliff diver makes when he hits the water at a slightly off angle.

And then the image was gone under the sea and Mitch could see nothing but foam in the place where he saw the flapping.

*It could have been a shark. It could have been.*

But Mitch Honeycutt knew it wasn't a shark that had dragged something under the water. A female something. Mitch started to shake violently.

He reached for the phone and was just about to call the emergency numbers when another motion drew his attention. The water in the area she had gone under was stirring again. It was spinning around itself like a cyclone and little splashes were coming *up* from the bottom. The water was launching up to the sky and Mitch literally gaped open-mouthed.

He dropped the phone from his hand when the man rose from the water to stand in the surf.

It was impossible. This *could not* be happening.

Mitch screamed when he looked to his left and saw another man rising from the water and standing in the surf. He looked farther to his left and then frantically to his right. As far as he could see, up and down the shore, people were emerging from the water and standing there, staring in at the beach. They weren't moving. They just stood there with the waves pounding off them.

Mitch Honeycutt screamed as he ran out of the hut and away from the beach. He would never forget, as long as he tried, what he saw tonight.

# CHAPTER THIRTY-EIGHT

Pat Smith stood at the bottom of a long gravel driveway. He was standing slightly to the side of the driveway and out of its immediate path, behind some foliage. To his left in crouched positions with their weapons drawn, were the four Navy Seals.

"We go," Pat whispered to Lieutenant Cummings.

She nodded an assent and then lowered her night vision goggles over her face, made a fist with her left hand to signal to the members of her team and moved forward into the underbrush.

The plan was a simple extraction. The details were fuzzy because the exact location within the house was unknown, and the Navy computer geeks had considerable trouble pulling up detailed plans of the house itself, which set Pat on high alert. If the government of Costa Rica didn't have the blueprints to the house in their database, it was because someone had paid someone else to keep the plans a secret. Whatever was going on in the house on the top of this hill wasn't for public viewing.

Pat and Lieutenant Cummings had agreed that the team would fan out in two details for a standard two-man approach. Cummings would lead one and Pat would lead the other. Cummings would work her way along the back of the house, and Pat would come in the front door. Since the occupiers of the house weren't expecting the Navy to show up on their doorstep this evening, the element of surprise still rested with Pat and Cummings.

Lieutenant Cummings looked back once more at Pat as she disappeared into the heavy jungle foliage followed closely by her second in command. She signaled to Pat that she would be radio non-com until the agreed upon time when they were both supposed to hit the house. Pat would approach the front door and distract them, while Cummings found another way in and searched the premises for Stickle.

It sounded simple enough when they drew it up on the flight down here, but standing there next to the driveway, Pat knew it wasn't ever that easy. He didn't especially like night operations anyway because of the visibility aspect, even with the night goggles, and to tell the truth he was getting too old for fieldwork. If Jon David hadn't been the one they were going after, he probably would've sat this one out or watched from the sidelines.

Pat took a deep breath and turned the goggles to max strength and then motioned for the other two seals to fall in closely behind him as he moved stealthily up the driveway.

⊠

Jon David was pressed up against a rock wall. He had his back firmly situated in a crevice, like he was trying to make himself part of the rock. His left hand was held palm out to Ana, who was right next to him. He looked back to see her intently watching him.

He frowned at her for a second. She wasn't nearly as concerned as he was about what might be around the next bend in the tunnel, and that fact alone bothered him. He whispered, "Which way to the outside, Ana?"

She cocked her head as if in reflection of a difficult math problem and then looked both left and right before pointing to the right passageway. She stepped around JD and decided she would lead for the next several minutes because she was simply more familiar with the tunnels. She still hadn't decided if she could completely trust JD, but he was the first man who had spent more than a cursory amount of time with her and hadn't tried to hurt her. She wasn't comfortable with that thought yet.

They ran as quickly as they could through the first tunnel with Ana in the lead before she suddenly slowed down and then stopped altogether. She glanced nervously ahead and then to JD. "This way will lead us to a locked gate at the end of the tunnel. There are bars on the door. I've been up to them but haven't gotten past them before."

"How many times have you tried?"

She shook her head and then looked down at the floor, suddenly embarrassed. "I don't know," she said softly like she was confessing a sin.

"It's okay, Ana. I'm sure you tried to get out of here as often as you could."

She looked up into his eyes and nodded. He took her at face value and she wasn't comfortable with that either. A flood of strange emotions was rapidly clouding her vision.

Jon David looked into her two different colored eyes. She was pretty in an innocent child kind of way and for some reason wore a red gown. The dress seemed as out of place in this dungeon as he felt. Her blonde hair was loose and hadn't been brushed in a while. High cheekbones and a dimple with a freckle in it. Small neck. One thing he was absolutely sure of was that she was completely capable of taking care of herself. He hadn't had time to even ask her why she was here in the first place.

"Do you know how long you've been here?" he asked.

She was about to answer when they both heard the growling.

⊠

Pat's first thought when they approached the locked gates was that he should just walk up and ring the doorbell and see what happened. He knew their approach wasn't expected but as often happened in this business, it was the unexpected that got people killed.

Motioning to the two seals beside him to fan out, Pat drew his nine-millimeter Beretta from its holster and circled the outside of the wall surrounding the complex. He had obtained infrared drawings from the site as soon as the radioman determined that Jon David's location was stable. He and Lieutenant Cummings had gone over the drawings until they were both certain of the number of potential threats in the building and the number of enemy combatants. It looked straight forward enough from his seat on the Lear Jet anyway.

There were only a handful of people in the compound, and their heat signatures were easy enough to follow. The radioman would be in constant contact if needed with both Pat and Cummings throughout the campaign, leading them through the inner hallways of the complex as well as alerting them to potential threats.

The only problem as far as Pat could tell was that he had the nagging feeling they were being led directly into the mouth of a hungry tiger. The house drawings were incomplete, and they easily managed to make their way up the side of this mountain. Two rights often as not made a wrong. And it made him all the more restless. It wasn't supposed to go this good.

The two seals dropped to their knees and did a quick area survey. The wall in front of them was ten feet tall and completely encircled the house. The top of the wall had several strands of barbed wire wrapped over it. This house said "Stay Out" from every direction.

One of the two men threw a nylon rope over the top and tightened it down and then hoisted the other man up. The Kevlar insulated suits they were wearing would keep the pinpricks of the barbed wire from penetrating their skin as they threw themselves over and onto the other side. The first man lifted Pat up and then followed him over and dropped down.

Pat stood completely still and just listened in the darkness along with the Navy Seals. It was just too easy.

⊠

The preparations were approaching a manic phase and as Greyson watched he could only smile. He hadn't felt this kind of excitement in many years and only vaguely remembered the last time. And that had produced a disaster as far as he was concerned.

He pointed to the sidewall and Limeh rolled his chair forward until he was situated at a vantage point that allowed him to see the entire room. The three aides who lived at the house and had worked for them for years were busy with their assigned tasks. They had no idea that they were each going to die on this night as the final battle began. It was only fitting.

"It's coming along beautifully, Mr. Limeh. How long until the prep work is complete and we can begin?"

Limeh surveyed the drawing on the floor. He had the aides pull the throw rug back from its place. The rug had been securely attached to the floor in the same position since the previous time. Under strict orders it hadn't been moved or altered in any way so that the painting on the floor wouldn't be smeared or smudged. Clarity was most important.

Limeh nodded, satisfied that the drawing was not an issue. "I was afraid that perhaps our artwork might have been damaged after so many years, Mr. Greyson. But we are in luck, I think," he said as he squinted at the various parts of the intricately drawn mural.

Greyson snorted under his breath. "It must be perfect. Perfect! Do you hear me? There can be no more screw-ups this time. I do not have the time or the energy left to witness another one."

"I know, Mr. Greyson. Nor do I," he said as he resumed his scrutiny of the mural. "I am certain of the timing of this event. We will not fail. Not this time."

Greyson pushed his chair forward to the edge of the mural that covered the center of the oversized room. A vivid array of colors, interspersed exactly at the right angles and proportionately where required, stared back at him. A medieval design, developed over the course of four years, and painstakingly pieced together by three different painters flown in from Italy, swam beneath his vision. He had covered various parts of the floor after each painter finished and then had each of the artists killed before they left the house to ensure their silence. Because of the way the layout had been developed, none of the three artists ever saw the complete picture. Each of them had no idea what they were drawing, only that it was to a precise image, with paints that were thicker than regular gloss colors.

The mural was exactly thirteen point three two meters in diameter, from one side of the wall to the other, and covered the entire floor. The border was point six six six of a meter wide and circular. Colored a vivacious red, it contained flecks of gold sprinkled throughout.

Inside the blood red circle were expertly drawn depictions of men, women and animals in various stages of decomposition. Half-men and half-women interwoven with beasts and drawings from another dimension. Animals with horns that should only have existed in fairy tales were depicted thrashing and violently tearing apart bleeding virgins. Men with tentacles for arms holding down other species of spiders crossed with women dressed as waiting sacrifices. Enormous teeth savoring bites of humans. Savoring each and every taste as they devoured men and women with equal malice. Quivering depictions of back-alley moments of hunger bordering on lust by demons from another dimension. Women screaming in agony during violent child birthing sessions and being ripped into shreds by vengeful children. And across it all were a pair of hairy, beast-like arms stretching the width and breadth of the drawing from side to side and clasped together as if they were holding an infant in a loving embrace.

All of the pictures sat encased in a black pentagram crisscrossed throughout the entire scene. An inverted pentagram. A symbol of malevolence that could evoke the blackest magic and images on this planet.

Greyson wheeled his chair into the center of the mural and twirled around like a child on a swing in a playground. He laughed and cackled over and over again like it was going to be the best day of his life. "Come to me Limeh, and join with me as we call forth the past and bring the future under our control. Together we can do what must be done." He possessed an energy that he hadn't displayed in years.

Limeh nodded and got caught up in the old man's excitement. They had worked so many years together for this night. So many wasted and missed opportunities would finally be ended with the culmination of this night. He trembled with anticipation.

Greyson moved his chair slightly from the exact center of the mural and stared gape-jawed at the machine as the aides rolled it on a set of golden casters. He was still in awe of its power. Of its possibilities. Slowly, almost lovingly, he reached out a gnarled hand and stroked the side of the machine.

Tonight was theirs.

⊠

Jon David heard the growl and although he'd heard animals growling in the woods when he was a boy, this was unlike anything he could describe. It was low and guttural, and came from somewhere deep inside the owner's throat. It held the distinct sound of malice. Whatever was doing the growling was letting JD and Ana know it had them in its sights and was just about to feast.

He immediately reached for the holster and again wished they hadn't taken his Beretta. It was almost an unconscious movement to locate the gun, even though he knew it wasn't there. He still stroked the holster with his right hand, like a worry stone. There was little comfort in an empty holster, but for some reason, Jon David felt like it helped.

"What was that?" he whispered in the tunnel.

"The ape. It's the apes," Ana whispered back. She had pressed up a little closer to him when the first growl sounded.

"What kind of apes?"

"I don't know. They're big and greasy-looking. And wet. I heard one of the old men call them half-apes once."

Jon David looked at her. He didn't like the sound of this at all. "Wet?"

She nodded with more force than was necessary. "That's what I always called it. They look wet. And they're not like regular gorillas. They're very intelligent and loyal. Something else? I think they're already dead." She said it as nonchalantly as if it were an everyday thing that JD might meet on the street.

"I was afraid it might be something like that. How do we kill them? I have a feeling they won't go down as easily as the guys back in the cell."

"No. They're stronger and he keeps them to hunt for him. We can't out run them."

JD nodded. *Can't out run them. Don't have a weapon. It doesn't look good*, he thought. *Not a very well thought out escape plan.*

"Let's try anyway, Ana. Come on," he ran ahead of her but held onto her hand.

She hesitated no more. She really had nowhere else to go and no one else to trust. This guy was as good as any. She took off behind him, running to keep up.

⊠

Lieutenant Cummings and her partner managed to scale the high outer wall and work their way up the side of the mountain and through the dense underbrush of the Costa Rica jungle. Some of the bushes were so tightly packed together she had to actually cut through the limbs with a bowie knife. There was no other way through it.

She stood next to the back wall of the house. The plans she'd gone over on the jet with Pat indicated no more than four live targets, and only one of them was Stickle. As far as she was concerned the other three were going to be collateral damage.

She opened her flip top on her heat sensor GPS unit and quickly located the four targets inside the house. Two of them were together in one room and two of them seemed to be running. Based on the speed of the two running, it quickly became apparent to Cummings that the two were urgently trying to get away. She paused for just a second when she realized that the other two weren't chasing them and seemed to be in no hurry at all. That meant they didn't know the two were running away or they didn't care. If they didn't care, that was a lot worse than if they didn't know. If they didn't care, it was because they knew the two wouldn't get very far.

She pointed to the GPS finder and located the two who were running to her partner. He nodded one quick, short nod. She immediately knew he understood they were going after them.

She scanned the side of the house for the closest entrance she could attain, and then her military mind calculated the time it would take to break through the window, and then find the targets. She was satisfied with the results of less than eight minutes start to finish, pulled her radio transmitter over to her face and snapped seven words off: "Delta One. Eight minutes to completion. Over."

She pushed her microphone back from her face and put her knife away when she sensed something wrong behind her. The hair on her neck stood up and she instantly tensed. Something was closing in on them from the jungles and not making any noise.

# CHAPTER THIRTY-NINE

As Jon David ran along the tunnels he knew two things for certain: one, he didn't know where he was running to or which passageway led out of this maze; and two, the constant sound of growling was getting closer with each passing moment.

He stopped, breathing hard. The air in the tunnels was musty and hurt his lungs. He was gasping as much from the running as he was from the musty air that hung suspended around him like old cigarette smoke. There was something dead and rotting laced underneath this place. He could smell it with each breath, but he could also *feel* it. Whatever was going on in this place, whatever depravity Ana had been subjected to over the years by their hosts, it wasn't natural. It seemed that death in this house was as much a part of the air as oxygen.

He pulled up and motioned for Ana to stop. She wasn't nearly as out of breath as he was and he knew this had to be from living under these conditions for so long. It was like drinking spoiled milk. Eventually you got used to the taste. "I need to rest for a second. I'm having trouble breathing."

She looked apprehensively behind them as the sound of padded paws hitting the dirt floor resounded over and over again. "They're getting close."

He nodded. "I know. I don't think we can outrun them anyway. This is as good a place as any to make a stand. It had to happen sometime. How many are there?" JD looked frantically around at the slick walls and the dirt flooring. He was desperately looking for something he could use as a weapon. A rock maybe or a spike sticking out of the wall. Anything that might give them a chance.

"Only one inside the house. The other ones patrol the outside. Sometimes they come inside to do work."

"So if we get out of these tunnels, we get to meet the others?"

Ana nodded and looked down at the rock and mud floor. She didn't really know what he expected her to say. "I just want out of this house forever."

The running sound of paws hitting the dirt slowed behind them. It was obvious to both JD and Ana that the half-ape had realized their quarry was close and slowed its pace. It was impossible to estimate the distance with the sounds echoing through the caverns. It was judging the prey.

JD whispered, "It's a skilled hunter. It knows we're right in front of it and it's positioning for the kill. We have to be ready." His voice was coming in short gasps between clenched teeth. He didn't like the odds.

Ana pushed him to the side for the second time in the last several minutes and then wedged backwards. With her feet scraping against the floor, she made sure the approach was from the front where she could see the half-ape coming and there wasn't any room for it to get to them from behind.

Jon David quickly scanned the area in the darkness. He saw a crevice about the size of his foot in the rock across from them. He looked up and saw it then. It was an idea, and the only one he had at the moment.

He pointed to Ana and then ran across the width of the tunnel as the growling from the half-ape completely stopped and the cavern was suddenly encased in a solitary quiet. It was more unsettling than the growling had been to both of them. At least when it was snarling, they knew approximately where it was located.

JD quickly planted his feet in the crevice in the wall and hoisted himself up. He grabbed a small ledge and cut his hand, but used the leverage to lift up off the ground. After a few more pulls and grunts, he started to slowly make progress and began climbing the side of the narrow cavern. There were just enough handholds in the rock face to give him a number of small but secure places to allow his hands and feet to find their supports.

He managed to get about nine feet up the side of the cave as Ana watched wide-eyed. It had never even occurred to her to go *up*; she had always thought about getting out by opening the doors in front of her until there weren't any doors left. She quickly got the hint. She walked up to where he first placed his hand and then looked up at him.

He motioned to her to start climbing. "Hurry. It could attack us at any time. Give me your hand and get moving," he hissed at her.

Her one blue eye and one green eye seemed to reflect a deep inner thought process going on as she stared at the rock wall. The light of the tunnel, dim but dancing repeatedly across the walls, fell on those eyes and suddenly reflected back at Jon David. She was highly intelligent and measured in her actions. She didn't react until she thought it through.

"I don't need to climb."

"What? Why not?" Jon David didn't like the sound of this. He had bought them a couple of minutes and he might be able to figure a way out of this while the half-ape stayed on the ground. It was all he felt they had at the moment. He knew it wouldn't be very long until the thing attacked them. He thought he might have a small but reliable advantage, being above the creature.

"It won't hurt me," she said as she looked up at him wedged against the rock.

JD suddenly got suspicious, like he had walked right into a trap and she led him here. He was almost afraid to ask. "Why not?"

Ana glanced back down for some reason, not wanting to look at him when she answered, "Because I'm its mother."

⌧

Lieutenant Cummings hand wrapped itself tightly around the bowie knife. Whatever was behind her had no heat signature and managed to get behind her and her partner without making a sound. She hadn't seen or heard the threat, but she knew it was there none-the-less. She had long ago learned to trust her senses. And right now they were screaming at her that she was in danger.

She slowly turned around, careful not to make a sound.

At that moment, *something* leaped from the trees and fell upon the two of them.

Cummings fell to the ground under a tremendous weight. It hadn't occurred to her that the threat could have been above her. The thought that it had no heat signature had made her stomach ball up into knots as soon as she realized it. Her only thought was self-preservation.

She hit the ground and immediately thrust upwards with the bowie knife. She felt something soft and pliable like putty give a small amount of resistance and then she heard a "popping" sound as the knife made a twelve-inch incision into soft flesh. She reached up and grabbed her attacker around his neck and immediately brought the knife deeper into his chest cavity. With a quick pull and then a tear, she ripped downward and cleanly sliced the attacker's heart in two sections. She pushed him aside and knew he was dead before his body fell to the dirt.

It was odd thought she had at that moment. For a reason that she couldn't explain, an idea hit her mind like someone had thrust the knife into her chest. It was a stabbing, piercing thought that made her recoil before she could react. Even after all of her years of training she couldn't stop the physics that assailed her mind. In the heat of this life and death battle, this idea shouldn't have been there, but yet it was crystal clear to her.

When she grabbed the neck of her assailant, the skin had been cold. Ice cold. *Morgue* cold.

She scrambled up and instantly looked for her partner. She knew he was under attack as well. He had managed to get on top of his attacker and was forcing him onto the ground under his weight. She was going to turn to help him when she saw the body on the ground next to her that she had just gutted begin to rise.

Her mind struggled with the absurdity of this situation. There was no doubt that she had cut his aorta and he should have bled out instantly. The human body could not possibly survive for more than a few seconds bleeding internally like that. Perhaps it could have flopped around for a moment or two before collapsing, but there was simply no way the man could get to his feet. It was impossible.

She crouched down and readied herself for another attack when she felt hands grab her from behind. She let out a small "yelp" of surprise as someone with enormous strength lifted her completely off the ground and spun her around.

His hands were ice cold.

⊠

Jon David's audible gasp of breath in the quiet cavern seemed as loud as a crowd roaring for a touchdown. He lowered his eyebrows into a frown as he tried to process this latest piece of information. "How?" was all that came out of his mouth.

"I don't really know. I don't understand it either," Ana said as she stepped back from the wall like she had somehow hurt Jon David and had a reason to be ashamed. It was strange reaction for her to make and she became aware of it without really knowing why. She just knew that what she said had startled the man in a way she didn't want to happen.

The half-ape chose that moment to move around the corner of the tunnel and locate the two of them. He looked first at Ana and almost nodded a greeting, and then his eyes roamed around the walls until they landed squarely on JD. With a grunt and recognition of its prey, the half-ape dropped to all fours and prepared to leap directly at Jon David.

JD scrambled up further, momentarily confused as to whether he should try and protect the girl or leave her there. She said she wasn't in any danger and the hairy thing that leaped at him totally ignored her and came after him.

JD grabbed for any section of rock that he could use to launch himself a little higher while he feverishly tried to think of a way out. He rapidly scanned all the sides of the cavern as he climbed, looking for any edges he might have missed or perhaps a loose rock that he could throw.

The half-ape growled once, a low signal of its intention to

attack, and then jumped as high as it could. It grabbed nothing but air with the first lunge and narrowly missed snatching JD's leg. Jon David turned and kicked out as hard as he could against the paw reaching for him. He impacted with its hand and there was a loud "smacking" sound as a couple of bones got twisted backwards. With a startled yelp like a puppy that lost its bone, the creature fell back to the floor. It rolled over immediately, made another sound and then crouched even deeper to leap higher. It wouldn't make the same mistake twice.

Jon David had run out of room to climb and was positioned against the ceiling. He was thrust into a small opening between the tunnel walls and the rock-like top. It was narrow enough that he couldn't climb in completely, but he could draw himself up enough that he might be able to avoid the creature for a couple of minutes. At least until the thing figured out how to climb the wall.

Jon David and the half-ape both paused like two fighters in a ring. It was the first chance JD had to clearly view the thing that had been pursuing them. He didn't much like what he saw.

The beast was crouched like a lion about to pounce in the jungle. It was sitting perfectly still, perched on its four legs, body tensed, muscles tightly clenched in anticipation of the impending fight. There wasn't any fat on the thing that JD could see and no weak places for him to possibly attack.

As far as he could tell the half-ape was perfectly named. It looked like it was very tall, nearly seven feet, and must have weighed close to three hundred pounds. It was covered from head to toe in a dark, thick, matted and greasy brown hair. "Wet" was an accurate word. There were strands of different color hair grown throughout the thick coat like someone had thrown a bucket of paint across it and the colors landed wherever they were comfortable.

JD recognized the stench he smelled since they entered the tunnels earlier. It was all over this creature. Every time the thing opened its mouth, a smell that would probably kill small animals wafted out across the cavern.

And it had teeth. A lot of teeth. White and sharp, and long like spikes, they glimmered in a wide-open mouth. There was no doubt about the intent of those incisors as far as JD could tell. The teeth were used to tear the flesh and bones off the victims and would tear him apart if they got the chance. The half-ape was a perfect fit for a killing machine.

Jon David tensed for the attack he knew was coming.

⊠

Pat didn't understand any of this. He and the two seals had met zero resistance and had progressed through the jungles like it was a summer cottage and he was going to the lake to visit relatives. No one stopped them, no one threatened them, and for some reason he could not understand, no one guarded this place. If whoever was pulling the strings to this whole operation was inside, he wasn't worried about anyone approaching. Tall walls and barbwire didn't cut it.

"Delta One. Eight minutes to completion. Over."

Pat answered into his microphone, "Roger. We go dark now." He listened for the "WILCO" answer that was standard Navy speak for "Will Comply". He heard a distinct sound like someone was ripping a branch off of a tree and then his earpiece went totally dead. Like the connection had been cutoff.

On alert now and understanding that Lieutenant Cummings had come under attack, he dropped to one knee and brought his Beretta up to shooting position. He clicked the gun off safety and pointed it at the house less than ten meters in front of him. The place was quiet and only two infrared images were displayed on his screen, but that didn't comfort him. He quickly swept the gun from his left to his right and covered all of the area in his immediate vision.

Pat let his left hand drop from the pistol and he waved a five-finger open palm signal behind his back. The two seals would interpret this as a command to fan out and take up offensive positions on either side of him. They would space themselves to the left and right, just a little behind to avoid friendly fire if he started shooting, but also close enough that they could guard his flank.

Pat lowered the pistol from the ready position slowly. He kept his eyes trained in front of him, but knew instantly that there was something wrong. He didn't hear the two men behind him move into position when he signaled. They would never ignore a direct order and if at all possible they would have either replied that they were unable to comply at present due to distress of some kind, or they would have just moved. Neither one of those things happened. That wasn't good. That meant something else had to have happened behind Pat's back.

Slowly, carefully, Pat turned his neck and tuned his senses to hear any sound he might have missed. Anything that might indicate where the two men had gone who stood next to him less than five seconds ago. He deliberately moved as stealthily as possible. No sound. No sudden movements. Not until he understood what was going on behind his back.

When he was turned around completely, with his gun pointed exactly one hundred and eighty degrees from where it was a moment ago, he let his eyes do a rapid scan. He did it like he had been taught so many years ago in basic training: left to right, up to down in small box patterns so as not to miss anything.

Both the men were gone.

Pat's fingers tensed a little more on the trigger of the gun and he readied himself. No Navy Seal could be taken without so much as a whimper so whatever had happened to his two men had to have been sudden and completely unexpected. And forceful. Very forceful. To keep the men quiet and move them at the same time would take super human strength or an utter surprise. Pat didn't think either one was possible.

Seeing nothing after completing his sweep he turned back to the house, still crouched with his pistol aimed. As he stayed perfectly still a thought occurred to him and he silently cursed himself for being so stupid.

Without moving his upper body, Pat let his eyes move upward to the trees above him.

☒

Lieutenant Cummings was hurled against the trunk of a tree with such force that she was momentarily dazed. She fell to the ground and put her right hand over her holster. She drew the pistol out and blindly aimed in the direction of the man who had thrown her across the jungle and into the base of the palm tree. With blood streaming into her eyes from a gash across her scalp, she fired three times rapidly in succession.

She heard a grunt and then a growling kind of noise. Even though dazed and aching, a small smile crept across her face when she realized the grunt was followed by the sound of liquid bubbling through a hole. The sound was so sweet to her because she knew at least one of the bullets hit the bastard. She hoped more than one had buried itself in his chest.

Pulling herself upright and then leaning against the tree, she wiped her brow with her sleeve and tried to focus on her attacker. She had no idea where her partner was, but at the moment she had to concentrate on making sure her assailant was dead. She was convinced he was going to kill her if she didn't get him first.

Blinking her eyes and struggling to maintain consciousness from the blow to her head, she looked up and in a startling moment of clarity, she knew she was going to die.

The thing in front of her was huge. It looked sort of like a gorilla but must have stood at over seven feet tall and weighed at least three to four hundred pounds. And it was enraged.

She gasped when she saw that all three of her shots hit it dead center in its massive chest, but even though the holes were there and clearly visible, there wasn't any blood. The thing wasn't going to bleed out. Not even close. It didn't even *slow* the thing down.

With strength of purpose that soldiers often find when all hope vanishes, she raised the gun to eye level and emptied the magazine dead center into the face of the ape-thing that was three feet in front of her. The creature staggered backwards and let out a hideous scream of pain, then threw itself forward and grabbed Cummings by her hair.

She swung the butt of her gun at its face but missed completely and the gun flew out of her hand and fell into the brush surrounding the two of them. The ape-thing lifted her off the ground and Cummings screamed as it brought her directly in front of its face.

She squirmed and furiously swung her fists at the single hand of the beast that had entangled itself in her hair. It clamped its grip tighter and she felt an arm the size of a human leg wrap completely around her torso. The ape-thing pulled her up to less than three inches from its monstrous face and two black eyes the size of almonds stared at Cummings. A cold, dead breath wafted out of its nostrils.

"Fuck you!" Cummings screamed and tried to head-butt the thing in the nose.

The ape-thing then did something she would not have thought possible: incredibly, the thing *laughed* at her.

Instead of defiance, Cummings actually started to sob. Blood soaking into her eyes, a huge, hairy arm encircling her, a stench she couldn't have imagined forcing its way into her lungs, and her own reflection looking back at her from black eyes.

The ape-thing opened its jaws and dozens of razor sharp teeth shined at Cummings. Teeth that were used for chewing and grinding and *eating*.

Cummings gave one last sob and a twist of struggle against the creature and then with a sudden flexing of its strong jawbones, the ape-thing bent its head to one side and clamped down on both sides of Cummings head.

She screamed for only a second as the teeth met in the middle of her brain and then ripped the front of her face completely off. It released her from its grasp and she fell to the ground as it chewed her head into bits small enough to swallow.

⊠

The creature leaped and rotated at the same time. It moved to its left and snarled like a wild animal, before reaching out with its enormous arms. Swinging both legs in the air and brushing the rock walls with just enough of the tips of its feet to propel it a couple of feet higher, it got to striking distance of its quarry.

Jon David waited until the last possible moment to launch across the top of the half-ape. With a perfectly timed move and the propulsion of his body weight he managed to avoid the long spike-like nails and hurled himself over the top of the creature. At one moment he was sitting in his crevice in the wall and as the half-ape climbed and aimed itself directly at his chest, JD managed to move out of the opening and use his leverage and his position above the creature to fly over the top. He pushed with his legs as hard as he could and just barely escaped the outstretched hairy arms.

For a brief second both beast and man hung suspended in mid-air. One was leaping up and grasping for the legs or any other hold it could get, and one was just trying to avoid the spike-like nails. Jon David twisted as he fell, and then prepared himself for the impact of the mud floor after falling almost ten feet. He hit and rolled against the wall and sprang up to a defensive position.

The creature screamed at missing its prey and slammed against the wall from its own momentum. It immediately spun its legs and got upright against the wall. Using an acrobatic move from years of leaping through jungle trees, the half-ape turned and moved at the same time and within seconds had gotten its feet under itself and pushed off against the wall. It pounced instantly and flew back down and straight at JD.

JD's eyes flew wide open at the move the creature made in mid-air as it looked physically impossible to twist and hurtle up and then back down without stopping its forward progress first. The beast was not only large but also very nimble.

Jon David rushed to get out of the way only to have the half-ape land directly on his back. He fell under both the three hundred pound weight and the force from the fall. He collapsed into a ball and tried to protect himself as best he could before it tore into his flesh.

Letting out a controlled yell of victory, it sat squarely on top of JD. It then grabbed him firmly around one of his legs and stood up, deciding to drag Jon David back through the tunnels.

JD kicked out to empty air, as the thing's arms were longer than his legs. He fought and grabbed for anything he could clutch, digging his fingernails under rocks and grasping at moss on the slimy walls, but the beast just pulled him along. For about ten feet, he was dragged unceremoniously along the ground.

Not really liking the struggle the man was putting up, the half-ape decided on a different approach as it suddenly flexed its hand and instantly clamped down hard on Jon David's ankle. Pain shot up through his leg and he howled once just long enough to satisfy the beast. The message the half-ape was sending was simple: continue to fight and kick and I will crush your leg into pieces. Jon David stopped fighting immediately, realizing not only the strength of his opponent, but also what an advantage it held. As it dragged JD deeper into the tunnel, for good measure and for true dominance of its quarry, the half-ape lifted Jon David up by one leg and swung him into the wall, bashing his head violently against the rock. Pain and white lights exploded in JD's head and he struggled for consciousness. The beast knew exactly what it was doing.

Jon David's head was bleeding from a cut over his eyebrow and he glanced one more time through weary eyes looking for Ana. She had remained quiet and partially in the shadows the entire time the thing was after him. Spotting her several paces behind the two of them, she looked like she had gone into some kind of a mental cocoon to protect herself. Her eyes were glazed over and he could only wonder what was going through her mind.

With a glance back down the tunnel the thing was dragging him into, JD noticed his nose had started to bleed again. *Oh shit*, he thought, *it's going to get worse* before passing out from the pain.

⊠

Pat Smith looked up into the trees above him. Any rookie in the service was taught to secure the perimeter not only left and right but also up and down. In every dimension because an attacker would use anything to gain an advantage. He had forgotten a basic premise of fieldwork: all areas had to be cleared.

Scanning across the leaves of the palm trees and then squinting into the thick brush, he spotted it after only a few moments. Sitting about thirty meters up and lounging lazily across a palm, a huge hairy thing that looked like part gorilla was sloppily eating some kind of dinner.

Pat's mouth clenched tightly when he focused on the green and black colored thing the beast was chewing into little bits. It was the pants leg of one of the two men who until just a second ago was standing behind him, guarding his flank.

Pat pulled the infrared camera up and quickly zeroed in for a closer detail as a sickening feeling worked itself into his stomach. He had never puked in the field, but he thought this might be a first time if what he thought was going on up in the trees turned out to be true. He snapped the infrared light off and flipped a switch to turn it into three hundred magnification binoculars. He adjusted the setting once for the falling light at this time of day and then swallowing the growing bile in the back of his throat, trained the lens on the image in the trees.

The thing in the trees, resting comfortably against a palm like it didn't have a care in the world, was quietly and succinctly *eating* one of his men.

Pat dropped the binoculars and immediately fell to his knees as he puked up a month's worth of greasy hamburgers. He hadn't eaten in several hours and had no idea how there could be this much solid food in his stomach left to eradicate, but still he threw up all over the nice green lawn of the house.

He stopped and composed himself and then realized he was out in the open and dove for cover under the brush behind him. He prayed the thing in the trees was too busy to notice him, but he didn't hold a lot of faith in that supposition. It had taken both of his men and for some strange reason the word *disposed* dropped into Pat's mind. Like his men had been dumped in a garbage heap and discarded.

He now knew why their approach had been so easy. Whatever the thing in the trees was, it was guarding the place from on high and whoever ran this place didn't need anything else watching out. He sat back against the wall of the house and tried to settle his stomach as he thought about his next move.

At that moment an idea popped into his mind. Something he hadn't thought of until now because of the horror he'd just witnessed. He steadied himself and flipped the infrared switch back to the "on" position and then retrained the glasses on whatever the thing was that was sitting in the trees.

His worst fears were realized when the infrared goggles didn't register the beast. The only heat signature that he got was from the partial leg it was holding. He took the goggles off and adjusted them to make sure they were working correctly and then made sure the gorilla-thing was still sitting there. He refocused the beam again and narrowed his vision to that single spot in the palm tree.

No reflection.

Whatever the thing was in the trees disposing of his men was not of this Earth and it wasn't alive. His heart sank when he immediately realized that his goggles were useless and there could have been literally hundreds of these things roaming around the grounds that they hadn't picked up before he and his team approached.

They were sitting ducks and by now most likely Cummings and her partner were dead. That left him and JD.

And whoever was pulling the puppet strings here.

He had made these kinds of decisions once or twice. Decisions that didn't really require thought so much as action. It wasn't something he relished but it was a responsibility he accepted. That was what his profile said about him for so many years: Pat Smith was willing to take the responsibility that went with the job.

He crawled as quietly as he could deeper into the thick brush and when he was safely out of earshot of the thing in the trees, he unclipped a top secret message transmitter from his belt, punched in a number known only to a handful of people on the face of the Earth, and then pressed a three digit code in to the keypad. He waited exactly thirty seconds for a confirmation code to come back through.

⊠

Off the coast of Costa Rica submerged in deep water, a United States Ohio class submarine named the *USS Wyoming* received an emergency transmission from the Pentagon in Washington, DC. The sub had been dispatched to this location yesterday during regular operations and simulated war games in the Pacific Ocean.

The captain of the sub, a capable man named Chad Stevens, confirmed his orders and then turned to his executive officer. "All hands on deck. Raise the ship to the surface and get me clear view of the topside. Prepare two tomahawks for immediate launch."

The executive officer knew the war games had been cancelled. He also knew better than to question this particular captain on any order let alone one this important. "Aye, sir," was all he said. He immediately relayed the order through the proper channels. Something huge must have happened to launch two missiles during peacetime. Something that could threaten the United States from this distance was not an everyday occurrence.

# Book Five

## Coronation

# CHAPTER FORTY

*I am Evil*

*Arise. Arise my children and let your presence be known. Come to the calling of your father. Of your master. It is time for the world of the living to know of our existence.*

*I am Evil and I am about to fulfill my greatest undertaking. I will lead you in a ceremony that will produce a new essence for you to follow. I will pass my strength and my will and my presence onto the next host. Onto the only being on the face of this puny world that can rightfully ascend to my position and receive my mantle.*

*For tonight, in the halls of Costa Rica, in the mansion of my fore bearers will be a creation. It will be an historic event that will cause the world to pause and give homage. And to tremble.*

*Tonight, with all eyes of the world cowering in fear, I will pass onto this world a perfect host. A perfect master. I will create a most divine being. I will give this world a leader who shall rise to be their king.*

*Tonight, you will commit untold events of pain, carnage and death. You will destroy all in your path and leave nothing in your wake. You will make the weak beings of this world afraid of the oceans and terrified of the trees. And you shall deliver scars unto them that will never be forgotten and will be recorded in the annals of time. Many years from now, when I have been reborn through this perfect host, the historians will bow in awe before us when they write of this night.*

*Tonight we will kill everyone who is in our path.*

*Tonight will be the Coronation of the King.*

*Tonight will be a Passage of magnificence.*

☒

All across the gold coast of Australia where the water meets the shores, people were screaming in both terror and fear. It started on the far north side of the island approximately one hundred kilometers from a little city called Karratha, and once they were discovered, they panic spread like a virus.

Monica Bowen and her husband knew nothing of the events in Costa Rica, or what was happening anywhere else for that matter. They were just tourists who came to the gold coast of Australia every year for the past twenty-three years to take in the beach and the sun. They were part-time locals as they liked to call themselves, having resided in Sydney for their entire lives, never seeing a reason to leave either Australia or New Zealand. The rest of the world didn't exist to them anymore than images on the television.

But this morning, when they arrived at their semi-private beach of white sand and idyllic palm trees, the same spot they had paid money to rent for the last sixteen of their twenty-three years visiting here, they were stunned to see three people standing in the water about fifty meters off the coast. The people, two men with a woman standing between them, stood in the water, staring at both Monica and her husband, Stan. While Monica stared back at the people who seemed not to notice the constant pounding of the ocean waves against them, she felt a cold terror grip her, even though it was almost thirty-two degrees Celsius this morning. She should have been looking for shade or running into the waves to cool off, but instead she stood frozen in place, deathly afraid for a reason she couldn't understand.

Monica put her hand out and reached for the comfort of her husband Stan, who inexplicably had backed up behind her. He normally took the lead and beat her into the water, but for some reason he was also hesitating.

She glanced once quickly at him and then at the three people in the water. She knew she shouldn't take her eyes off of them.

Her first thought was that it was some kind of television or kid's prank, to see how the tourists reacted to this kind of thing. But then she noticed that the three people in the water weren't *right*. When she thought about it, no other word seemed to work at the moment. There was something just not quite right about them.

Their clothes were very shredded and tattered, and seemed to be attached to their bodies like they'd been wearing them for many years. They hung off their scrawny bodies at strange angles. There was no other way she could describe it. The clothes were an older style, clothes Monica hadn't seen worn anywhere and only glimpsed in picture books in libraries.

But their faces. That was the worst.

Their faces were covered in scales and barnacles like they'd been attached to the bottom of a boat for centuries. Like the people had been submerged for years and had risen out of the water this very morning. One had something crawling across his face like it was feeding off of him.

Monica shivered and silently made a sign of the cross. She was about to turn and get out of there when the taller of the two men suddenly made a beckoning motion with his hand. He lifted a scaly and green-looking fist and incredibly called her to join them.

She was riveted to the spot for only a second before she broke the trance and turned to run. She dropped Stan's hand and hurried for the safety of their car. She knew Stan would be close behind her.

She ran as fast as her sixty years would allow, pounding her feet against the sand, before she looked back at the water. She stopped dead in her tracks when she saw her husband of so many years, the love of her life, her soul mate, running *towards* the water.

Monica stood open-mouthed, unable to believe what she was seeing. Stan leaped into the surf and fought against a series of rising waves with perfect freestyle swimmer's strokes, until he closed in on the woman.

Monica screamed at him as if her life depended on it because for some reason, she was convinced Stan was leaving her forever. "Jesus, Mary Mother of God! Stan! Please come back. Stanley!" She screamed his formal name only when she was mad at him or terrified.

Stan kept swimming at the woman and as Monica watched helplessly from the shore the other two men converged on Stan and without any resistance, Stan was pulled under the surf. There was a splash and then foam and Stanley Bowen was gone.

⊠

The news reports started coming in across the wires as fast as the world could post it on Facebook or Tweet about it. All across the western coast of Australia, people were running into the surf and disappearing. There were numerous reports of surfers being dragged under the water screaming. Several small boats capsized and their people struggled only to be pulled down to the ocean's floor. Piers and docks were toppled and anyone standing on them was taken. Other reports came in that claimed people were standing off the shore, in the middle of the ocean, like they had somehow mysteriously risen from the bottom.

Reporters rushed to the ocean's fronts and the Australian Navy, along with the Coast Guard and the Army, were dispatched to calm the rising panic. The only dilemma being that no one was sure exactly where or how to protect the swimmers or the surfers or the boaters because the attacks were random and up and down the entire coast. People were being dragged into the water faster than the word could get to them. Most people on beaches didn't carry cell phones into the water and several thousand drowned before the morning newscast could warn them.

⊠

The voice that screamed out like a lion roaring in the jungle made Jon David's throbbing headache pound all the more. He was just barely able to register words with the voice, but it seemed to permeate the room and echo off the walls. It was a thunderous voice that would not be ignored, but JD had no idea who it was or what he needed. Whoever was speaking was loud, he was sure of that. And it didn't really appear that the voice was speaking directly to JD, just screaming into the air.

Jon David was groggy and his left leg was swollen and hurt like hell. He remembered the half-ape grabbing it and dragging him. He also remembered the thing pinching his ankle so that he couldn't run even if he could get the beast to release its grip. He tried to shake his head and clear his thought process when he realized he was tied down and his head was still bleeding.

He lifted his head to look at the nylon straps that bound him. He was tied to some kind of gurney and it was pretty secure. He wasn't going anywhere anytime soon. He laid his head back down and tried to control the panic that was creeping into his stomach. Blood was running into his eyes and seeping through his hair. If he was going to get out of this one, he was going to have to be clear headed and think his way through it.

He twisted his body a little to the left only to be immediately stabbed by a sharp pain directly in his side, under his ribs. He didn't remember getting kicked or anything during his meager escape attempt. As sharp as the pain in his side was, he figured he should have had a decent memory to correlate it.

He was able to move his left arm enough to reach up and tenderly rub the place where his ribs hurt. He was shocked to discover a round hole with a lever of some kind attached. He gingerly probed the opening with his fingers, testing the limits of the hole, making sure he didn't turn the lever. The hole wasn't bleeding and was as smooth as a piece of molded plastic.

Panic now taking over, JD struggled and thrust and fought against the straps. He tried to sit up and see whatever it was that was in his ribcage. Whatever was there was an *opening*. He didn't like the sound of that one bit.

"You may relax your struggling, Mr. Stickle. Gunther is quite adept at simple tasks and the straps that bind you to the table will not yield."

Jon David let the thought of breaking free go for a moment as he concentrated on the voice that was speaking to him. His head hurt like hell and the blood made his vision blur. He'd heard that voice before but couldn't quite place it. Then it came it him: the old man at the top of the pit. "Every time I wake up around here, I seem to hear your voice, Greyson. If we're going to keep waking up together, then you're going to have to get better looking and drop the perverted leering old man routine. That get you off does it?" JD turned his head to the sound of the voice.

Greyson didn't seem amused. He wheeled his chair into a position that allowed JD to see him from the table. He sat in front of him, just out of JD's reach for a full minute before speaking. "The problem with people like you is that you have never considered your own mortality. You think that you will always win out, always escape, and always live to fight another day. I can assure, that idea is not only stupid, it's also your weakness."

Jon David rested his head against the table and turned to look at the man. He was dressed in a suit that looked like a faded tuxedo without the bow tie. He was dressed for an event, which was evident. Whatever the event was, JD knew it involved him and the hole in the side of his chest. "Prom night is it, Greyson? I bet a sick bastard like you had to take your mother, if you even have one."

A look of pure hatred flashed across Greyson's face for just a moment and then he immediately regained his composure. He wouldn't let this ant, this weakling, this *human*, interrupt his careful planning. "You may taunt me if it makes you feel more secure, Mr. Stickle. We are almost ready anyway and soon you'll be nothing but a memory. Mr. Limeh, if you please?"

Limeh appeared from out of the sight and grabbed the handles of the old man's wheelchair. With a smiling glance back at Jon David, he turned the chair on a sharp arc and then moved it out of the way.

"I wondered where you were, Limeh," JD said into the air. He couldn't see them anymore but he could hear them moving around. "I could smell you. And Gimpy here can't seem to get around without you pushing his dead legs."

Jon David heard Limeh chuckle softly. The joke wasn't funny and the sound of the laugh caused a ripple of terror to run the length of JD's spine. He had to think fast and act faster.

JD looked to his left deciding to concentrate on the layout of the room and locate the exits. He hadn't bothered to check as he should have as soon as he woke up, which was a tactical error. Any operative caught in an unfamiliar locale would assess the situation from both a location standpoint and a physical one. He should have pinpointed the exits sooner. He silently cursed himself for his grogginess.

JD looked to his immediate right and was astonished to see the box from the blueprints he'd recovered on the *USS Nevada* sitting less than six feet away from him. It was softly glowing a singular golden light and a barely audible humming noise was emanating from the inside.

JD quickly scanned the box from top to bottom and side to side. The picture of the *SS Waratah* was facing him and although it looked the same as the drawing, he couldn't be completely sure. There was something odd about seeing it larger than the image. He obviously wasn't as clear-headed as he would have liked. The fear that had been bubbling just beneath his skin began to surface.

He drew in a sharp breath and tried to concentrate. *What have I missed? The answer is here, Jon David,* he thought. *Think. Think!*

An idea came to him. It wasn't a good idea at all and he knew Greyson would see through it instantly but it was all he had. "Hey Greyson. What happened to Ana?"

From the other side of the box a soft voice answered his question. "I'm here, Jon David."

JD raised his head at the sound of her voice and didn't like what he heard. The voice was small and tinny, and seemed resigned, not like the tough woman he met earlier. She'd seen this game before. He understood instantly why she hated this place.

"Soon, Mr. Stickle, the ceremony will begin and we'll get you out of those straps and into the next level," Greyson called from out of sight.

"Can't wait, buddy. Really." JD laid his head back down and looked up at the ceiling. He focused on the shapes hanging above him. He'd noticed them before but not really thought about it. Like a shadow, they were just in the background of his conscious. With a sudden start, he saw that the shapes were bodies, or rather, partial bodies. With jerky motions and quiet rattles, the bodies were swaying rhythmically back and forth. Small gyrations that grew with each swing, like a pendulum, and the movements became more exaggerated with each passing moment.

Until now, JD had been more concerned with his escape then what was going on above him and its relationship to his predicament, but staring at the moving bodies now, he could see the two were intermixed. A series of multicolored flashing lights began to cascade off the bodies, adding an eerie vision to the whole thing that looked like something out of a Halloween contest. The strobe lights blinked and danced alternately red, green, black and orange and bounced around the room constantly rebounding off the bodies like pinballs in a machine. The entire room was suddenly lit up.

He was strapped down to a table with a hole in his chest, a box was glowing next to him, a woman was on the other side of the box in distress, partial bodies that looked like they were long dead were swinging above him and an old psycho was pulling the levers. *It can't get much worse*, he thought.

"You got my attention, Greyson. What's going on?" he asked while desperately trying to untie the straps. Greyson had been right: Gunther did a good job.

At that moment, the voice that woke Jon David up bellowed throughout the room:

*I Am Evil.*

# CHAPTER FORTY-ONE

Pat Smith remained hidden in the thick brush covering the west side of the house. He had checked on the gorilla in the trees a couple of times with his binoculars just to make sure the thing was still there, and satisfied that it was, he went back to patiently waiting for the incoming text.

This was a bad situation and he could see no other way out. The radio was dead and he assumed that Cummings and her partner were also dead. He didn't wish to think about what might have happened to them. There wasn't any way to communicate with the outside world and get reinforcements. He had come to a foreign country during peacetime and under covert orders had infiltrated a house without the local government's approval or notification. If it got out that a Navy Seal team and their commander had been wiped out on foreign soil without authorization, the United States would have a lot of explaining to do. He knew that his entire department and this operation would be denied and the top brass would claim they went rogue and were acting without orders.

That meant they were completely on their own. And he was in command.

By law he was required to carry an emergency satellite transmitter that only sent and received certain kinds of encoded texts. The kinds of texts that changed the way nations interacted. The kinds of texts that started wars and only a few people even knew existed, let alone had the authority to transmit. He'd already used that one.

He looked back down at the receiver in his hand when it started to vibrate. The message said a very simple four words: eight minutes, thirty seconds.

Pat pushed the button on his stopwatch marking the time, and then stood up. He had to get to Jon David if they had any chance to get out of this alive.

⊠

Captain Chad Stevens stood on the bridge of the *USS Wyoming*. He was wearing ear protectors and scanning the sky above and the ocean in front of the sub through his binoculars. He had earlier issued the order to prepare the launch when it came in complete with verification code. Whatever was on that hill in the mountains of Costa Rica, the United States government had deemed its removal a top priority.

The light was fading fast to darkness and as he rapidly scanned the horizon for any enemy combatants that might possibly intercept his sub and cause a delay in his mission, he could only wonder what was going on to cause this state of emergency. He had spent many years in the service of his country and though he rarely questioned orders of any kind, the orders he was holding in his fist were still unnerving. He read them for the sixth time in the last minute and then turned to his executive officer, who accompanied him onto the deck. "It's a go. Launch the tomahawks immediately on the coordinates."

"Aye, sir," the exec answered and then rushed to relay the message. In a matter of less than four seconds there was the deafening sound of rocket engines at full throttle followed by the high-pitched whistle scream of the launch.

Captain Stevens traced the second tomahawk through his binoculars as long as he could by the red vapor trail it left. He shook his head and hoped he hadn't just started World War Three with a nation that wasn't even on alert. His missiles would find their mark within fifty meters and after impact there wouldn't be anything left of the mountain, let alone the target.

He turned to his exec. "How long to impact?"

Making some fast calculations and then double-checking them against the launch data, he said, "Eight minutes, thirty seconds, sir."

Stevens nodded. "Relay that information to the brass and get it

244

to the team on the ground. They better get out of there now."

"Aye, sir," the young man said as he silently prayed for the people he knew they were just about to incinerate.

⊠

*I am Evil.*

*I have called you from the waters and from the depths to witness the Coronation of a new king. To witness the passage of the mantle and to begin a new world order as I lead you against all the puny, pathetic nations on the face of this planet. Together we shall take over and rule the world.*

*Behold the time has come for the birth of a new king!*

*Behold my Coronation!*

"What the hell are you up to now Greyson?" Jon David called across the room. He was desperately biding for time with any ploy he could think of trying. So far he hadn't been very successful and the straps were still in place, Ana was still out of sight and probably in trouble, and he really had no idea what was going on.

"I suppose I can answer a question or two of yours until I'm no longer amused. Your time is short and my time is just beginning. As you waste precious time trying to think of a way out of this, the army that I have been preparing and putting in place for two hundred years is rising up from the depths of the seas. Soon, the entire world will know what we are and that we take what we want. From now on, there will be a new world order. It has begun." He motioned to the golden box. "It will take only a few more moments to prepare the 'Creator' anyway. We might as well entertain ourselves."

"The Creator? That's what you call this thing? You've out done yourself, Greyson. Got a God complex going on also?"

"It doesn't matter to us what you think, Mr. Stickle. That isn't why you were brought here. Not at all."

JD pursed his lips against the pain being delivered by the slit over his eyebrow and the hole in his ribs. "Is Ana okay? I can't see her, but she didn't sound like herself."

Greyson laughed loudly. He acted like he'd heard the best joke of his life. "She is fine, Mr. Stickle. Aren't you, Margana?"

When no answer came from the other side of the box, JD called out softly, "You alright? Ana? Can you hear me?"

"I'm okay. I've been here before. It's not so bad."

"Is Margana your real name?" JD asked.

"So I've been told. Don't worry too much, Jon David. It doesn't really hurt and I'll survive. It was nice of you to promise to take me out of here, though."

Greyson laughed all the harder at that comment. "Bravado is so rare these days, Mr. Stickle, and such a pleasure to witness first hand. I can only imagine what a gentleman you must be under other circumstances."

JD ignored him. "It's not too late, Ana. Don't give up just yet. Things have a way of changing."

He couldn't see her but she started to cry quietly on her side of the box. She was strapped down the same as he was, but she felt hopelessness and a depth of despair that she didn't know existed. She didn't answer him, preferring to stay quiet and will her mind to take her away from this hell she lived.

"Okay, asshole, let's try it again. What's up with the box?" JD asked. He'd had just about enough of this whole thing and was getting madder by the minute.

"I'll save that answer for just a second. Your file says you're most intelligent. We shall see if you can figure it out. Because you are at a disadvantage and cannot see her though, I will tell you she is strapped down exactly the same way you are at the moment."

Jon David's nose started to bleed faster than it had ever bled.

⊠

Pat looked up at the streaming colors of lights coming out of the main window in the front of the house. He would have guessed it was some sort of parlor or something from the location, but the way it was lit up made it seem like Mardi Gras was going on inside. There was a rainbow of colors bouncing off the window and flashes of light coming out like bursts from a pulse gun. The lights ricocheted off the window and the ledge and then focused in several different spots like laser beams fixating on a target.

Pat glanced down at his watch and checked his time. Satisfied that he had used less than two minutes and still had over six to get Jon David and himself out, he decided to risk the possibility of exposure long enough to look in the window. Perhaps, with any luck at all, he could quickly locate the room JD was in and make a try to get him out.

Pat stood up and moved to a position directly next to the window where all the lights were bouncing off the pane. He flipped his infrared locater on and aimed it at the side of the house. In a moment he located three separate targets all in the room just on the other side of this wall but for some reason the machine also registered a partial reflection. Pat scratched his head and redirected the locater to make sure it was reading the images correctly. Satisfied nothing was wrong with the machine, he shook his head. Just like the thing in the trees that hadn't shown up on his infrared tracker, whatever was in the room with Jon David was only partially warm-blooded.

He drew his pistol and released the safety. He was going to have to attempt an immediate rescue. He had exactly five and one half minutes left until this entire area was burning from the tomahawks.

⊠

Gunther grunted softly while he performed the work. The task didn't require any deep thinking, only a measure of dexterity and deftness. He grasped a clear, plastic six-inch tube from a small table. Gunther pulled the hose two or three times until he was satisfied that it was straight, and then he grabbed a second hose and did the same thing.

Jon David's fingers traced the outline of the plastic tube with the little lever on the side of his chest. He had a sinking feeling that he knew where the hoses were going to be connected.

"You know Greyson, I really don't have time for this kind of thing. Perhaps you can speed it up?" Jon David asked into the air. He could no longer see Greyson or his wheelchair in the area, but he could feel the old man's presence in the room. He felt the man was stationed somewhere closer to Ana but almost exactly between the two of them. He didn't know why he felt this way, but he was sure it was right. It felt right.

"Ah! Marvelous, Mr. Stickle. I see that your nose is bleeding again. Your blood is as advertised."

*That's it*, thought JD. *I know what they want.*

Gunther roughly grabbed the gurney JD was strapped to and with a "click" and a "snap" connected the clear hose to the hole in JD's ribs. The half-ape then strapped down JD's hands tighter so he couldn't reach the lever any more. With another grunt of task completion, Gunther disappeared to the other side of the box and JD heard the same two sounds of connection. Presumably, the other hose was going to bleed Ana dry.

"This doesn't make a lot of sense to me, Greyson. How did you find out about me? How could you possibly know about my blood? Why am I here?" JD asked. He noticed that the faster the lights bounced around the room, the more the bodies hanging from the ceilings vibrated. They were seriously creepy.

There was an audible "clicking" sound of several switches being thrown one at a time and with a final "whoosh" and another series of hinges unclipping and chains rattling, Jon David felt his gurney start to slowly move.

He lifted his head as far as he could possibly strain and looked down at the floor. He was shocked to see the lights reflecting off glittering tiles of what looked like one continuous mural of people, animals, and things he didn't recognize engaged in some kind of vicious act. Everywhere he looked, something on the floor was torturing, maiming, decapitating, or eating something or someone else. Some of the pictures were impossible to decipher, but many were detailed drawings. Many of the animals were recognizable, but the rest of the depictions were beyond JD's scope of knowledge. Whatever they were supposed to represent, he had but one thought: *it was hideous*.

He instantly remembered the borders on the blue prints contained faces and eyes. Screaming mouths and body parts that didn't look quite right and mesmerized him to the point of losing control.

He looked down again and saw the same hideous faces staring up at him. The smiles were tighter. The eyes were blacker. The teeth were sharper. The organs were more vibrant. The drawings were so real they looked almost alive.

*Creepy and hideous*, he thought. *Oh Shit*.

As the floor began to rotate, JD saw the beginning of his blood flow into the clear plastic tube, and drip slowly to cover the floor. This was beyond the scope of trouble. He had to get out of there now. He didn't understand the inner workings of the ceremony that Greyson was dressed up for, but he knew he was the main feast.

"Gunther," Greyson said, "Adjust Mr. Stickle's lever to spray a finer mist."

The half-ape appeared again and fiddled with the side of Jon David's hose and in a minute, the blood was no longer dripping but rather spraying a fine mist.

"Do not despair, Mr. Stickle. We need your marvelous blood. Every time your heart beats until your blood is completely drained, the mist will be thrown across the floor and onto the Creator. Inside the Creator, a truly *magnificent* engineering marvel, are the souls of all the people we have taken over the years. And something else, actually. A friend of yours. Someone you would recognize who was chosen from thousands for specific reasons. You are the central part of a greater cause that you cannot possibly comprehend."

Jon David watched horrified, as everything Greyson said was true. He could have timed his heartbeats by the spray of the deep red mist out of the side of his chest.

"How did we come to know of you and the possibilities you

could offer us? It is quite simple really. In just a minute, I'm sure you'll figure it out. The table you're on is starting a slow rotation around our machine. The speed of the floor will pick up greatly as the Creator accelerates to full strength. Your blood will be mixed with Ana's and the two of you will anoint my host, giving him life. You will soon pass out from the centrifugal force and the drainage of your life's blood into our machine. I suggest you keep your eyes open as long as you can as the ceremony commences. I believe you'll find someone you know on the other side of the room, when the table gets to that side, as well as some of the answers you so desperately seek."

Jon David wasn't sure of many things, but he knew for a fact he was going to kill Greyson with his bare hands before this was over. He heard the first ear-piercing scream and he instinctively looked down at the floor. He was shocked to see the drawings had come to life and all the terrifying figures were now flexing, moving, adjusting, or stretching with an intensity and vigor that seemed beyond comprehension. They were merely hideous paintings before, now with every spray of his blood on top of them, their gyrations and thrusting motions intensified.

And one by one, the mouths with sightless eyes started to scream.

"Your magnificent blood gives them life, Mr. Stickle," Greyson said admiring the floor.

The table had rotated around the golden box almost ninety degrees while Greyson spoke and JD watched the depiction of the *Mary Celeste* come into view from the end of the machine. As the floor moved him to the side of the room that he hadn't been able to see, he knew one of the answers would be waiting.

☒

Pat had seen enough. The room was lit up and in the center of the floor sat the box he'd seen from the blue prints so long ago that JD had found in Brown's apartment. The floor was rotating and the only explanation was that the box was some kind of mechanical instrument and it was now turned on. He couldn't see JD, but he could see a woman strapped to a table with a hose draining blood from her like an IV in a hospital. He traced the flow of her blood and watched as it filtered onto the tile floor.

He had no intention of waiting to see what *that* was going to produce. He glanced to the left and saw an old man in a wheelchair with one hand placed firmly on the box and the other hand pointing to the floor. He seemed to be in some kind of a trance and his mouth was moving like he was talking, although Pat couldn't hear what was being said.

Pat was just about to break the glass and end the party when the floor finally rotated enough to let Jon David come into view. The spinning floor speed was increasing in small increments and Pat gasped when he realized that JD was also strapped down with a hose draining his blood away quickly.

# CHAPTER FORTY-TWO

Jon David blinked his eyes and cleared his throat. He stared with an open mouth like a bucket of cold water had been poured over his head. His emotions ran a gauntlet that he didn't know he even possessed, and like a roller coaster off the rails, he flew up and down with each breath he took. In one minute he was struggling against the nylon straps desperately looking for a way out of the situation, while at the same time watching his blood being syphoned off and worrying about Ana across from him, and in the next minute he felt like someone hit him with a tree trunk.

As the floor completed its first half rotation of one hundred and eighty degrees and JD could finally see the side of the room that had been so conveniently hidden, he understood exactly what Greyson said about some of his answers.

He stifled a cry from coming out of his throat when the body first came into his sight. Crumpled up against the wall, lying on its side and staring open-eyed and point blank into space for all time, with wet clothes and slicked back grimy hair, was the body of Jon David's fourteen-year old brother, Jay.

Jon David hadn't seen him since that day on the shores of the West Bay in Traverse City over thirty years ago. The undertow took Jay and the police had dragged the bay only to bring back empty nets to his father, who stood watch on the shore every day until the nightfall came and the police halted their search.

He looked just as JD remembered him. Same clothes, same dimple on his cheek. JD quickly scanned Jay's open collar and there it was, hanging limply from his neck, the same tiny gold necklace that their father had given both of them the Christmas before Jay drowned.

Jon David blinked back tears of pain and sorrow at the same time as he felt an inferno grow beneath his skin like he had never experienced in his life. The son-of-a-bitch had taken his brother from him and now was sucking the very blood out of his arteries. "Over my ass," he hissed through clenched teeth.

He tore his eyes from the sight of his crumpled and disfigured brother and searched the floor for Greyson. He was going to kill the bastard right now.

"I see you recognize your brother from how many years ago? What was it, Mr. Stickle? Thirty years at least? He was fourteen when we took him. We had no idea at the time, of course, that his blood was somehow different than the others. He was but a number until the first time we hooked him up on the same bed you're lying on. Hell, I think we even used the same hose."

Greyson removed his hand from caressing the machine. "Mr. Limeh? It's time to go to full power. I can see the blood of Mr. Stickle has intensified itself and is now at full strength. If you please?"

"Certainly, Mr. Greyson," Limeh, who until this moment had disappeared, moved to the last set of controls and threw two more switches before he seemed satisfied. "Done."

"You see, Mr. Stickle, when we first tried your brother's blood, we found out that it was missing something. It wasn't until the first one was produced we realized the Creator, the magnificent machine you are attached to at this very moment, had a flaw. It was your brother's very rich, red, vibrant blood that brought life to the first one. Before that, the results were failures. Utter failures."

JD was listening but was furiously straining against the nylon restraints. If it was humanly possible he was going to break them and get to that bastard. And then carry his brother out of there.

"The flaw, we later learned, and this is where Captain Joe Brown and his incredible intelligence came to assist us, was in the blood itself. To create the being, the *person* we wanted, from this machine we had to use blood that was *alive*. Living, breathing, flowing-red blood that had to be as vibrant as the being we were creating. The blood from your brother, although it enabled us to make the first prodigy from the machine, was not perfect because, he was quite simply, dead as hell when we hooked him up to it."

Greyson fell into a quiet moment of reflection thinking about the first experiments and the problems that they created. "Some of the beings we created were abominable. That's about the only word that truly describes them. Uncontrollable monsters. We had to kill them before they killed us."

Limeh continued from that point like they had the same thought process going on. He moved over to where Greyson had leaned back up against the machine and was actually embracing it. "But we kept trying, Mr. Stickle. We were sure that through trial and error we could produce the next one to take our place. The one who will lead our army."

The room was starting to spin faster and faster and JD collapsed back against the table, exhausted from the blood spraying from him and the effort he was exerting. Every time he rounded the corner, every time he got within eyeshot of his brother, he stopped all attempts to break the straps and just stared at the boy who left him so many years ago.

"We did not give up. We took from the places where no one would miss the people and we brought them here and used their souls, indeed their very essences, to make our being. To create our new leader. We took from ships and islands and people who didn't matter and wouldn't be missed. And we tried to make the one. The perfect one to lead us."

He shook his head and laid a hand on his old friend, Greyson. They had been together so many years and this would be the last night. After tonight, they would both move on. "The first one was wrong for so many reasons, but was still able to assist us. Quite nicely actually."

JD could barely focus because the room was spinning around and around and he was close to giving up. His subconscious took over and from somewhere deep inside came the question, "Where is the first one now?"

Greyson lifted his head and then chuckled. "You're not really that smart, are you? The file was obviously wrong on a couple of counts, eh? Tsk, tsk." He shook his head as if dismissing a lesser employee from the factory line before firing him. "She's lying across from you and hooked up to the machine with you. Margana was the first."

# CHAPTER FORTY-THREE

Greyson was embracing the golden machine as if it were a long lost child. He was hugging it and sobbing in the ecstasy of the moment. He grasped the edges and using an upper body strength he hadn't possessed in at least twenty years, he pulled himself to a standing position against the side of the machine. It was the moment that he had been waiting for his entire life. "Margana was the first. She was also the most feral. We didn't get the mix of blood and, how do I say it, other things, correct until a couple of attempts after her. We then hooked her up to the Creator," he rubbed the box as if it might break at any minute, "and she produced the half-apes that so perfectly guard this place. Like Gunther. They are not intelligent, but they are strong and undoubtedly loyal, as you've seen."

He threw his hands into the air and leaned backwards and then opened his mouth as if to scream. He stared in defiance at the Creator absorbing Jon David Stickle's very life's blood with every heartbeat. With a concentration bordering on a personal nirvana, he reveled in the true nature of who he was as he bellowed into the air:

*I AM EVIL! This is the moment we have been waiting for two centuries to arrive. The Creator will make the perfect host. The perfect Leader. All will bow before his power. Before his majesty. Before our new king.*

A blinding light emanating from someplace deep inside Greyson's core beamed out through his open mouth and then through his eye sockets as something sinister came out. It willed him to throw his arms wide open and proclaim to the witnesses once again:

*I AM EVIL! I command the lowers to rise up and begin an unholy war against the highers. Arise, my children. Come into your own world.*

The lights were beaming and bouncing around the room as the bodies on the ceiling joined in an unholy rhythm of lustful violence with the mutating and screaming faces on the floor. Hearts beat and arms flapped to unimaginable rhythms. Lungs belched and arteries flowed sinister things across and over the paintings of beasts consuming humans in painful displays of evisceration. They were all there to witness. All there to contribute. A seed that could only be spawned in Hell was taking place and a birth from a place that should not have existed was awakening.

JD had gone beyond the stage of madness and even though he was close to losing consciousness, his anger controlled his emotions. He would not let this man beat his family. He silently willed his blood to turn to blackness and kill the very being it was trying to create. Clamping his jaw shut and focusing all of his energy into his flowing bloodstream, Jon David imagined that his churning hot, throbbing, deep red and darkly rich blood was now an acid-like substance that would kill anything it touched. He gritted his teeth and fought both the rapidly spinning movement of the table and the flow of his life to the creature in the machine. If he died now, then he would send death through the plastic hose to this creature.

He would not let his man have his family.

Jon David's eyes flew open at the thought of his family. With his death, the Stickles would be no more. He looked at the blood spurting across the box and dripping down to the floor and concentrated on pain and acid. He stared defiantly down at his life's essence and then noted with satisfaction that for some reason the blood was bubbling like it had started boiling before leaving the tubing.

His family. His legacy.

He snapped his head to the right as a thought hit him that he couldn't believe he'd missed before. JD's mind was racing. *How can I be so stupid? It's all about my family. Christ, it's been right in front of me the whole time.*

He had an idea and now he had a chance, if only he had the time.

*I am Evil and I am your father. Arise my son and join with me in our divine purpose. Together as one we will rule this puny world and rid the entire system of their need for existence. Come alive now and stand. Take your place as the leader of our army. Join with me!*

Greyson was completely transfixed on the body and the machine and had become totally oblivious to anything else happening. The machine was glowing like a hot fire was building inside and the lid had opened and above the rim, a body had started to rise. The body must have been the one he was praying to, because until this moment, it had been completely submerged inside the machine and hidden from view.

Greyson started to melt and smoke was willowing out of the open pores of his skin and burning up his flesh as he hailed the arrival of the new king.

In that precise moment, Jon David realized the power of his blood. It had taken him thirty-nine years to get to this place where he understood exactly what his dark gift entailed: his blood had the power to keep his family *alive*.

He tried the only thing he had left. He spoke into the insanity happening all around him. He spoke into the blinding lights and the creature that was beginning to ascend from the machine and the screaming, vengeful images under his table. He spoke into the darkness of the minds surrounding him and the evil of this night.

But mostly, he spoke to her.

"Ana," Join David said softly but knew she could hear him. "Ana. I'm sorry for not noticing sooner."

She was beyond the ability to comprehend his every word, but she heard his voice, as if it were speaking to her from inside her head instead of the other side of the room. "What? What are you talking about?" she whispered back.

Jon David heard her, as clearly as if they were the only ones alive on Earth and this was their moment. "I should have noticed sooner. You have my brother's blood flowing through you. The blood of our father. That means you are my sister. That means you are my family."

# CHAPTER FORTY-FOUR

Jon David concentrated solely on Ana while the madness around him ramped up to a fury that could only be measured by a seismograph. The floor was alive with undulating bodies of grotesque forms screaming in every dimension and from every orifice that could be imagined. The laser lights were whizzing across the ceiling so fast a distinct "whine" could be heard from them. They reflected off the floor and traced the bodies hanging from the ceiling. The golden box was levitating slightly above the floor like it had risers under it and the body that came from its insides and was being fed with JD's blood was slowly beginning to stand upright. All the movement was of a purely sinister nature.

Jon David focused on the only thing he had left. The only chance to survive this onslaught of depravity. The only thing that might save him and keep his sanity. "Ana. Listen to me. I am your only true blood brother. My family's blood courses through your veins and comes from our father."

Ana was having a hard time believing any of the words that somehow crossed the madness and managed to be clearly heard. She had no idea how she could understand this man she had only met this night, but for some reason, she felt a calmness descend over her when he talked to her. She had no family. This was an entirely new thing to her. The feeling was spreading across her like the ray of sunshine she so desperately dreamed of touching someday. Like the sand between her toes and the wind in her face when she ran on a beach she had only imagined, this man brought a feeling that she did not want to release. Her life had been such a singular hell, she could not afford to pass this opportunity, even if he was playing her. She decided almost instantly to trust him.

"Brother." It seemed a strange word. "What do you need from me?" she asked.

"Quickly. We are almost out of time," Jon David was fully aware that if the body managed to stand upright and gather more strength, the ceremony would be complete and all would be lost, including their lives. "You are the mother of Gunther. Tell him to release us and help us get out of here."

She had never disobeyed the old men before and this was not an easy step to take. "I am afraid, Jon David."

"I will get us out of here. I promise you, Ana we will go far away where you can be anything you want to be and do anything you want to do. I'll take you with me. To our home. But we must act quickly. I will not let them hurt you."

She turned her head to locate Gunther, who was sitting idly by the machine, ignoring everything that was going on around him. With a whip of her head and screech of an inhuman sound, Gunther stood up and immediately came to Ana. She used a language that only he understood and within a matter of seconds, he was untying her and then he moved across to do the same to Jon David.

Pat had been completely mesmerized outside the window from the craziness of the scene unfolding in front of him. Jon David was in peril, some woman he had never seen before was talking to an ape like she owned him, and an old man was pointing at a body that was rising out of the box like Lazarus. Even the damn floor was writhing. It was a picture straight out of a movie.

He stole one more glance at his stopwatch to make sure he had the time to even attempt a rescue and then with four and one half minutes left, he hit the outer pane with the butt end of his Beretta, shattering the glass into a thousand pieces. Pat quickly leaped through the open window, scraped and cut himself in several places on the broken glass, and then rolled up to a defensive position with his pistol drawn.

Without any hesitation he trained the gun on the lone standing man, the only threat he perceived at this point and the only one he could easily take out, and shot him cleanly through the chest. Limeh looked up in complete amazement having been in the shadows during the whole ceremony, clutched his chest, and toppled to the floor.

Greyson's attention was completely immersed in the body struggling to stand up. He didn't see or hear Pat break the glass and didn't notice when Limeh fell to the ground in a pool of blood. His attention was fixated solely on the Creator and the thing it was creating. The body fought for its survival as a purplish aura resonated out from the center of its chest and began glowing. With a jerk and a thrust, the body was beginning to move in flopping strides. It was only going to be a minute before the ceremony was complete and it became fully alive.

Greyson's face was sinking into his skull and melting so badly that large chunks of flesh were falling off with searing sounds like a skillet would make while frying eggs. His fingers pointed at the jerking body and his hands reached out of their sleeves to touch the assembly. His head was thrown back and his heart was beating so strongly that the skin surrounding his rib cage was pulsating and shaking with every beat.

*I am Evil and this is my son. I have created you and we are one in the same. Come to me now. Grasp my hand and inherit all that I am. Together we shall be the most powerful force of Evil nature has ever envisioned. We shall rule the world!*

The words coming out of Greyson were like gibberish to Jon David and were taking on the volume of a jet plane. Every time he pronounced something anew, the walls started to tremble and plaster fell in large chunks and splattered on the mutating and screaming figures on the floor that were in such a devotion to their blood-letting they never hesitated as the roof caved. As soon as his hands were free, JD yanked the hose away from his body, stopping the spray and cutting off the loss of his blood.

Ana had jumped up and pulled the hose out as well and then she screeched another series of unintelligible sounds and Gunther turned back to her. She pointed to the door and ran.

*NO! You cannot interrupt the ceremony at this point! It cannot be done! I command you to stop! I command you! Kill them! Kill them all!*

The body that had risen managed to stand up straight. It was becoming stronger with each passing minute. Levitating a couple of feet above the box that created it, the man flung its arms wide open as a milky substance ran down its flesh and pooled back inside the box.

Greyson screamed. His head began expanding and contracting like he had no skull. His facial features had become indistinct and completely smooth like they had been sanded off and the skin stretched so tightly across his face that it was like cellophane wrapping. The blood pounding in his paper-thin arteries began to spew across the floor to replace the loss of JD's and Ana's. He grabbed both sides of his head and screamed repeatedly as the floor started to shake uncontrollably.

*You cannot stop the flow of your blood! It must be complete! I am above you and I will kill you unmercifully. I am evil! I am evil and you have betrayed me! You will be consumed by my army and die a thousand deaths.*

It had gotten so loud that Jon David could hear little else. There was the screeching sound of gears and metal breaking and crashing into each other and the floor slowed to a stop while he regained his footing. He grabbed Gunther's arm and pointed at the glowing purple body and the half-ape nodded like it understood.

"Jon David! For Christ sakes. We have to get out of here now!" Pat emptied a magazine of bullets into Greyson's chest but the shots passed right through and came out the other side. Pat could see a spray pattern of shots hitting the wall directly behind Greyson.

Jon David hadn't noticed Pat until now and had no idea how he managed to show up at this exact moment, but he was thankful that he was here. In their time together, Pat had a habit of doing just that.

"I have to do this, Pat. Take Ana and get out of here. I'll catch up!"

Pat looked at the girl that JD pointed at and shook his head in agreement. He made a "T" symbol with his hand, like he was signaling for a timeout and then held up three fingers.

Jon David nodded. He understood instantly that the "T" meant Pat had called in a tomahawk missile and he had three minutes to get away. He pointed to the doorway and Pat and Ana ran towards it. "I'll be right behind you Ana, don't worry. Go with this man until I catch up to you."

She didn't know this man either, but her brother said it was all right, so she accepted it. She wouldn't follow him for long though, because she decided that once she got out of the front door, if Jon David didn't appear in a couple of minutes, she was going back to get him. She screeched one more time at Gunther before sprinting out the door close behind Pat.

Greyson had somehow regained partial control of his collapsing body. He spent years preparing for this night and he had to know if the ceremony was completed before the hoses were pulled out. He tried to lift his arms to touch the jerking body levitating above the machine. As Greyson stretched, there was a primeval scream and then a growl of malice that came from the disfigured, milky face of Captain Joe Brown.

Greyson worked what was left of his facial muscles into a smile. It had been born and was alive.

Jon David gasped in astonishment when he recognized Brown's face on the levitating body. He'd lost a lot of blood and his head was still bleeding. He had to fight every second to stay coherent. He wasn't sure if his blood could regenerate itself fast enough to keep him alive, but he knew he had to stop this monstrosity of nature from coming to life if at all possible. He would take the creature from the old man even though it might kill him in the process.

Fighting to control his movements and not lose consciousness, JD decided to rely on the half-ape to get them out of here after this was finished. He concentrated on a single movement and motioned to Gunther. Pulling his arms apart and flexing his hands open and closed, he motioned to the body. Gunther grunted an acceptance and leaped into the box. He grabbed the ankles of the emerging man and as the purple light turned to a deep crimson color, the half-ape and the body with Joe Brown's face seemed to meld together as one.

*No! You cannot! You cannot interrupt this moment! You cannot touch this perfection!*

Jon David turned to face the abomination of an old man. Having nothing else left to try he lunged directly at Greyson and knocked him clear of the box and apart from his creation. Greyson screamed a venomous yell and fell to the floor while Jon David fought to separate himself from the old man. He did not want to touch the bastard again.

The half-ape clutched the body and violently ripped the legs of the newest creation as far apart as it could. There was a tearing sound and a scream of pure pain that came from the depths of hell, and the emerging man was split from his groin to his neck. Gunther's muscles bulged as it pulled the body in half, and a growl of satisfaction came out of the half-ape's mouth. It had killed and was now celebrating.

With a nonchalant toss of his bulging arms, the body was hurled in two different directions.

Pat screamed, "Now JD! We have to go now!"

Jon David motioned to the ape to go to the door, and running as fast as he could, JD took off, unsteady in his balance but confident in his intent. He was regaining some strength in his legs. In a matter of seconds, he had crossed the room and ran through the door and out into the jungle. Looking back over its shoulder as he fled the mansion, he took one last look at his brother Jay's corpse.

Greyson's eyes sought out the fleeing form of JD and the half-ape and followed them with unrivaled hatred. He raised his arm and pointed at their backs as if he was targeting them. A flopping half-body of a man was wiggling beneath his feet.

"We have to go! Faster, JD! Faster!" Pat led the way down the driveway and through the open gates and as far away as the four of them could run. The half-ape managed to scoop Ana up and was carrying her in its arms, and was easily outdistancing the other two.

Suddenly, there was the piercing scream of a sonic boom and then in an instant the entire jungle was lit up in a hailstorm of fire as the first of two tomahawk missiles found their target. The second one impacted within three seconds of the first and the four of them were hurtled into the air like gravity had been suspended and they were twigs in the wind.

Pat landed first, almost fifty meters from where he started with a sickening "thud". He hit his back against a tree and he was knocked unconscious. Ana was flung into some heavy brush and landed without serious damage. Jon David fell on top of the ape and the two of them rolled several times from the force of the impact until finally coming to rest about thirty meters from Ana. As the two of the collided and then rolled, JD heard the distinct sound of bones breaking.

JD lay still where he fell, momentarily dazed. He shook his head and tried to figure out where he was when Ana came across and reached out a tentative hand to help him to his feet. He winced and fell back down and she responded by pulling back. She was on alert again and stood ready to flee from him.

"Sorry, Ana. I think my ankle is broken. It hurts to stand on it. My fault for scaring you."

She smiled then, a small sheepish kind of grin that felt good to her. It wasn't something she had done very often. She knelt down next to the still form of Gunther. "He was never bad to me. He only did what they commanded."

JD stood up but was careful to put his weight on the good leg. He looked back up at the burning house and jungle. The heat from the fire singed his face. "They're gone, I think. No one could have survived." He pointed at Gunther. "He must have broken his neck when we fell. It could have just as easily been me."

"I don't think it's your turn today, Jon David," she said.

"Not today anyway. Someday." He looked across at a very limp but moaning Pat Smith. "Let's get him to a hospital. Whoever fired those Hawks will be close by. I'm sure they'll pick us up."

He hopped across to Ana and put his arm around her shoulder for support. "Let's go home," he said at the same time that he noticed his nose had quit bleeding.

# Book Six

## Conclusion

# CHAPTER FORTY-FIVE

Things couldn't get much better for Mark Lowry. He was sitting at the pool, having just finished a full body massage that included a happy ending from a stunning Asian dressed in a skimpy skirt, ordered lobster bisque from the lounge, and was on his third martini.

His money was hidden in three different offshore accounts in the Bahamas, Switzerland, and Belize. He dispersed all the funds to various accounts under pseudo-names with little trouble. A couple of simple keystrokes on his laptop and he could move the money and use it as he wished. The latest thing on his list today was booking an around the world cruise.

Reminding himself to make a call to a travel agent before the afternoon was finished, he downed the last of the martini, looked for and didn't see the waiter approaching with his meal, and decided to take one last dip in the ocean before lunch. He stood up from the lounge chair and dropped his towel on the beach, walked down to the surf and strode into the waves.

He swam for a few moments before deciding the rays of the beating sun might be burning him, and even though he was a strong swimmer from his years in the Navy, he dog paddled back towards the shore. He couldn't have been more than a hundred yards out and it would only be a minute before he was downing another martini with his lobster bisque.

He felt his left leg scrape across a coral reef and he cursed. The damn beaches were supposed to be cleared by the locals so this kind of thing didn't happen and the tourists that came to this five star luxury resort never got hurt. He would speak to the manager as soon as he got to the beach.

He kept his body upright in the water as his other leg struck something solid that was too firm to be a reef this close to the shore. He quit dog paddling for a moment longer as he tentatively tried to touch the bottom with his feet. He could just as easily stand up and walk the rest of the way because the water was so shallow.

He felt his toes sink into the soft sand under the water, and relaxed. He wiggled his toes a little deeper, giggling at the absurd notion that a reef was this close to the beach, and started to walk.

He was suddenly stopped when he felt an arm encircle his ankle. In the next instant, another set of fingers entwined themselves around his other leg.

Lowry screamed a curt, short, yelp of terror. He frantically tried to yank his legs free, but the viscosity of the water made his movements slow and not nearly as forceful as they would have been out of the water. He held his breath and ducked under the surface long enough to try and free his ankles from the hands. He hit, scratched, and pried at the fingers.

When he couldn't hold his breath any longer and had to come up for air, he screamed as loud as possible. The wind was blowing a little more than twenty knots today and his voice barely carried to the beach. It never came close to being heard up on the shore.

Panicking and on the fringe of hysteria, Lowry tried to kick out and break free, only to have the hands clamp down even tighter. He couldn't believe what was happening, but as he strained to look through the four feet of water and see what was gripping him, he was startled to see a face appear in the sand.

And it was smiling at him.

Lowry started shaking from mortal fear as all of the sudden the hands pushed up and then immediately pulled violently down. Lowry was raised up about two feet, just high enough to make a bigger splash, and then he was dragged under the water and deep into the depths of the sandy bottom.

⌧

Jon David sat at the window looking out into the blackness of the night. He was spending his third night in the Naval Hospital outside Washington, DC and try as he might, he couldn't shake an unpleasant feeling. His nose hadn't bled since he and Ana returned. He sent her on ahead to Michigan under naval escort and learned this morning that she arrived safely at his beach house.

Pat was in the room down the hall recovering from a broken vertebra that would heal but he'd be wearing a cast for the next three months at least. If he had collided with that tree a fraction lower on his back, he would have been paralyzed.

JD was thankful that the worst thing he had to deal with was a left over scar on his right side that the doctors sewed up. It would leave a four-inch reminder there for the rest of his life.

But that wasn't what was bothering him. Yesterday he had a junior officer bring the original blueprints he found in Brown's apartment to his room. He'd been studying them ever since.

He knew. He just couldn't let it go.

He made a decision as he drew the blinds down on his window and then wheeled his chair down to Pat's room. It took him only three minutes to reach the door, and he pushed it open with his foot. He could have walked, the ankle was never broken, only sprained, but he rather liked the feeling of having to sit for a while.

"Are you awake, Pat?" he asked. A single light at the foot of the bed lit the room in the soft glow all hospital rooms seem to emit, but he couldn't see Pat's face so he wasn't sure. He figured he'd be awake at this time of night. Pat never slept.

"Of course, JD. Come on in. I could use the company."

"No thanks, Pat. I'm just here to tell you I'm leaving."

Pat didn't say anything for a full minute before answering. "I figured. When?"

"I have to go now. I need to see for myself."

"They're dead, Jon David."

"I hope you're right."

# CHAPTER FORTY-SIX

"The first one was hidden in the anchor hanging from the *SS Waratah*," Jon David said softly.

The conn deck of the *USS Nevada* was as ice cold as the last time he was there. It seemed like so long ago since the first time he saw the hanging men on the sub. The Navy finally decided to remove the bodies. The sub was going to be decommissioned and the incident put under the heading of "Unexplained Events".

He walked unafraid among the rows of the men. They still hung rigidly in the same positions, with only the body of Joe Brown missing. The freezing temperatures had preserved them. There was no more listing or moving. They hung stiffly, waiting to be removed and buried properly. The Navy was going to move them first thing in the morning.

He walked back to the front and faced the men, listening for movement to confirm his suspicions. He stood completely still before trying again.

"On the *Mary Celeste*, it was hidden on the left mast. The lighthouse from Flannan Isle had it on the top section, just under the light. It was your ego, if you're wondering what gave you away. And your choice of Captain Brown was a mistake," JD said into the deathly stillness.

When no one answered, a single quick thought that perhaps he'd been wrong tried to surface, but Jon David quickly pushed it away. He knew he was right.

"Come on out, Mr. Limeh," JD said.

From the very back of the sub's conn deck, came a voice that was cold like death. It was deep, and hollow, and filled with hatred. "You are most intelligent after all, Mr. Stickle."

The voice echoed strongly off the metal walls of the sub and resonated long after he quit speaking. For a moment, there was utter stillness in the sub. JD took that time to move towards the ladder nearest the exit to the conn.

"Your egos were always the problem. You ultimately thought you could never be defeated. So you signed the box with four hidden 'Ls', like an artist would sign a painting. You guys were so proud of what you created; you had to let the world know."

"Please continue, Mr. Stickle. I am quite enjoying this. I haven't had a worthy opponent for the longest time. To which guys are you referring?" The voice seemed to be testing and pushing.

"The Nazis, of course, Limeh."

A long, desperate and deliberate laughter ensued. "I wondered why no one figured it out for so long. How did *you* do it?"

Jon David stood perfectly still, trying to pinpoint the voice. It would matter in this endgame.

"It was easy enough. I noticed it when you had me tied to the table. I kept looking over at the machine and at that picture of the *SS Waratah*. That's when I spotted the hidden 'L'. Rotating me on the table made me look at the other three pictures. After I had the first one, I saw the other three on the sides of the box, cleverly hidden. I put it together while lying in the hospital. Four L's? Four L's laid at just the right angle make a swastika. I should have seen it sooner than I did. I was blinded by your monstrosity. I should have picked it up sooner from the blueprints."

"Is that the best you can do, Mr. Stickle? I had hoped for so much more. Do you hear the clock ticking, Mr. Stickle? I believe they call it an atomic clock these days. It is a perfect metaphor for the end of your life. Your life is ticking away."

It was so quiet that JD could have heard a rat scurrying at the back of the sub. There was only the constant tick-tick-ticking that Limeh noticed. Other than that, he could only hear himself breathe.

JD moved to the perfect place for retreating in case he had to get out of the sub fast. He stood at the bottom of a sharply angled ladder that the Navy used to load its missiles. He could scamper up that ladder and close the hatch in a matter of seconds.

"No one here but you and I, Mr. Stickle. It ends tonight." As he spoke, a shroud of ice fog started to radiate up from the floor.

"I can't figure out why you used Joe Brown. What happened on board this ship?" JD could see the fog developing every time Limeh spoke. It was making it harder to see in the cramped quarters of the conn deck.

A long, low venomous chuckle carried up to Jon David. There was a definite threat in the laughter. Not even slightly veiled, it carried death.

"That idiot. I offered him immortality in exchange for his expertise in molecular biology. I chose him to fix the Creator. It produced Ana and the apes. But he couldn't do it and then he betrayed me."

Jon David understood then. He about had the whole thing figured out anyway. He just wanted Limeh's confirmation. "He surprised you. He was brilliant. He figured out what the four L's meant and realized he was helping the Nazi's, didn't he? Then he double-crossed you."

"Bravo, Mr. Stickle. Bravo."

Jon David continued, scanning every crevice and straining his eyes against the thickening fog. It had risen steadily while they talked and the visibility had dropped to mere meters. "How did you do it? How'd you kill these men?"

"I assisted Captain Brown. They were weak. I held their minds. He was supposed to bring their souls to me."

"It was the muscle stimulant I found in his house, wasn't it? He altered it somehow and used it on the men. My guess is he somehow turned it into a muscle paralyzer, to hold them still. Something like that. But instead of bringing them to you, he hung each one of them to keep you from getting them. You needed them alive this time. You didn't get the souls you wanted. Couldn't complete the job without them."

JD carefully slid his foot up a rung of the ladder. "The men aren't smiling. They're *grimacing*. From the pain of a muscle paralyzer. That's why they had bits of broken teeth on the front of their shirts. Brown killed them to save their souls. He wasn't going to give you his men."

"I have spent my eternity in passage, but even I have to play by the rules of physics. I needed Brown's brilliance and his physical being. I have grown weary of moving from animals to humans and back again. Human bodies cannot be counted on; they tend to wear out after fifty years. I devised the perfect plan and chose Captain Brown carefully. He was going to be my last passage. He was going to be the perfect host. The souls of dead men had not worked thus far to produce my army. Brown was supposed to bring me a cargo of live souls and this submarine."

Jon David braced himself to run up the ladder as quickly as he could. As soon as he verified where Limeh was on the ship he was gone. "But he killed himself and the crew. He was the only one actually smiling. He made a pact with the devil and found a way out."

There was no movement that Jon David could sense and a creeping fear was working its way into the pit of his stomach. The fog was as thick as any he had ever seen. He could see the floor beneath his feet and the outlines of the men. A soft light from the rear of the conn deck bathed the area in a yellowish glow.

Coming here and facing this kind of evil, was a risk from the beginning. JD kept talking, using the dialogue to gauge his adversary's position. "And Greyson was a sham the whole time. A shill. A figurehead so no one noticed you in the background. You controlled him and used him as well. It was your voice talking through him the whole time. One more thing and we're done here, Limeh."

Tick-tick-tick. Cold, deathly silence.

"You are correct. We are done here. But not like you envision. You have stolen my host from me, but then you presented yourself to me. With richness in your blood that will serve me very well." The voice emanated from all corners of the sub. It seemed as if Limeh had gotten behind him somehow. He was coiled like a snake and just about ready to strike.

JD whirled around and checked his six o'clock position. There was nothing on the ladder leading out. He had to locate the voice.

"The submarine was as important to you as Brown. You needed nuclear capability to attack the gold coast of Australia. Like you said, it's physics. Dead men in the water couldn't get the job done. This whole thing was about you needing the power of a nuclear sub. And of course, the gold. It was also about the money."

The voice stopped for second like it was thinking about what Jon David said. "I wanted to control the gold. Cutting off one of the few remaining precious metals would have the world at my mercy. Shut down the flow of money and the world's infrastructure would crumble."

"Gold, an army of undead guarding the shores, and a nuclear submarine. Quite a day's work." Jon David knew it was time. He couldn't guarantee Limeh would hold off any longer.

"You were just a different approach. With Brown dead when he arrived, I had to try another method to pass to him. You blood is not like others. The ceremony was working when you interrupted it."

"Sorry to disappoint you."

The venom from the next words was thick enough to cut. "I knew you would come here. I knew I would take you next. You cannot leave events unfinished. It is in the Stickle blood."

In the center of the conn, directly where Brown's body had once hung, a pair of blood red, beady little eyes pierced the fog like lasers cutting through a piece of metal. The eyes were alight with fierceness and a vengeance. They would not be denied.

Jon David held the stare as the red eyes focused into his. He wasn't going to back down this time. The ice fog swirled just enough to catch glimpses of Limeh. The sound of the incessant ticking in the sub was all that could be heard while the two of them measured each other one last time before attacking.

"Two problems, Mr. Limeh," JD said as he tensed for the inevitable.

"I no longer need to speak to you. Your time is up, Mr. Stickle," he laughed a deep belly laugh. He was going to kill JD and take the sub.

"Problem one. There is no Mr. Limeh. It's an anagram. And not a very good one as it only took me about fifteen minutes to figure it out. Mr. Limeh rearranged spells 'Himmler'. As in Heinrich Himmler. I imagine he built this machine for you. He and his engineers were so far ahead of the rest of the world and deeply into the occult. Since he's been dead for so many years, just who are you?"

The chuckle gave way silence. "I am Heinrich Himmler. I kept his body and his soul. He was truly pure evil. We merged as one. I keep him alive. You will keep us both alive. All of my hosts live within me."

"Hang on Himmler. You forgot problem number two," Jon David said as he continued stepping up the rungs of the ladder while Himmler spoke.

"And what is that?" The eyes had a slightly amused look in them as if their prey was about to be eaten.

"You don't know shit about nuclear submarines. Atomic clocks don't make a ticking sound."

Jon David rushed up the ladder as fast as he could go. He knew the timer on the C-4 explosive he laid on the foredeck when he first got there was close to zero. He kicked the hatch closed and quickly swung the lock shut before securing it with a metal bar through the handle. It fit perfectly and he wedged it down before turning and running away.

He was about forty yards away when the first of the two explosions rocked the dry dock of the New York Port Authority. The sub was consumed in flames and burned for three days before the fire department got it under control. Parts of the *USS Nevada* scattered into little bits that flew skyward with the wind. The C-4's efficiency resulted in the sub being declared a total hull loss.

As he stood and watched the smoke and flames, JD couldn't help but hope that he got the bastard.

# CHAPTER FORTY-SEVEN

"It's over now, Pat," JD said into his cell phone. He was sitting in his favorite rocker on his porch on the shore of Lake Michigan. The clouds had parted and even though it was only forty-seven degrees, the sun made it feel considerably warmer.

"Jon David! Let's go for a swim!" Ana yelled at him from the water. She spent every day since being brought here on the beach. Not even a cold north breeze could keep her out of the surf. After being in captivity for thirty years, she wasn't going to let a little thing like freezing temperatures stop her.

He laughed at her running though the foam of the waves. It was going to be difficult at times, but he looked forward to watching the wonderment in her face as she got to see the world. He promised himself that he would show her whatever she wanted to see. "I'll be there in a minute." Her spontaneity brought out the kid in him.

"A small amount of C-4 explosive set at just the right spot took the *Nevada* down. They couldn't find enough of her to drag the pieces back. What was left intact sunk to the bottom of the harbor," Pat said. He let it sit for a minute and then continued. "Only someone with an extensive understanding of submarines and their construction could've known exactly where to put that bomb. I doubt we'll ever know the whole story about it." In truth, Pat knew exactly what happened. "The only good news is that now the Navy has an 'official' explanation as to what happened to the fathers and sons who died on board. The official report will say 'core meltdown'. That works for them and gives some kind of closure to the families, I guess. It's better than nothing."

"I guess." Jon David was busy making sure Ana didn't get too far out in the waves. He was acting like her father, but he didn't really care. She was his responsibility now. One he actually relished.

"So we're done until the next time, JD?" Pat asked rather

hopefully. He was afraid that Jon David Stickle might leave the country and never help him out again. He could certainly understand it if he did, but that still didn't stop him from wanting him around.

"Don't push it, Pat. It's going to take some time and I'm not sure about it at all right now. I'll call you next time."

"Understood, JD. One question though. How did you figure out the truth about Limeh, er, I mean Himmler? How could you have known that?"

He thought about not telling Pat but after just a second, he knew there wasn't anything that could be changed. "It was simple, Pat. Really. I'm looking at the answer as we speak." Ana had just come up from under the frigid water and was splashing around like a three year old. JD couldn't help but laugh. The water had to be freezing.

"I don't understand, JD. Take it slow for me."

"Ana. Remember her real name is Margana?"

"Sure. What about it?"

"Well, Pat. You should read more books. 'Margana' spelled backwards is 'Anagram'."

Pat drew in a sudden, sharp gasp of breath.

"Mr. Limeh was an anagram for Himmler. He named his daughter after he renamed himself. When I realized what her name was and the relationship between them, the rest was easy."

Jon David hung up his cell phone stood up on his porch and then tossed the phone as far out into the surf as possible. He took his shoes off and headed for the water.

He was going swimming in the frigid water with his sister.

# CHAPTER FORTY-EIGHT

The reports were coming in across the wire furiously for three days and then they just stopped. The media didn't know what or what not to believe. People in the water dragging others under and drowning them. Strange disappearances. Faces swimming just below the surf.

With no new reports, the media quickly lost interest and the Australian Navy could not confirm or deny the existence of the "water people", but a lot of people had gone missing over the last several days. That was the only fact in the entire case.

If there ever were any people in the water, then they just left one day as quietly as they arrived. Officially, it never happened and the Prime Minister promised a thorough investigation into the matter when time and funds permitted.

For three days and three nights, Monica Bowen sat on the beach. Her husband of thirty-seven years had disappeared into the foam and the water of the surf when those things first appeared.

The Australian Navy was so busy just trying to log the number of missing persons in the last few days, an event unprecedented in Australia's history, they had only time enough to give a cursory look along the beach and in the different coves and inlets for her husband. He was just one of several that in a short time would be declared officially lost at sea, most likely due to the strong currents.

Monica cried herself to sleep every night and awakened the same way. Without her Stanley by her side, she was debating the merits of living.

And the way he ran towards the water when she was running from those abominations of nature or whatever they were called was so unlike him. The Navy hadn't said a word but the Internet was alive with crazy reports of people rising out of the ocean all over the world, and other people disappearing just as fast. It was impossible to tell fact from fiction. It made no sense to Monica and she didn't really care. Her husband was gone, that was the fact.

She stood up and wiped her eyes for the hundredth time since this horror happened. Adjusting her sunglasses, she vowed never to go in the water again and she turned to head home to Sydney.

She took one step when something made her turn around and look one last time. Perhaps she would see his body floating to the shore and she could at least take him home with her. Seeing nothing, she shook her head at the stupidity of her thought process and decided to leave. She would look back no longer.

Fleeting thoughts of a happier time made her pause and reflect. She would go on and make Stanley proud of her. It was all she had left.

A gentle breeze picked up and knocked her hat off. She stooped over and picked the hat up and then brushed the sand out of the brim. As she put it back on and adjusted it to shield her eyes from the sun, she gasped.

In front of her, no more than thirty meters away, stumbling towards her like he had been on a three-day drinking binge, was Stanley. He made a motion like he wasn't sure he could stand up and then pitched face-forward into the sand.

She screamed and rushed over to him. She turned him over and immediately fell to the ground hugging him.

Unsure of how it happened, but with tears flowing freely down her cheeks, she hugged him so tightly she wanted to crush him. In the span of a few moments, her life had been reborn.

She threw her arms around his neck and didn't really care that his skin felt unnaturally cold. He had come back to her and she could fix the rest.

He struggled to sit up and then put his arm around her neck, pulling her in closer. He let his fingers wind their way through her soft, black hair until he dug a little deeper and softly scratched the back of her head. Embracing her, he pulled her in tightly to his chest.

Stanley nestled once in her neck before drawing her close to speak to his beloved wife. His voice was raspy and hoarse as he whispered into her ear, "I am Evil."

Coronation

<u>*A Note to the Readers*</u>

*Flannan Isle*, *The Mary Celeste*, and the *SS Waratah* are all actual nautical mysteries that have never been solved. In each case, unusual circumstances dictated a compelling disappearance of the people involved, and no trace has ever been found. There are many theories, of course, as to what happened in each case, but the mystery still lives.

In order to facilitate the telling of *Coronation*, and for a variety of reasons, I altered the dates and some of the facts involved, but wherever possible, I stuck to the truth as much as I could and still tell this story.

Any mistakes, either in the facts or the telling of the story, or discredits to the actual people involved, are entirely my fault.

Since there have never been any traces found, this is just one theory of what happened...

Lee F. Jordan
March 2012

www.ingramcontent.com/pod-product-compliance
Lightning Source LLC
Chambersburg PA
CBHW010442100726
47904CB00008B/2443